# The
# Best
# of
# Benedict
# Kiely

# The
# Best
# of
# Benedict
# Kiely

## A SELECTION OF STORIES

AFTERWORD BY ANTHONY GLAVIN

NEW ISLAND

THE BEST OF BENEDICT KIELY
First published in 2019 by
New Island Books
16 Priory Office Park
Stillorgan
County Dublin
Republic of Ireland

www.newisland.ie

Print ISBN: 978-1-84840-751-0
eBook ISBN: 978-1-84840-752-7

Typeset by JVR Creative India
Cover design by Byren Meam
Cover (author) photograph by Albert Fenton
Printed by TJ International Ltd, Padstow, Cornwall

New Island received financial assistance from The Arts Council (An Comhairle Ealaíon), Dublin, Ireland.

New Island Books is a member of Publishing Ireland.

# Benedict Kiely
# 1919–2007

Benedict Kiely was born near Dromore, County Tyrone, on 15 August 1919, the sixth child of Thomas and Sara Alice Kiely. His family moved to Omagh, County Tyrone, when he was only one, and here he spent his formative years.

As a schoolboy, he dutifully read the essays of Addison, Belloc, Chesterton, Hazlitt and Lamb; for pleasure, he read Zane Gray and Edgar Wallace. As a teenager, Benedict began to feel the urge to become a writer. He had a keen interest in the work of George Bernard Shaw, H. G. Wells and Jonathan Swift. In 1936, after completing his education in Omagh, Benedict went to work as a sorting clerk in Omagh Post Office. However, he soon realised that the post office would not provide him with the life of the scholar which he so desired. So, in the spring of 1937 he left Omagh and began a new life in Emo Park, Portarlington, County Laois, where he decided he would train as a Jesuit priest. It was after a lengthy convalescence from a spinal ailment that he decided that the religious life was not for him, later saying 'My vocation evaporated within a week. Somebody with influence in the highest quarters was praying for the Jesuits, so I was removed. But a finer crowd of men I never met.' He then enrolled for an arts degree at University College, Dublin (UCD), where he was involved in the production of a poetry broadsheet and was a member of the literature society.

By the time his first novel, *Land Without Stars*, was published in 1946, Benedict was a leaderwriter on the *Irish Independent* – his instructions were to 'avoid coming to any conclusion about anything.' In 1950 he resigned. The banning of his novel *In a Harbour Green* (1949) had not endeared him to the management, and later books, including *Honey Seems Bitter* and

*There Was an Ancient House*, were also banned. A friend suggested he would be happier at the *Irish Press*, where he then spent almost fifteen years as literary editor. He retired from full-time journalism in the mid-1960s, became a visiting professor of creative writing at several American universities, and later lectured at UCD.

RTÉ Radio's 'Sunday Miscellany' featured Benedict as a regular contributor to short talks, mostly on literature and other Irish topics, for over quarter of a century between the 1970s and 1990s. He was awarded honorary doctorates by the National University of Ireland and Queen's University, Belfast. In 1996 he received the highest honour of Aosdána, the Irish artists' body, when he was elected a Saoi in recognition of his contribution to literature.

On 9 February 2007 Benedict Kiely died in Dublin after a short illness. He was eighty-seven.

# Praise for Benedict Kiely

# Complete List of Works by Benedict Kiely

## NOVELS

Nothing Happens in Carmincross (1985)
Proxopera: A Tale of Modern Ireland (1977)
The Captain with the Whiskers (1960)
There Was an Ancient House (1955)
The Cards of the Gambler (1953)
Honey Seems Bitter (1952)
Call for a Miracle (1950)
In a Harbour Green (1949)
Land Without Stars (1946)

## NON-FICTION

A Raid into Dark Corners and Other Essays (1999)
God's Own Country (1993)
Yeats' Ireland (1989)
Ireland from the Air (1985)
All the Way to Bantry Bay and Other Irish Journeys (1978)
Modern Irish Fiction: A Critique (1950)
Poor Scholar: A Study of the Works and Days of
William Carleton (1947)
Counties of Contention (1945; 2004, with an
introduction by John Hume)

SHORT STORIES
Selected Stories (2011)
The Collected Stories of Benedict Kiely (2001)
The Trout in the Turnhole (1996)
A Letter to Peachtree (1987)
The State of Ireland: A Novella and
Seventeen Short Stories (1981)
A Cow in the House (1978)
A Ball of Malt and Madame Butterfly (1973)
A Journey to the Seven Streams (1963)


AUTOBIOGRAPHY
The Waves Behind Us: A Memoir (1999)
Drink to the Bird: An Omagh Boyhood (1992)

# Contents

# The Dogs in the Great Glen

The professor had come over from America to search out his origins and I met him in Dublin on the way to Kerry where his grandfather had come from and where he had relations, including a grand-uncle, still living.

'But the trouble is,' he said, 'that I've lost the address my mother gave me. She wrote to tell them I was coming to Europe. That's all they know. All I remember is a name out of my dead father's memories: the great Glen of Kanareen.'

'You could write to your mother.'

'That would take time. She'd be slow to answer. And I feel impelled right away to find the place my grandfather told my father about.

'You wouldn't understand,' he said. 'Your origins are all around you.'

'You can say that again, professor. My origins crop up like the bones of rock in thin sour soil. They come unwanted like the mushroom of *merulius lacrimans* on the walls of a decaying house.'

'It's no laughing matter,' he said.

'It isn't for me. This island's too small to afford a place in which to hide from one's origins. Or from anything else. During the war a young fellow in Dublin said to me: "Mister, even if I ran away to sea I wouldn't get beyond the three-mile limit".'

He said, 'But it's large enough to lose a valley in. I couldn't find the valley of Kanareen marked on any map or mentioned in any directory.'

'I have a middling knowledge of the Kerry mountains,' I said. 'I could join you in the search.'

'It's not marked on the half-inch Ordnance Survey map.'

'There are more things in Kerry than were ever dreamt of by the Ordnance Survey. The place could have another official name. At the back of my head I feel that once in the town of Kenmare in Kerry I heard a man mention the name of Kanareen.'

We set off two days later in a battered, rattly Ford Prefect. Haste, he said, would be dangerous because Kanareen might not be there at all, but if we idled from place to place in the lackadaisical Irish summer we might, when the sentries were sleeping and the glen unguarded, slip secretly as thieves into the land whose legends were part of his rearing.

'Until I met you,' the professor said, 'I was afraid the valley might have been a dream world my grandfather imagined to dull the edge of the first nights in a new land. I could see how he might have come to believe in it himself and told my father – and then, of course, my father told me.'

One of his grandfather's relatives had been a Cistercian monk in Mount Melleray, and we went there hoping to see the evidence of a name in a book and to kneel, perhaps, under the high arched roof of the chapel close to where that monk had knelt. But, when we had traversed the corkscrew road over the purple Knockmealdowns and gone up to the mountain monastery through the forest the monks had made in the wilderness, it was late evening and the doors were closed. The birds sang vespers. The great silence affected us with something between awe and a painful, intolerable shyness. We hadn't the heart to ring a doorbell or to promise ourselves to return in the morning. Not speaking to each other we

2

retreated, the rattle of the Ford Prefect as irreverent as dicing on the altar-steps. Half a mile down the road the mute, single-file procession of a group of women exercitants walking back to the female guest-house underlined the holy, unreal, unanswering stillness that had closed us out. It could easily have been that his grandfather never had a relative a monk in Mount Melleray.

A cousin of his mother's mother had, he had been told, been a cooper in Lady Gregory's Gort in the County Galway. But when we crossed the country westwards to Gort, it produced nothing except the information that apart from the big breweries, where they survived like birds or bison in a sanctuary, the coopers had gone, leaving behind them not a hoop or a stave. So we visited the woods of Coole, close to Gort, where Lady Gregory's house had once stood, and on the brimming lake-water among the stones, we saw by a happy poetic accident the number of swans the poet had seen.

Afterwards in Galway City there was, as there always is in Galway City, a night's hard drinking that was like a fit of jovial hysteria, and a giggling ninny of a woman in the bar who kept saying, 'You're the nicest American I ever met. You don't look like an American. You don't even carry a camera. You look like a Kerryman.'

And in the end, we came to Kenmare in Kerry, and in another bar we met a talkative Kerryman who could tell us all about the prowess of the Kerry team, about the heroic feats of John Joe Sheehy or Paddy Bawn Brosnan. He knew so much, that man, yet he couldn't tell us where in the wilderness of mountains we might find the Glen of Kanareen. Nor could anybody else in the bar be of the least help to us, not even the postman who could only say that wherever it was, that is if it was at all, it wasn't in his district.

'It could of course,' he said, 'be east over the mountain.'

Murmuring sympathetically, the entire bar assented. The rest of the world was east over the mountain.

With the resigned air of men washing their hands of a helpless, hopeless case the postman and the football savant directed us to a roadside post office twelve miles away where, in a high-hedged garden before an old grey-stone house with latticed windows and an incongruous, green, official post office sign there was a child, quite naked, playing with a coloured, musical spinning-top as big as itself, and an old half-deaf man sunning himself and swaying in a rocking-chair, a straw hat tilted forwards to shade his eyes. Like Oisin remembering the Fenians, he told us he had known once of a young woman who married a man from a place called Kanareen, but there had been contention about the match and her people had kept up no correspondence with her. But the day she left home with her husband that was the way she went. He pointed. The way went inland and up and up. We followed it.

'That young woman could have been a relation of mine,' the professor said.

On a rock-strewn slope, and silhouetted on a saw-toothed ridge where you'd think only a chamois could get by without broken legs, small black cows, accurate and active as goats, rasped good milk from the grass between the stones. His grandfather had told his father about those athletic, legendary cows and about the prov-erb that said: Kerry cows know Sunday. For in famine times, a century since, mountain people bled the cows once a week to mix the blood into yellow maize meal and provide a meat dish, a special Sunday dinner.

The road twisted on across moorland that on our left sloped dizzily to the sea, as if the solid ground might easily slip and slide into the depths. Mountain shadows melted like purple dust into a green bay. Across a ravine set quite alone on a long, slanting, brown knife blade of a mountain, was a white house with a red door. The rattle of our pathetic little car affronted the vast stillness. We were free to moralise on the extent of all space in relation to the trivial area that limited our ordinary daily lives.

The two old druids of men resting from work on the leeward side of a turf-bank listened to our enquiry with the same attentive, half-conscious patience they gave to bird-cries or the sound of wind in the heather. Then they waved us ahead towards a narrow cleft in the distant wall of mountains as if they doubted the ability of ourselves and our conveyance to negotiate the Gap and find the Glen. They offered us strong tea and a drop out of a bottle. They watched us with kind irony as we drove away. Until the Gap swallowed us and the hazardous, twisting track absorbed all our attention we could look back and still see them, motionless, waiting with indifference for the landslide that would end it all.

By a roadside pool where water-beetles lived their vicious secretive lives, we sat and rested, with the pass and the cliffs, overhung with heather, behind us and another ridge ahead. Brazenly the sheer rocks reflected the sun and semaphored at us. Below us, in the dry summer, the bed of a stream held only a trickle of water twisting painfully around piles of round black stones. Touch a beetle with a stalk of dry grass and the creature either dived like a shot or, angry at invasion, savagely grappled with the stalk.

'That silly woman in Galway,' the professor said.

He dropped a stone into the pool and the beetles submerged to weather the storm.

'That day by the lake at Lady Gregory's Coole. The exact number of swans Yeats saw when the poem came to him. Upon the brimming water among the stones are nine and fifty swans. Since I don't carry a camera nobody will ever believe me. But you saw them. You counted them.'

'Now that I am so far,' he said, 'I'm half-afraid to finish the journey. What will they be like? What will they think of me? Will I go over that ridge there to find my grandfather's brother living in a cave?'

Poking at and tormenting the beetles on the black mirror of the pool, I told him, 'Once I went from Dublin to near Shannon Pot, where the river rises, to help an American woman find the house where her dead woman friend had been reared. On her deathbed the friend had written it all out on a sheet of notepaper: "Cross the river at Battle Bridge. Go straight through the village with the ruined castle on the right. Go on a mile to the crossroads and the labourer's cottage with the lovely snapdragons in the flower garden. Take the road to the right there, and then the second boreen on the left beyond the schoolhouse. Then stop at the third house on that boreen. You can see the river from the flagstone at the door."

'Apart from the snapdragons it was exactly as she had written it down. The dead woman had walked that boreen as a barefooted schoolgirl. Not able to revisit it herself she entrusted the mission as her dying wish to her dearest friend. We found the house. Her people were long gone from it but the new tenants remembered them. They welcomed us with melodeon and fiddle and all the neighbours came in and collated the long memories of the townland. They feasted us with cold ham and chicken, porter and whisky, until I had cramps for a week.'

'My only grip on identity,' he said, 'is that a silly woman told me I looked like a Kerryman. My grandfather was a Kerryman. What do Kerrymen look like?'

'Big,' I said.

'And this is the heart of Kerry. And what my grandfather said about the black cows was true. With a camera I could have taken a picture of those climbing cows. And up that hill trail and over that ridge is Kanareen.'

'We hope,' I said.

The tired cooling engine coughed apologetically when we abandoned it and put city-shod feet to the last ascent.

'If that was the mountain my grandfather walked over in the naked dawn coming home from an all-night card-playing then, by God, he was a better man than me,' said the professor.

He folded his arms and looked hard at the razor-cut edges of stone on the side of the mountain.

'Short of too much drink and the danger of mugging,' he said, 'getting home at night in New York is a simpler operation than crawling over that hunk of miniature Mount Everest. Like walking up the side of a house.'

He was as proud as Punch of the climbing prowess of his grandfather.

'My father told me,' he said, 'that one night coming home from the card-playing my grandfather slipped down fifteen feet of rock and the only damage done was the ruin of one of two bottles of whisky he had in the tail-pockets of his greatcoat. The second bottle was unharmed.'

The men who surfaced the track we were walking on had been catering for horses and narrow iron-hooped wheels. After five minutes of agonised slipping and sliding, wisdom came to us and we took to the cushioned

grass and heather. As we ascended the professor told me
what his grandfather had told his father about the market town he used to go to when he was a boy. It was a
small town where even on market days the dogs would sit
nowhere except exactly in the middle of the street. They
were lazy town dogs, not active, loyal and intelligent like
the dogs the grandfather had known in the great glen. The
way the old man had described it, the town's five streets
grasped the ground of Ireland as the hand of a strong
swimmer might grasp a ledge of rock to hoist himself out
of the water. On one side was the sea. On the other side
a shoulder of mountain rose so steeply that the Gaelic
name of it meant the gable of the house.

When the old man went as a boy to the town on a
market day it was his custom to climb that mountain, up
through furze and following goat tracks, leaving his shiny
boots, that he only put on, anyway, when he entered the
town, securely in hiding behind a furze bush. The way he
remembered that mountain it would seem that twenty
minutes active climbing brought him halfways to heaven.
The little town was far below him, and the bay and the
islands. The unkempt coastline tumbled and sprawled to
left and right, and westwards the ocean went on for ever.
The sounds of market-day, voices, carts, dogs barking,
musicians on the streets, came up to him as faint, silvery
whispers. On the tip of one island two tall aerials marked
the place where, he was told, messages went down into
the sea to travel all the way to America by cable. That
was a great marvel for a boy from the mountains to hear
about: the ghostly, shrill, undersea voices; the words
of people in every tongue of Europe far down among
monstrous fish and shapeless sea-serpents that never saw
the light of the sun. He closed his eyes one day and it
seemed to him that the sounds of the little town were the

voices of Europe setting out on their submarine travels. That was the time he knew that when he was old enough he would leave the Glen of Kanareen and go with the voices westwards to America.

'Or so he said. Or so he told my father,' said the professor.

Another fifty yards and we would be on top of the ridge. We kept our eyes on the ground, fearful of the moment of vision and, for good or ill, revelation. Beyond the ridge there might be nothing but a void to prove that his grandfather had been a dreamer or a liar. Rapidly, nervously, he tried to talk down his fears.

'He would tell stories for ever, my father said, about ghosts and the good people. There was one case of an old woman whose people buried her – when she died, of course – against her will, across the water, which meant on the far side of the lake in the glen. Her dying wish was to be buried in another graveyard, nearer home. And there she was, sitting in her own chair in the chimney corner, waiting for them, when they came home from the funeral. To ease her spirit they replanted her.'

To ease the nervous moment I said, 'There was a poltergeist once in a farmhouse in these mountains, and the police decided to investigate the queer happenings, and didn't an ass's collar come flying across the room to settle around the sergeant's neck. Due to subsequent ridicule the poor man had to be transferred to Dublin.'

Laughing, we looked at the brown infant runnel that went parallel to the path. It flowed with us: we were over the watershed. So we raised our heads slowly and saw the great Glen of Kanareen. It was what Cortez saw, and all the rest of it. It was a discovery. It was a new world. It gathered the sunshine into a gigantic coloured bowl. We accepted it detail by detail.

'It was there all the time,' he said. 'It was no dream. It was no lie.'

The first thing we realised was the lake. The runnel leaped down to join the lake, and we looked down on it through ash trees regularly spaced on a steep, smooth, green slope. Grasping from tree to tree you could descend to the pebbled, lapping edge of the water.

'That was the way,' the professor said, 'the boys in his time climbed down to fish or swim. Black, bull-headed mountain trout. Cannibal trout. There was one place where they could dive off sheer rock into seventy feet of water. Rolling like a gentle sea: that was how he described it. They gathered kindling, too, on the slopes under the ash trees.'

Then, after the lake, we realised the guardian mountain; not rigidly chiselled into ridges of rock like the mountain behind us but soft and gently curving, protective and, above all, noble, a monarch of mountains, an antlered stag holding a proud horned head up to the highest point of the blue sky. Green fields swathed its base. Sharp lines of stone walls, dividing wide areas of moorland sheep-grazing, marked man's grip for a thousand feet or so above sea-level, then gave up the struggle and left the mountain alone and untainted. Halfways up one snow-white cloud rested as if it had hooked itself on a snagged rock and there it stayed, motionless, as step by step we went down into the Glen. Below the cloud a long cataract made a thin, white, forked-lightning line, and, in the heart of the glen, the river that the cataract became, sprawled on a brown and green and golden patchwork bed.

'It must be some one of those houses,' he said, pointing ahead and down to the white houses of Kanareen.

'Take a blind pick,' I said. 'I see at least fifty.'

They were scattered over the glen in five or six clusters.

'From what I heard it should be over in that direction,' he said.

Small rich fields were ripe in the sun. This was a glen of plenty, a gold-field in the middle of a desert, a happy laughing mockery of the arid surrounding moors and mountains. Five hundred yards away a dozen people were working at the hay. They didn't look up or give any sign that they had seen two strangers cross the high threshold of their kingdom but, as we went down, stepping like grenadier guards, the black-and-white sheepdogs detached themselves from the haymaking and moved silently across to intercept our path. Five of them I counted. My step faltered.

'This could be it,' I suggested with hollow joviality. 'I feel a little like an early Christian.'

The professor said nothing. We went on down, deserting the comfort of the grass and heather at the side of the track. It seemed to me that our feet on the loose pebbles made a tearing, crackling, grinding noise that shook echoes even out of the imperturbable mountain. The white cloud had not moved. The haymakers had not honoured us with a glance.

'We could,' I said, 'make ourselves known to them in a civil fashion. We could ask the way to your grand-uncle's house. We could have a formal introduction to those slinking beasts.'

'No, let me,' he said. 'Give me my head. Let me try to remember what I was told.'

'The hearts of these highland people, I've heard, are made of pure gold,' I said. 'But they're inclined to be the tiniest bit suspicious of town-dressed strangers. As sure as God made smells and shotguns they think we're inspectors from some government department: weeds, or warble-fly or horror of horrors, rates and taxes. With equanimity they'd see us eaten.'

He laughed. His stride had a new elasticity in it. He was another man. The melancholy of the monastic summer dusk at Mount Melleray was gone. He was somebody else coming home. The white cloud had not moved. The silent dogs came closer. The unheeding people went on with their work.

'The office of rates collector is not sought after in these parts,' I said. 'Shotguns are still used to settle vexed questions of land title. Only a general threat of excommunication can settle a major feud.'

'This was the way he'd come home from the gambling cabin,' the professor said, 'his pockets clinking with winnings. That night he fell he'd won the two bottles of whisky. He was only eighteen when he went away. But he was the tallest man in the glen. So he said. And lucky at cards.'

The dogs were twenty yards away, silent, fanning out like soldiers cautiously circling a point of attack.

'He was an infant prodigy,' I said. 'He was a peerless grandfather for a man to have. He also had one great advantage over us – he knew the names of these taciturn dogs and they knew his smell.'

He took off his white hat and waved at the workers. One man at a haycock raised a pitchfork – in salute or in threat? Nobody else paid the least attention. The dogs were now at our heels, suiting their pace politely to ours. They didn't even sniff. They had impeccable manners.

'This sure is the right glen,' he said. The old man was never done talking about the dogs. They were all black-and-white in his day, too.'

He stopped to look at them. They stopped. They didn't look up at us. They didn't snarl. They had broad shaggy backs. Even for their breed they were big dogs. Their long tails were rigid. Fixing my eyes on the white cloud I walked on.

'Let's establish contact,' I said, 'before we're casually eaten. All I ever heard about the dogs in these mountains is that their family tree is as old as the Red Branch Knights. That they're the best sheepdogs in Ireland and better than anything in the Highlands of Scotland. They also savage you first and bark afterwards.'

Noses down, they padded along behind us. Their quiet breath was hot on my calves. High up and far away the nesting white cloud had the security of heaven.

'Only strangers who act suspiciously,' the professor said.

'What else are we? I'd say we smell bad to them.'

'Not me,' he said. 'Not me. The old man told a story about a stranger who came to Kanareen when most of the people were away at the market. The house he came to visit was empty except for two dogs. So he sat all day at the door of the house and the dogs lay and watched him and said and did nothing. Only once, he felt thirsty and went into the kitchen of the house and lifted a bowl to go to the well for water. Then there was a low duet of a snarl that froze his blood. So he went thirsty and the dogs lay quiet.'

'Hospitable people.'

'The secret is touch nothing, lay no hand on property and you're safe.'

'So help me God,' I said, 'I wouldn't deprive them of a bone or a blade of grass.'

Twice in my life I had been bitten by dogs. Once, walking to school along a sidestreet on a sunny morning and simultaneously reading in *The Boy's Magazine* about a soccer centre forward, the flower of the flock, called Fiery Cross the Shooting Star – he was redheaded and his

surname was Cross – I had stepped on a sleeping Irish ter-
rier. In retaliation, the startled brute had bitten me. Nor
could I find it in my heart to blame him, so that, in my
subconscious, dogs took on the awful heaven-appointed
dignity of avenging angels. The other time – and this was
an even more disquieting experience – a mongrel dog had
come up softly behind me while I was walking on the
fairgreen in the town I was reared in and bitten the calf
of my leg so as to draw spurts of blood. I kicked him but
not resenting the kick, he had walked away as if it was
the most natural, legitimate thing in heaven and earth for
a dog to bite me and be kicked in return. Third time, I
thought, it will be rabies. So as we walked and the silent
watchers of the valley padded at our heels, I enlivened the
way with brave and trivial chatter. I recited my story of
the four wild brothers of Adrigole.

'Once upon a time,' I said, 'there lived four brothers
in a rocky corner of Adrigole in west Cork, under the
mountain called Hungry Hill. Daphne du Maurier wrote
a book called after the mountain, but divil a word in it
about the four brothers of Adrigole. They lived, I heard
tell, according to instinct and never laced their boots
and came out only once a year to visit the nearest town
which was Castletownberehaven on the side of Bantry
Bay. They'd stand there, backs to the wall, smoking, saying nothing, contemplating the giddy market-day throng.
One day they ran out of tobacco and went into the
local branch of the Bank of Ireland to buy it and raised
havoc because the teller refused to satisfy their needs. To
pacify them the manager and the teller had to disgorge
their own supplies. So they went back to Adrigole to live
happily without lacing their boots, and ever after they
thought that in towns and cities the bank was the place
where you bought tobacco.

'That,' said I with a hollow laugh, 'is my moral tale about the four brothers of Adrigole.'

On a level with the stream that came from the lake and went down to join the valley's main river, we walked towards a group of four whitewashed, thatched farmhouses that were shining and scrupulously clean. The track looped to the left. Through a small triangular meadow a short-cut went straight towards the houses. In the heart of the meadow, by the side of the short-cut, there was a spring well of clear water, the stones that lined its sides and the roof cupped over it all white and cleansed with lime. He went down three stone steps and looked at the water. For good luck there was a tiny brown trout imprisoned in the well. He said quietly, 'That was the way my grandfather described it. But it could hardly be the self-same fish.'

He stooped to the clear water. He filled his cupped hands and drank. He stooped again, and again filled his cupped hands and slowly, carefully, not spilling a drop, came up the moist, cool steps. Then, with the air of a priest, scattering hyssop, he sprinkled the five dogs with the spring-water. They backed away from him, thoughtfully. They didn't snarl or show teeth. He had them puzzled. He laughed with warm good nature at their obvious perplexity. He was making his own of them. He licked his wet hands. Like good pupils attentively studying a teacher, the dogs watched him.

'Elixir,' he said. 'He told my father that the sweetest drink he ever had was out of this well when he was on his way back from a drag hunt in the next glen. He was a great hunter.'

'He was Nimrod,' I said. 'He was everything. He was the universal Kerryman.'

'No kidding,' he said. 'Through a thorn hedge six feet thick and down a precipice and across a stream to make sure of a wounded bird. Or all night long waist deep in an icy swamp waiting for the wild geese. And the day of this drag hunt. What he most remembered about it was the way they sold the porter to the hunting crowd in the pub at the crossroads. To meet the huntsmen halfways they moved the bar out to the farmyard. With hounds and cows and geese and chickens, it was like having a drink in Noah's Ark. The pint tumblers were set on doors lifted off their hinges and laid flat on hurdles. The beer was in wooden tubs and all the barmaids had to do was dip and there was the pint. They didn't bother to rinse the tumblers. He said it was the quickest-served and the flattest pint of porter he ever saw or tasted. Bitter and black as bog water. Completely devoid of the creamy clerical collar that should grace a good pint. On the way home he spent an hour here rinsing his mouth and the well-water tasted as sweet, he said, as silver.'

The white cloud was gone from the mountain.

'Where did it go,' I said. 'Where could it vanish to?'

In all the wide sky there wasn't a speck of cloud. The mountain was changing colour, deepening to purple with the approaching evening.

He grasped me by the elbow, urging me forwards. He said, 'Step on it. We're almost home.'

We crossed a crude wooden stile and followed the short-cut through a walled garden of bright-green heads of cabbage and black and red currant bushes. Startled, fruit-thieving birds rustled away from us, and on a rowan tree a sated, impudent blackbird opened his throat and sang.

'Don't touch a currant,' I said, 'or a head of cabbage. Don't ride your luck too hard.'

He laughed like a boy half-hysterical with happiness. He said, 'Luck. Me and these dogs, we know each other. We've been formally introduced.

'Glad to know you dogs,' he said to them over his shoulder.

They trotted behind us. We crossed a second stile and followed the short-cut through a haggard, and underfoot the ground was velvety with chipped straw. We opened a five-barred iron gate, and to me it seemed that the noise of its creaking hinges must be audible from end to end of the glen. While I paused to rebolt it he and the dogs had gone on, the dogs trotting in the lead. I ran after them. I was the stranger who had once been the guide. We passed three houses as if they didn't exist. They were empty. The people who lived in them were above at the hay.

Towards the fourth thatched house of the group we walked along a green boreen, lined with hazels and an occasional mountain ash. The guardian mountain was by now so purple that the sky behind it seemed, by contrast, as silvery as the scales of a fish. From unknown lands behind the lines of hazels two more black-and-white dogs ran, barking with excitement, to join our escort. Where the hazels ended there was a house fronted by a low stone wall and a profusion of fuchsia. An old man sat on the wall and around him clustered the children of the four houses. He was a tall, broad-shouldered old man with copious white hair and dark side whiskers and a clear prominent profile. He was dressed in good grey with long, old-fashioned skirts to his coat – formally dressed as if for some formal event – and his wide-brimmed black hat rested on the wall beside him, and his joined hands rested on the curved handle of a strong ash plant. He stood up as we approached. The stick fell to the ground. He stepped over it and came towards us. He was as tall or, without the slight stoop of age, taller than the professor. He put out his two hands and rested them on the professor's shoulders. It wasn't an embrace. It was an appraisal, a salute, a sign of recognition.

He said, 'Kevin, well and truly we knew you'd come if you were in the neighbourhood at all. I watched you walking down. I knew you from the top of the Glen. You have the same gait my brother had, the heavens be his bed. My brother that was your grandfather.'

'They say a grandson often walks like the grandfather,' said the professor.

His voice was shaken and there were tears on his face. So, a stranger in the place myself, I walked away a bit and looked back up the Glen. The sunlight was slanting now and shadows were lengthening on mountain slopes and across the small fields. From where I stood the lake was invisible, but the ashwood on the slope above it was dark as ink. Through sunlight and shadow the happy haymakers came running down towards us; and barking, playing, frisking over each other, the seven black-and-white dogs, messengers of good news, ran to meet them. The great Glen, all happy echoes, was opening out and singing to welcome its true son.

Under the hazels, as I watched the running haymakers, the children came shyly around me to show me that I also was welcome. Beyond the high ridge, the hard mountain the card-players used to cross to the cabin of the gambling stood up gaunt and arrogant and leaned over towards us as if it were listening.

It was moonlight, I thought, not sunlight, over the great Glen. From house to house, the dogs were barking, not baying the moon, but to welcome home the young men from the card-playing over the mountain. The edges of rock glistened like quartz. The tall young gambler came laughing down the Glen, greatcoat swinging open, waving in his hand the one bottle of whisky that hadn't been broken when he tumbled down the spink. The ghosts of his own dogs laughed and leaped and frolicked at his heels.

# The Heroes in the Dark House

'They were gone in the morning,' the old man said.

His name was Arthur Broderick, and the young folk-tale scholar sat quietly, listening for the story that had been promised him.

'Lock, stock and barrel,' said the old man. 'The whole U.S. garrison, off for the far fields of France. Jeeps, guns, and gun-carriers. In the dump behind the big camp at Knocknashee Castle the handful of caretakers they left behind slung radio sets and bicycles and ran a gun-carrier with caterpillar wheels over the lot, and as good as made mash of them. Very wasteful. War's all waste. Those bicycles would have kept every young boy in the county spinning for the next five years.'

Like the plain girl that nobody wanted, Mr Broderick's nine-times rejected manuscript-folk-tales set down with such love and care in high-spined script lay between them on an antique drawing-room table. The table's top, solid oak and two inches thick, was shaped like a huge teardrop pearl with the tip abruptly nipped off.

'Oak,' Mr Broderick said through the smoke. 'Solid oak and two centuries old. In 1798, in the year of the Rising, it was the top of a bellows in a smithy. Look here where the British yeomanry sawed the tip off it so that the rebels could no longer use it for the forging of the pikes. When I was the age of yourself I converted it into a table. Sixty years ago last July.'

Around them in the ancient, musty, tapestried room the wreathing smoke might have come from the fires of 1798. Birdsong outside, sunshine, wind in the creepers were as far away as Florida. The greedy, nesting jackdaws held the flues as firmly as ever at Thermopylae or the Alamo or Athlone, or a score of other places all around the battered globe, unforgotten heroes had held passes, bridgeheads or gun-burned walls. And unforgotten heroes had marched through the smoke in this room: Strong Shawn, the son of the fisherman of Kinsale, triumphant, with the aid of white magic, crossed the seven-mile strand of steel spikes, the seven-mile-high mountain of flames, the seven miles of treacherous sea, and came gloriously to win his love in a castle courtyard crowded with champions and heroes from the four sides of the world; the valiant son of the King of Antua fought with Macan Mor, son of the King of Soracha, in the way that they made rocks of water and water of rocks, and if the birds came from the lower to the upper world to see wonders it was to see these two they came.

Mr. Broderick went on with his tale. All night long through the village below the old, dark, smoky house that had once been a rectory the lorries had throbbed and thundered on the narrow, twisted street and above, in the upper air, the waves of planes had swept east towards Europe.

'They were gone in the morning,' he said. 'Lock, stock and barrel. There was never a departure like it since the world was made. For quick packing, I heard afterwards, they drove the jeeps up the steep steps of the courthouse below. It reminded me of the poem about the three jolly gentlemen in coats of red who rode their horses up to bed.'

'They were gone,' he said, 'like snow off a ditch.'

It was as much as the young scholar could do to see him for smoke. But with an effort that would have done credit to Macan Mor or Shawn of Kinsale he managed to control his coughing.

In the old dizzy chimney the jackdaws were so solidly entrenched that at times Mr. Broderick had found it hard to see the paper he transcribed the folk-tales on. The smoke no longer made him cough, but at eighty-five his eyes were not as keen as they had been when he was in his prime and from the saddle of a galloping hunter could spot, in passing, a bird's nest in a leafy hedgerow. Lovingly he transcribed the tales in the high, spidery handwriting that – like himself, like his work for Sir Horace Plunkett in the co-operative creameries, his friendship with Thomas Andrews who had built the *Titanic* and gone bravely with it to Wordsworth's incommunicable sleep – belonged to a past, forgotten time. For years of his life he had followed these tales, the people who told them, the heroes who lived in them, over miles of lonely heathermountain, up boreens that in rain became rivulets, to crouch in mountain cabins by the red hearth-glow and listen to the meditative voices of people for whom there was only the past.

Peadar Haughey of Creggan Cross had sat on the long, oaken settle with his wife and three daughters and dictated to him the adventures of the son of the king of Antua, as well as the story of the giant of Reibhlean who had abducted from Ireland a married princess. Giants as a rule preferred unmarried princesses. Peadar told the story in Irish and English. His wife and daughters understood only English but together they rocked in unison on the settle and sang macaronic songs in a mixture of both languages. That simple world had its own confusions.

At times in his smoky house he found it hard to separate the people in the tales from the people who told them.

Bed-ridden Owen Roe Ward, in a garret in a back-lane in the garrison town ten miles away, had told him the story of the King of Green Island and other stories that were all about journeys to the end of the earth in search of elixirs that could only be won by herculean labours. Hewing trees for hire in a tangled plantation whose wood had once paid for the travels and other activities of D'Orsay and Lady Blessington, Owen had brought down on his hapless spine a ton-weight of timber. Paralysed in his garret he travelled as he talked to find life-giving water in the well at the world's end.

A woman of eighty by the name of Maire John (she still sang with the sweet voice she had at twenty and displayed the fondness for embracing men that, according to tradition, had then characterised her) had told him of the three princesses who sat in the wishing chair. One wished to marry a husband more beautiful than the sun. The second wished to marry a husband more beautiful than the moon. The third stated her honest but eccentric preference for the White Hound of the Mountain. It was a local heather-flavoured version of the marriage of Cupid and Psyche, and Maire John herself was a randy old lady who would, in the days of silver Latin, have delighted Apuleius.

The stories had come like genii, living, wreathing from holes in the wall behind smoky hearths, or from the dusty tops of dressers, or from farmhouse lofts where ancient, yellow manuscripts were stored. By Bloody Bridge on the Camowen River (called so because of no battle, but because of the number of fine trout killed there) he had heard from Pat Moses Gavigan a completely new version of the story of Fionn MacCumhail and the enchanted Salmon of Wisdom.

Plain and mountain and river-valley, the places he knew were sombre with the sense of family, and folk-tales grew as naturally there as grass. Heroes, princesses, enchanters good and bad, he had marshalled them all, called them to order in his own smoky room, numbered them off right to left, made his roll-call, described them in that high-spined handwriting he had studied so laboriously in the old manuscripts. Properly thus caparisoned they would go out into the twentieth century. He made his own of them. He called them his children. He sent them out to the ends of the earth, to magazine editors and publishing houses. They came back rejected to him, as if being his children they could have no life when torn away from him. Then one day in the smoky room under the power of the squabbling enchanters of jackdaws he had the bitterness of discovering that his children had betrayed him. In a Dublin newspaper he read the review of the young scholar's book:

'The scholar who has compiled, translated and edited these folk-tales has a wise head on young shoulders. Careful research and a wide knowledge of comparative folklore have gone into his work. He has gleaned carefully in the mountainous area ten miles north of the town where he was born. He presents his findings with an erudite introduction and in an impeccable style…'

The smoke wreathed around him. The reviewer's weary sentences went on like the repetition of a death-knell:

'His name is worthy to rank with that of such folk-lorists as Jeremiah Curtin. Particularly notable is his handling of the remarkable quest tale of the King of Green Island…'

Mr. Broderick couldn't blame the three princesses for leaving the wishing chair and making off with a younger man. That scholar, wise head on young shoulders, could be Cupid, more beautiful than the sun and the moon: he might even be that enigmatic character, The White Hound of the Mountain. But Shawn of Kinsale could have been kinder to old age, and so could all those battling heroes or venturesome boys who crossed perilous seas, burning mountains and spiked strands.

He wrote to the young scholar at the publisher's address: 'While I am loath to trade on your time, I have, it would seem, been working or wandering about in the same field and in the same part of the country. We may share the acquaintanceship of some of the living sources of these old tales. We certainly have friends in common in the realms of mythology. Perhaps my own humble gatherings might supplement your store. So far I have failed to find a publisher for them. If you are ever visiting your home town you may care to add a few miles to the journey to call on me. My congratulations on your achievement. It gratifies me to see a young man from this part of the country doing so well.'

A week later he took up his stick one day and walked down the winding, grass-grown avenue. An ancestor was rector here long years ago, he thought, as in the case of William Yeats, the poet, who died in France on the eve of this war and who had an ancestor a rector long years ago in Drumcliffe by the faraway Sligo sea. Mr. Broderick's house had been the rectory. When the church authorities judged it a crumbling, decaying property they had given it to Mr. Broderick for a token sum – a small gesture of regard for all that in an active manhood he had done for the village. Crumbling and decaying it was, but peace, undisturbed, remained around the boles of the trees, the tall gables and old tottering chimneys, the shadowy bird-rustling walks.

Now, as he walked, yews gone wild and reckless made a tangled pattern above his head.

Weeks before, from the garrison town in the valley, war had spilled its gathering troops over into this little village. Three deep, burdened with guns and accoutrements, they slouched past Mr. Broderick on the way down the hill to their courthouse billet. Dust rose around them. They sang. They were three to six thousand miles from home, facing an uncertain future, and in reasonably good humour. A dozen or so who knew Mr. Broderick from the tottering house as the old guy who made souvenirs out of blackthorn and bog oak, waved casual, friendly hands. Beyond and behind them as they descended was the blue cone of Knocknashee Hill where the castle was commandeered and where a landlord had once stocked a lake with rainbow trout that like these troops had been carried across the wide Atlantic. The soldiers' dust settling around him in wreaths and rings, Mr. Broderick went down the road to collect his mail at the post-office. There had been no troops in this village since 1798 when the bellows had been mutilated and the soldiers then, according to the history books, had been anything but friendly.

The long red-tiled roofs and white walls of the co-operative creamery, the sheen of glasshouses from the slopes of the model farm were a reminder to Mr. Broderick of the enthusiasms of an active past. People had, in his boyhood, been evicted for poverty in that village. Now every year the co-operative grain store handled one hundred and fifty thousand tons of grain. An energetic young man could take forty tons of tomatoes out of an acre and a quarter of glasshouses, and on a day of strong sunshine the gleam of the glasshouses would blind you. Crops burst over the hedges as nowhere else in that part of the country. It was good, high, dry land that took less harm than most places from wet seasons and flooding, and the cattle were as heavy and content as creamy oxen in French vineyards.

Over the hedge and railings by the parish church the statue of the old Canon, not of Mr. Broderick's persuasion, raised a strong Roman right arm. The pedestal described the Canon as a saintly priest and sterling patriot and to anybody, except Mr. Broderick, that raised right arm might have been minatory. To Arthur Broderick it was a kind memory of hero and co-worker, it was an eternal greeting in stone.

'Arthur,' the statue said, 'yourself and myself built this place. There was a time when you'd have clambered to the top of a telegraph pole if somebody'd told you there was a shilling there would help to make the village live. You did everything but say mass and I did that. You got little out of it yourself. But you saw they were happy and strong. Look around you. Be proud and glad. Enjoy your dreams of lost heroes in the mist. No young man can steal from you what you want to give away.'

High above the dead stone Canon the Angelus bell rang. Before him, down the cobbled footwalk, so steep that at times it eased itself out with a sigh into flat, flagged steps, went a tall soldier and a small young woman. Mr. Broderick knew her. She was one of the eighteen Banty Mullans, nine male, nine female, all strawheaded and five feet high, the males all roughs, and the females, to put it politely, taking in washing for the Irish Fusiliers in the town below. She was ill-dressed, coarse-tongued and vicious. She carried in her left hand a shiny gallon buttermilk-can. Stooping low, the tall warrior eased the handle of the can from the stumpy, stubborn fingers and, surprised at a gentlemanly gesture that could never have

28

come from a pre-war fusilier trained in the old Prussian school and compelled in public to walk like clockwork, she asked with awe, 'Aren't you feared the sergeant will see you?'

'In this man's army,' he said.

He could be a Texan. It was diverting to study their accents and guess at States.

'In this man's army, sister, we don't keep sergeants.'

Suddenly happy, Arthur Broderick tripped along behind them, kicked at a stray pebble, sniffed at the good air until his way was blocked by the frail, discontented figure of Patrick who kept the public house beside the post-office and opposite the courthouse, and who sold the bog oak and blackthorn souvenirs to thirsty, sentimental soldiers.

'Lord God, Mr. Broderick,' said Patrick. 'Do you see that for discipline? Carrying a tin can like an errand boy.'

'But Patrick, child, it's idyllic. Deirdre in the hero tale couldn't have been more nobly treated by the three Ulster brothers, the sons of Uisneach. Hitler and Hirohito had to bring the doughboys over here before one of the Banty Mullans was handled like a lady.'

'Mr. Bee,' said Patrick, 'we all know you have odd ideas on what's what. But Mr. Bee, there must be a line of demarcation. Would you look across the street at that for soldiering?'

In sunshine that struggled hard, but failed, to brighten the old granite walls and Ionic columns of the courthouse the huge, coloured sentry had happily accepted the idea that for that day and in that village he did not have to deal with the Wehrmacht. Unlike the courthouse he looked as if he had been specially made by the sun. He sat relaxed on a chair, legs crossed, sharing a parcel of sandwiches with a trio of village children. Behind him on a stone ledge, his weapon of war was a votive offering at the feet of a bronze statue of a famous hanging judge who, irritated by the eczema of the droppings of lawless, irreverent birds, scowled like the Monster from Thirty Thousand Fathoms. Then clattering down the courthouse steps, came fifty young men, very much at ease. Falling into loose formation they went jauntily down the hilly street to the cookhouse at the bottom of the village. To the rhythm of their feet they played tunes with trays and table utensils.

'Their morale is high,' said Mr. Broderick.

Dark, hollow-cheeked, always complaining, persecuted by a corpulent wife, Patrick resented the young warriors with every bone in his small body. Some local wit had once said that he was a man constitutionally incapable of filling a glass to the brim.

'Those fellows, Mr. Bee, are better fed than yourself or myself.'

'They're young and growing, Patrick. They need it more. Besides, doesn't the best authority tell us an army marches on its belly?'

'They're pampered. Starve the Irish, Lord Kitchener said, and you'll have an army.'

'Ah, but Patrick the times have changed. I had the pleasure of serving under Lord Kitchener. But he never impressed me as a dietician.'

'Soft soles on their boots,' said Patrick, 'and their teeth glued together with chewing gum and all the girls in the country running wild since they came.'

'Life,' said Mr. Broderick, 'we can't suppress. Every woman worth breathing loves a warrior who's facing death.'

'Once upon a time,' Patrick said, 'your old friend, the Canon, made a rake of a fellow kneel at the church gate with a horse collar round his neck to do public penance for his rascalities with the girls.'

'Lothario in a leather frame, Patrick.'

Mr. Broderick laughed until his eyes were moist, at the memory and at the unquenchable misery in the diminutive, unloved, unloving heart of hen-pecked Patrick.

'Today, Patrick, there wouldn't be enough horse collars to go round. The horse isn't as plentiful as it was. The Canon had his foibles. He objected also to tam o'shanters and women riding bicycles. That was so long ago, Patrick. We'll drink to his memory.'

Everything, he thought as he left the public house and stepped on to the post-office, was so long ago. Patrick could hardly be described as part of the present. His lament was for days when heroes went hungry, when the fusiliers in the town below were forbidden by rule to stand chatting on the public street, were compelled to step rigidly, gloves like this, cane like that under the oxter – like a stick trussing a plucked chicken in a poulterer's shop. Patrick in his cave of a pub was a comic, melancholy, legendary dwarf. His one daring relaxation was to brighten the walls of his cave with coloured calendars of pretty girls caught with arms full of parcels and, by the snapping of some elastic or the betrayal of some hook or button, in mildly embarrassing situations. With startled but nevertheless smiling eyes they appealed to Patrick's customers.

'Your souvenirs sell well, Mr. Bee,' Patrick said. 'The pipes especially. But the sloe-stone rosary beads too. Although it puzzles me to make out what these wild fellows want with rosary beads.'

'They may have mothers at home, Patrick, who like keepsakes. They're far from home. They're even headed the other way.'

At the post-office the girl behind the brass grille said, 'Two letters, Mr. Broderick.'

He read the first one. The young scholar said that he had read with great interest of Mr. Broderick's interest in and his collection of folktales. He realised that folktales were often, curiously enough, not popular fare but he still considered that the publishers lacked vision and enterprise. He had only had his own book published because of the fortunate chance of his meeting a publisher who thought that he, the young scholar, might some day write a book that would be a moneymaker. The young scholar would also in the near future be visiting his native place. He thanked Mr. Broderick for his kind invitation and would take the liberty of calling on him.

The second letter came from an old colleague in the city of Belfast. It said: 'Arthur, old friend, yesterday I met a Major Michael F. X. Devaney – it would seem he has Irish ancestry – who has something or other to do with cultural relations between the U.S. troops and ourselves. He's hunting for folk-tales, local lore, to publish in book-form for the army. I thought of you. I took the liberty of arranging an appointment and of loaning him a copy of some of the stories you once loaned me.'

Mr. Broderick went to Belfast a few days later to keep the appointment. From the window of the major's office the vast, smoky bulk of the domed City Hall was visible. He turned from its impressive Victorian gloom to study the major, splendidly caparisoned as any hero who had ever lived in coloured tales told by country hearths.

'Mr. Broderick,' said the major, 'this is real contemporary.'

'Old tales, major, like old soldiers.'

'This spiked strand and burning mountain. I was in the Pacific, Mr. Broderick. This seven miles of treacherous sea. A few pages of glossary, Mr. Broderick. A few explanatory footnotes. How long would that take you?'

'A month, major. Say a month.'

'We'll settle for a month. Then we'll clinch the deal. These tales are exactly what we want, Mr. Broderick. Tell the boys something about the traditions of the place.'

He took the train home from the tense, overcrowded city to the garrison town in the valley. The market-day bus brought him up over the ridge to his own village. All that warm night the lorries on the steep street robbed him of his sparse, aged sleep as the troops moved; and they were gone in the morning, lock, stock and barrel, and on the far French coast the sons of the Kings of Antua and Soracha grappled until they made rocks of water and water of rocks, and the waves of the great metal birds of the air screamed over them.

High in the sky beyond Knocknashee one lone plane droned like a bee some cruel boy had imprisoned in a bottle to prevent it from joining the swarm. At his hushed doorway sad Patrick the publican looked aghast at the newspaper headlines and more aghast at the cold, empty courthouse that once had housed such thirsty young men.

'You'd swear to God,' he said, 'they were never here at all.'

Arthur Broderick left him to his confusion. He walked home under twisted yews, up the grass-grown avenue to his own smoky house. The heroes had gone, but the heroes would stay with him for ever. His children would stay with him for ever, but, in a way, it was a pity that he could never give his stories to all those fine young men.

'Come in,' Mr. Broderick said to the young scholar, 'you're welcome. There's nothing I'm prouder of than to see a young man from these parts doing well. And we know the same people. We have many friends in common.'

'Shawn of Kinsale,' the young scholar said, 'and the son of the King of Antua.'

'The three princesses,' said Mr. Broderick, 'and the White Hound of the Mountain.'

He reached out the hand of welcome to the young scholar.

'Publishing is slow,' the young man stammered. 'They have little vision...'

'Vision reminds me,' Mr. Broderick said. 'Do you mind smoke?'

He opened the drawing-room door. Smoke billowed out to the musty hallway.

'My poor stories,' he said. 'My poor heroes. They went away to the well at the world's end but they always came back. Once they came very close to enlisting in the U.S. army. That's a story I must tell you sometime.'

The manuscript of his tales lay between them on the table that had once been part of the rebel's bellows. Around them in the smoke were the grey shadows of heroic eighteenth-century men who, to fight tyranny, had forged steel pikes. And eastwards the heroes had swept that earth-shaking summer, over the treacherous mined sea, over the seven miles of spiked strand, over the seven and seventy miles of burning mountain.

# A Journey to the Seven Streams

My father, the heavens be his bed, was a terrible man for telling you about the places he had been and for bringing you there if he could and displaying them to you with a mild and gentle air of proprietorship. He couldn't do the showmanship so well in the case of Spion Kop where he and the fortunate ones who hadn't been ordered up the hill in the ignorant night had spent a sad morning crouching on African earth and listening to the deadly Boer guns that, high above the plain, slaughtered their hapless comrades. Nor yet in the case of Halifax nor the Barbadoes where he had heard words of Gaelic from coloured girls who were, he claimed, descended from the Irish transported into slavery in the days of Cromwell. The great glen of Aherlow, too, which he had helped to chain for His Majesty's Ordnance Survey, was placed inconveniently far to the South in the mystic land of Tipperary, and Cratloe Wood, where the fourth Earl of Leitrim was assassinated, was sixty miles away on the winding Donegal fjord called Mulroy Bay. But townlands like Corraheskin, Drumlish, Cornavara, Dooish, The Minnieburns and Claramore, and small towns like Drumquin and Dromore were all within a ten-mile radius of our town and something of moment or something amusing had happened in every one of them.

The reiterated music of their names worked on him like a charm. They would, he said, take faery tunes out

of the stone fiddle of Castle Caldwell; and indeed it was
the night he told us the story of the stone fiddle and the
drowned fiddler, and recited for us the inscription carved
on the fiddle in memory of the fiddler, that he decided to
hire a hackney car, a rare and daring thing to do in those
days, and bring us out to see in one round trip those
most adjacent places of his memories and dreams.

'In the year 1770 it happened,' he said. 'The landlord
at the time was Sir James Caldwell, Baronet. He was also
called the Count of Milan, why, I never found anybody
to tell me. The fiddler's name was Dennis McCabe and by
tradition the McCabes were always musicians and jesters
to the Caldwells. There was festivity at the Big House
by Lough Erne Shore and gentry there from near and
far, and out they went to drink and dance on a raft on
the lake, and wasn't the poor fiddler so drunk he fiddled
himself into the water and drowned.'

'Couldn't somebody have pulled him out, Da?'

'They were all as drunk as he was. The story was that
he was still sawing away with the bow when he came
up for the third time. The party cheered him until every
island in Lough Erne echoed and it was only when they
sobered up they realised they had lost the fiddler. So
the baronet and Count of Milan had a stone fiddle taller
than a man made to stand at the estate gate as a monument to Dennis McCabe and as a warning for ever to
fiddlers either to stay sober or to stay on dry land.

'Ye fiddlers beware, ye fiddler's fate,' my father recited.
'Don't attempt the deep lest ye repent too late. Keep to
the land when wind and storm blow, but scorn the deep
if it with whisky flow. On firm land only exercise your
skill; there you may play and safely drink your fill.'

Travelling by train from our town to the seaside
you went for miles along the green and glistening

Erne shore but the train didn't stop by the stone fiddle nor yet at the Boa island for the cross-roads' dances. Always when my father told us about those dances, his right foot rhythmically tapped and took music out of the polished steel fireside fender that had Home Sweet Home lettered out on an oval central panel. Only the magic motor, bound to no tracks, compelled to no fixed stopping places, could bring us to the fiddle or the crowded cross-roads.

'Next Sunday then,' he said, 'as certain as the sun sets and rises, we'll hire Hookey and Peter and the machine and head for Lough Erne.'

'Will it hold us all?' said my mother. 'Seven of us and Peter's big feet and the length of the driver's legs.'

'That machine,' he said, 'would hold the twelve apostles, the Connaught Rangers and the man who broke the bank at Monte Carlo. It's the size of a hearse.'

'Which is just what it looks like,' said the youngest of my three sisters who had a name for the tartness of her tongue.

She was a thin dark girl.

'Regardless of appearance,' he said, 'it'll carry us to the stone fiddle and on the way we'll circumnavigate the globe: Clanabogan, and Cavanacaw, Pigeon Top Mountain and Corraduine, where the barefooted priest said Mass at the Rock in the penal days and Corraheskin where the Muldoons live ...'

'Them,' said the third sister.

She had had little time for the Muldoons since the day their lack of savoir faire cost her a box of chocolates. A male member, flaxen-haired, pink-cheeked, aged sixteen, of those multitudinous Muldoons had come by horse and cart on a market day from his rural fastnesses to pay us a visit. Pitying his gaucherie, his shy animal-in-a-thicket appearance, his outback ways and gestures, she had grandly reached him a box of chocolates so as to sweeten his bitter lot with one honeyed morsel or two or, at the outside, three; but unaccustomed to towny ways and the mores of built-up areas the rural swain had appropriated the whole box.

'He thought,' she said, 'I was a paleface offering gifts to a Comanche.'

'But by their own hearth,' said my father, 'they're simple hospitable people.

'And Cornavara,' he said, 'and Dooish and Carrick Valley and your uncle Owen, and the two McCannys the pipers, and Claramore where there are so many Gormleys every family has to have its own nickname, and Drumquin where I met your mother, and Dromore where you' (pointing to me) 'were born and where the mail train was held up by the I.R.A. and where the three poor lads were murdered by the Specials when you' (again indicating me) 'were a year old, and the Minnieburns where the seven streams meet to make the head waters of the big river. Hookey and Peter and the machine will take us to all those places.'

'Like a magic carpet,' said my mother – with just a little dusting of the iron filings of doubt in her voice.

Those were the days, and not so long ago, when cars were rare and every car, not just every make of car, had a personality of its own. In our town with its population of five thousand, not counting the soldiers in the barracks, there were only three cars for hire and one of them was the love-child of the pioneer passion of Hookey Baxter for the machine. He was a long hangle of a young fellow, two-thirds of him made up of legs, and night and day he was whistling. He was as forward-looking as Lindbergh and he dressed like Lindbergh, for the air, in goggles, leather jacket and helmet; an appropriate costume, possibly, considering Hookey's own height and the altitude of the driver's seat in his machine. The one real love of his young heart was the love of the born tinkerer, the instinctive mechanic, for that hybrid car: the child of his frenzy, the fruit of days spent deep in grease giving new life and shape to a wreck he had bought at a sale in Belfast. The original manufacturers, whoever they had been, would have been hard put to it to recognise their altered offspring.

'She's chuman,' Peter Keown would say as he patted the sensitive quivering bonnet.

Peter meant human. In years to come his sole recorded comment on the antics of Adolf Hitler was that the man wasn't chuman.

'She's as nervous,' he would say, 'as a thoroughbred.'

The truth was that Peter, Hookey's stoker, greasemonkey and errand boy, was somewhat in awe of the tall rangy metal animal, yet wherever the car went, with the tall goggled pilot at the wheel, there the pilot's diminutive mate was also sure to go. What living Peter earned he earned by digging holes in the street as a labouring man for the town council's official plumber so that, except on Sundays and when he motored with Hookey, nobody in the town ever saw much of him but the top of his cloth cap or his upturned face when he'd look up from the hole in the ground to ask a passer-by the time of day. Regularly once a year he spent a corrective month in Derry Jail, because his opportunities as a municipal employee and his weakness as a kleptomaniac meant that good boards, lengths of piping, coils of electric wire, monkey wrenches, spades, and other movable properties faded too frequently into thin air.

'A wonderful man, poor Peter,' my father would say. 'That cloth cap with the turned up peak. And the thick-lensed, thin-rimmed spectacles – he's half-blind – and the old tweed jacket too tight for him, and the old Oxford-bag trousers too big for him, and his shrill voice and his waddle of a walk that makes him look always like a duck about to apologise for laying a hen-egg. How he survives is a miracle of God's grace. He can resist the appeal of nothing that's portable.'

'He's a dream,' said the third sister. 'And the feet are the biggest part of him.'

'The last time he went to Derry,' said my brother, 'all the old women from Brook Street and the lanes were at the top of the Courthouse Hill to cheer him as he passed.'

'And why not?' said my mother. 'They're fond of him and they say he's well-liked in the jail. His heart's as big as his feet. Everything he steals he gives away.'

'Robin Hood,' said the third sister. 'Robbing the town council to pay Brook Street.'

'The Council wouldn't sack him,' said my eldest sister, 'if he stole the town.'

'At the ready,' roared my father. 'Prepare to receive cavalry.'

In the street below the house there was a clanking, puffing, grinding tumult.

'God bless us, look at Peter,' said my father. 'Aloft with Hookey like a crown prince beside a king. Are we all ready? Annie, Ita, May, George, yourself ma'am, and you the youngest of us all. Have we the sandwiches and the flasks of tea and the lemonade? Forward.'

A lovelier Sunday morning never shone. With the hood down and the high body glistening after its Saturday wash and polish, the radiator gently steaming, the car stood at the foot of the seven steps that led down from our door. The stragglers coming home from early mass, and the devout setting off early for late mass had gathered in groups to witness our embarkation. Led by my father and in single file, we descended the steps and ascended nearly as high again to take our lofty places in the machine.

There was something of the Citroën in the quivering mongrel, in the yellow canvas hood now reclining in voluminous ballooning folds, in the broad back-seat that could hold five fair-sized people. But to judge by the radiator, the absence of gears, and the high fragile-spoked wheels, Citroën blood had been crossed with that of the Model T. After that, any efforts to spot family traits would have brought confusion on the thought of the greatest living authorities. The thick slanting glass windscreen could have been wrenched from a limousine designed to divert bullets from Balkan princelings. The general colour-scheme, considerably chipped and cracked, was canary yellow. And there was Hookey at the wheel, then my brother and father, and Peter on the outside left where he could leap in and out to perform the menial duties of assistant engineer; and in the wide and windy acres of the back seat, my mother, myself and my three sisters.

High above the town the church bell rang. It was the bell to warn the worshippers still on their way that in ten minutes the vested priest would be on the altar but, as it coincided with our setting out, it could have been a quayside bell ringing farewell to a ship nosing out across the water towards the rim of vision.

Peter leaped to the ground, removed the two stones that, blocked before the front wheels, acted as auxiliaries for the hand brake. Hookey released the brake. The car was gathering speed when Peter scrambled aboard, settled himself and slammed the yellow door behind him. Sparing fuel, we glided down the slope, back-fired twice loudly enough to drown the sound of the church bell, swung left along John Street and cleared the town without incident. Hands waved from watching groups of people but because this was no trivial event there were no laughs, no wanton cheers. The sound of the bell died away behind us. My mother expressed the hope that the priest would remember us at the offertory. Peter assured her that we were all as safe as if we were at home in bed. God's good green Sunday countryside was softly all around us.

Squat to the earth and travelling at seventy you see nothing from cars nowadays, but to go with Hookey was to be above all but the highest walls and hedges, to be among the morning birds.

'Twenty-seven em pee haitch,' said Hookey.

'Four miles covered already,' said Peter.

'The Gortin Mountains over there,' said my father. 'And the two mountains to the north are Bessy Bell and Mary Grey, so named by the Hamiltons of Baronscourt, the Duke of Abercorn's people, after a fancied resemblance to two hills in Stirlingshire, Scotland. The two hills in Stirlingshire are so called after two ladies of the Scottish court who fled the plague and built their hut in the wild wood and thatched it o'er with rushes. They are mentioned by Thomas Carlyle in his book on the French Revolution. The dark green on the hills by Gortin Gap is the new government forestry. And in Gortin village Paddy Ford the contractor hasn't gone to mass since, fifteen years ago, the parish priest gave another man the job of painting the inside of the sacristy.'

'No paint no prayers,' said the third sister.

'They're strange people in Gortin,' my mother said.

'It's proverbial,' said my father, 'that they're to be distinguished anywhere by the bigness of their backsides.'

'Five miles,' said Peter. 'They're spinning past.'

'Running sweet as honey,' said Hookey.

He adjusted his goggles and whistled back to the Sunday birds.

'Jamie Magee's of the Flush,' said my father.

He pointed to a long white house on a hill slope and close to a waterfalling stream.

'Rich as Rockefeller and too damned mean to marry.'

'Who in heaven would have him,' said the third sister.

'Six miles,' said Peter.

Then, with a blast of backfiring that rose my mother a foot in the air, the wobbling yellow conveyance came to a coughing miserable halt. The air was suddenly grey and poisoned with fumes.

'It's her big end, Hookey,' said Peter.

'She's from Gortin so,' said the third sister.

The other two sisters, tall and long-haired and normally quiet girls, went off at the deep end into the giggles.

'Isn't it providential,' said my mother, 'that the cowslips are a glory this year? We'll have something to do, Henry, while you're fixing it.'

Hookey had been christened Henry, and my mother would never descend to nicknames. She felt that to make use of a nickname was to remind a deformed person of his deformity. Nor would she say even of the town's chief inebriate that he was ever drunk: he was either under the influence or he had a drop too many taken. She was, my mother, the last great Victorian euphemiser.

'We won't be a jiffy, ma'am,' said Hookey. 'It's nothing so serious as a big end.'

The three sisters were convulsed.

The fields and the roadside margins were bright yellow with blossom.

'Gather ye cowslips while you may,' said my father.

He handed the ladies down from the dizzy heights. Peter had already disembarked. Submitting to an impulse that had gnawed at me since we set sail I dived forwards, my head under Hookey's left elbow, and butted with both fists the black, rubber, punch-ball horn; and out over the fields to startle birds and grazing cattle went the dying groan of a pained diseased ox.

'Mother of God,' said my father, 'that's a noise and no mistake. Here boy, go off and pick flowers.'

He lifted me down to the ground.

'Screw off the radiator cap, Peter,' said Hookey.

'It's scalding hot, Hookey.'

'Take these gauntlet gloves, manalive. And stand clear when you screw it off.'

A geyser of steam and dirty hot water went heavenwards as Peter and my brother, who was always curious about engines, leaped to safety.

'Wonderful,' said my father to my brother, 'the age we live in. They say that over in England they're queued up steaming by the roadsides, like Iceland or the Yellowstone Park.'

'Just a bit overheated,' said Hookey. 'We won't be a jiffy.'

'Does it happen often?' said my father.

Ignoring the question, descending and opening the bonnet to peer and poke and tinker, Hookey said, 'Do you know a funny thing about this car?'

'She's chuman,' said Peter.

'You know the cross-roads at Clanabogan churchyard gate,' Hookey said. 'The story about it.'

'It's haunted,' said my father.

'Only at midnight,' said Peter.

As was his right and custom, my father stepped into the role of raconteur. 'Do you know that no horse ever passed there at midnight that didn't stop – shivering with fear? The fact is well attested. Something comes down that side road out of the heart of the wood.'

Hookey closed over the bonnet, screwed back the radiator cap and climbed again to the throne. He wiped his hands on a bunch of grass pulled for him and handed to him by Peter. Slowly he drew on again his gauntlet gloves. Bedecked with cowslips and dragging me along with them the ladies rejoined the gentlemen.

'Well, would you credit this now,' Hookey said. 'Peter and myself were coming from Dromore one wet night last week.'

'Pouring rain from the heavens,' said Peter, 'and the hood was leaking.'

'A temporary defect,' said Hookey. 'I mended it. Jack up the back axle, Peter, and give her a swing. And would you credit it, exactly at twelve o'clock midnight she stopped dead at the gate of Clanabogan churchyard?'

With an irony that was lost on Hookey my mother said, 'I could well believe it.'

'She's chuman,' said Peter.

'One good push now and we're away,' said Hookey. 'The slight gradient is in our favour.'

'Maybe,' he said to my father and brother, 'you'd lend Peter a hand.'

Twenty yards ahead he waited for the dusty pushers to climb aboard, the engine chug-chugging, little puffs of steam escaping like baby genii from the right-hand side of the bonnet. My father was thoughtful. He could have been considering the responsibilities of the machine age particularly because when it came to team pushing Peter was more of a cheer leader, an exhorter, a counter of one two three, than an actual motive force.

'Contact,' said Hookey.

'Dawn patrol away,' said Peter. 'Squadron Leader Baxter at the joystick.'

He mimicked what he supposed to be the noises of an aeroplane engine and, with every evidence of jubilation, we were once again under way; and a day it was, made by the good God for jubilation. The fields, all the colours of all the crops, danced towards us and away from us and around us; and the lambs on the green hills, my father sang, were gazing at me and many a strawberry grows by the salt sea, and many a ship sails the ocean. The roadside trees bowed down and then gracefully swung their arms up and made music over our heads and there were more birds and white cottages and fuchsia hedges in the world than you would readily imagine.

'The bride and bride's party,' sang my father, 'to church they did go. The bride she goes foremost, she bears the best show...'

'They're having sports today at Tattysallagh,' said Hookey.

'But I followed after my heart full of woe, for to see my love wed to another.'

We swept by a cross-roads where people and horses and traps were congregated after the last mass. In a field beside the road a few tall ash plants bore fluttering pennants in token of the sports to be.

'Proceed to Banteer,' sang my father, 'to the athletic sporting and hand in your name to the club comm-i-tee.

'That was a favourite song of Pat O'Leary the Corkman,' he said, 'who was killed at Spion Kop.'

Small country boys in big boots, knickerbockers, stiff celluloid collars that could be cleaned for Sunday by a rub of a wet cloth, and close-cropped heads with fringes like scalping locks above the foreheads, scattered before us to the hedges and the grass margins, then closed again like water divided and rejoining, and pursued us, cheering, for a hundred yards. One of them, frantic with enthusiasm, sent sailing after us a half-grown turnip, which bounced along the road for a bit, then sought rest in a roadside drain. Looking backwards I pulled my best or worst faces at the rustic throng of runners.

'In Tattysallagh,' said my father, 'they were always an uncivilised crowd of gulpins.'

He had three terms of contempt: Gulpin, Yob and, when things became very bad he became Swiftian, and described all offenders as Yahoos.

'Cavanacaw,' he said, 'and that lovely trout stream, the Creevan Burn. It joins the big river at Blacksessiagh. That there's the road up to Pigeon Top Mountain and the mass rock at Corraduine, but we'll come back that way when we've circumnavigated Dooish and Cornavara.'

We came to Clanabogan.

'Clanabogan planting,' he said.

The tall trees came around us and sunlight and shadow flickered so that you could feel them across eyes and hands and face.

'Martin Murphy the postman,' he said, 'who was in the survey with me in Virginia, County Cavan, by Lough Ramor, and in the Glen of Aherlow, worked for a while at the building of Clanabogan Church. One day the vicar said to him: "What height do you think the steeple should be?" "The height of nonsense like your sermons," said Martin, and got the sack for his wit. In frosty weather he used to seal the cracks in his boots with butter and although he was an abrupt man he seldom used an impolite word. Once when he was aggravated by the bad play of his wife who was partnering him at whist he said: "Maria, dearly as I love you, there are yet moments when you'd incline a man to kick his own posterior".

'There's the church,' my father said, 'and the churchyard and the haunted gate and the cross-roads.'

We held our breath but, with honeyed summer all around us and bees in the tender limes, it was no day for ghosts, and in glory we sailed by.

'She didn't hesitate,' said Peter.

'Wonderful,' said the third sister.

It was more wonderful than she imagined for, as the Lord would have it, the haunted gate and cross-roads of Clanabogan was one of the few places that day that Hookey's motor machine did not honour with at least some brief delay.


'I'd love to drive,' said my brother. 'How did you learn to drive, Hookey?'

'I never did. I just sat in and drove. I learned the basic principles on the county council steamroller in Watson's quarries. Forward and reverse.'

'You have to have the natural knack,' Peter explained.

'What's the cut potato for, Hookey?' asked my brother.

'For the rainy day. Rub it on the windscreen and the water runs off the glass.'

'It's oily you see,' said Peter.

'Like a duck's back,' said the third sister.

'Where,' said my father – sniffing, 'do you keep the petrol?'

'Reserve in the tins clipped on the running board. Current supply, six gallons. You're sitting on it. In a tank under the front seat.'

'Twenty miles to the gallon,' said Peter. 'We're good for more than a hundred miles.'

'Godalmighty,' said my father. 'Provided it isn't a hundred miles straight up. 'Twould be sad to survive a war that was the end of better men and to be blown up between Clanabogan and Cornavara. On a quiet Sunday morning.'

'Never worry,' said Hookey. 'It's outside the bounds of possibility.'

'You reassure me,' said my father. 'Twenty miles to the gallon in any direction. What care we? At least we'll all go up together. No survivors to mourn in misery.'

'And turn right here,' he said, 'for Cornavara. You'll soon see the hills and the high waterfalls.'

We left the tarred road. White dust rose around us like smoke. We advanced half a mile on the flat, attempted the first steep hill and gently, wearily, without angry fumes or backfiring protests, the tremulous chuman car, lying down like a tired child, came to rest.

'We'll hold what we have,' said Hookey. 'Peter … pronto. Get the stones behind the back wheels.'

'Think of a new pastime,' said the third sister. 'We have enough cowslips to decorate the town for a procession.'

With the sweet face of girlish simplicity she asked, 'Do you buy the stones with the car?'

'We'd be worse off without them,' Hookey muttered.

Disguised as he was in helmet and goggles it was impossible to tell exactly if his creative soul was or was not wounded by her hint of mockery, but my mother must have considered that his voice betrayed pain for she looked reprovingly at the third sister and at the other two who were again impaled by giggles, and withdrew them out of sight down a boreen towards the sound of a small stream, to – as she put it – freshen up.

'Without these stones,' Peter panted, 'we could be as badly off as John MacKenna and look what happened to him.'

'They're necessary precautions,' said Hookey. 'Poor John would never use stones. He said the brakes on his car would hold a Zeppelin.'

The bonnet was open again and the radiator cap unscrewed but there was no steam and no geyser, only a cold sad silence, and Hookey bending and peering and probing with pincers.

'She's a bit exhausted,' Peter said.

'It's simple,' Hookey said. 'She'll be right as rain in a jiffy. Going at the hill with a full load overstrained her.'

'We should walk the bad hills,' Peter explained.

'Poor John MacKenna,' Hookey said, 'was making four fortunes drawing crowds to the Passionist monastery at Enniskillen to see the monk that cures the people. But he would never use the stones, and the only parking place at the monastery is on a sharp slope. And one evening when they were all at devotions doesn't she run backways and ruin all the flower-beds in the place and knock down a statue of Our Lord.'

'One of the monks attacked him,' said Peter, 'as a heathen that would knock the Lord down.'

'Ruined the trade for all,' said Hookey. 'The monks now won't let a car within a mile of the place.'

'Can't say as I blame them,' said my father.

'Poor John took it bad,' said Hookey. 'The lecture he got and all. He was always a religious man. They say he raises his hat now every time he passes any statue: even the Boer War one in front of the courthouse.'

'So well he might,' said my father.

Suddenly, mysteriously responding to Hookey's probing pincers, the very soul of the machine was again chug-chugging. But with or without cargo she could not, or, being weary and chuman, would not assault even the first bastion of Cornavara.

'She won't take off,' said Hookey. 'That run to Belfast and back took the wind out of her.'

'You never made Belfast,' said my father, 'in this.'

'We did, Tommy,' said Peter apologetically.

'Seventy miles there and seventy back,' said my father incredulously.

'Bringing a greyhound bitch to running trials for Tommy Mullan the postman,' said Hookey.

'The man who fishes for pearls in the Drumragh river,' said Peter.

They were talking hard to cover their humiliation.

'If she won't go at the hills,' my father said, 'go back to the main road and we'll go on and picnic at the seven streams at the Minnieburns. It's mostly on the flat.'

So we reversed slowly the dusty half-mile to the main road.

'One night in John Street,' Peter said, 'she started going backways and wouldn't go forwards.'

'A simple defect,' Hookey said. 'I remedied it.'

'Did you turn the other way?' asked the third sister.

Artlessly, Peter confessed, 'She stopped when she knocked down the schoolchildren-crossing sign at the bottom of Church Hill. Nipped it off an inch from the ground, as neat as you ever saw. We hid it up a laneway and it was gone in the morning.'

My father looked doubtfully at Peter. He said, 'One of those nice shiny enamelled pictures of two children crossing the road would go well as an overmantel. And the wood of the post would always make firewood.'

Peter agreed, 'You can trust nobody.'

Hurriedly trying to cut in on Peter's eloquence, Hookey said, 'In fact the name of Tommy Mullan's bitch was Drumragh Pearl. Not that that did her any good at the trials.'

'She came a bad last,' burst out the irrepressible Peter.

'And to make it worse we lost her on the way back from Belfast.'

'You what?' said my father.

'Lost her in the dark where the road twists around Ballymacilroy Mountain.'

My mother was awed, 'You lost the man's greyhound. You're a right pair of boys to send on an errand.'

''Twas the way we stepped out of the car to take the air,' said Hookey.

By the husky note in his voice you could guess how his soul suffered at Peter's shameless confessions.

'And Peter looked at the animal, ma'am, and said maybe she'd like a turn in the air too. So we took her out and tied her lead to the left front wheel. And while we were standing there talking didn't the biggest brute of a hare you ever saw sit out as cool as sixpence in the light of the car. Off like a shot with the bitch.'

'If the lead hadn't snapped,' Peter said, 'she'd have taken the wheel off the car or the car off the road.'

'That would have been no great exertion,' said my father. 'We should have brought a greyhound along with us to pull.'

'We whistled and called for hours but all in vain,' said Peter.

'The hare ate her,' said the third sister.

'Left up the slope there,' said my father, 'is the belt of trees I planted in my spare time to act as a wind-breaker for Drumlish schoolhouse. Paddy Hamish, the labouring man, gave me a hand. He died last year in Canada.'

'You'd have pitied the children on a winter's day,' my mother said, 'standing in the playground at lunchtime taking the fresh air in a hilltop wind that would sift and cut corn. Eating soda bread and washing it down with buttermilk. On a rough day the wind from Lough Erne would break the panes of the windows.'

'As a matter of curiosity,' my father said, 'what did Tommy Mullan say?'

'At two in the morning in Bridge Lane,' said Peter, 'he was waiting for us. We weren't too happy about it. But when we told him she was last in the trials he said the bloody bitch could stay in Ballymacilroy.'

'Hasn't he always the pearls in the river,' my mother said.

So we came to have tea and sandwiches and lemonade in a meadow by the cross-roads in the exact centre of the wide saucer of land where seven streams from the surrounding hills came down to meet. The grass was polished with sunshine. The perfume of the meadowsweet is with me still. That plain seemed to me then as vast as the prairies, or Siberia. White cottages far away on the lower slopes of Dooish could have been in another country. The chief stream came for a long way through soft deep meadowland. It was slow, quiet, unobtrusive, perturbed only by the movements of water fowl or trout. Two streams met, wonder of wonders, under the arch of a bridge and you could go out under the bridge along a sandy promontory to paddle in clear water on a bottom as smooth as Bundoran strand. Three streams came together in a magic hazel wood where the tiny green unripe nuts were already clustered on the branches. Then the seven made into one, went away from us with a shout and a song towards Shaneragh, Blacksessiagh, Drumragh and Crevenagh, under the humpy crooked King's Bridge where James Stuart had passed on his way from Derry to the fatal brackish Boyne, and on through the town we came from.

'All the things we could see,' said my father, 'if this spavined brute of a so-called automobile could only be persuaded to climb the high hills. The deep lakes of Claramore. The far view of Mount Errigal, the Cock of the North, by the Donegal sea. If you were up on the top of Errigal you could damn' near see, on a clear day, the skyscrapers of New York.'

In his poetic imagination the towers of Atlantis rose glimmering from the deep.

'What matter,' said my mother. 'The peace of heaven is here.'

For that day that was the last peace we were to experience. The energy the machine didn't have or wouldn't use to climb hills or to keep in motion for more than two miles at a stretch, she expended in thunderous staccato bursts of backfiring. In slanting evening sunlight people at the doors of distant farmhouses shaded their eyes to look towards the travelling commotion, or ran up whinny hills for a better view, and horses and cattle raced madly around pastures, and my mother said the country would never be the same again, that the shock of the noise would turn the milk in the udders of the cows. When we came again to the crossroads of Tattysallagh the majority of the spectators, standing on the road to look over the hedge and thus save the admission fee, lost all interest in the sports, such as they were, and came around us. To oblige them the right rear tyre went flat.

'Peter,' said Hookey, 'jack it up and change it on.'

We mingled unobtrusively with the gulpins.

'A neat round hole,' said Peter.

'Paste a patch on it.'

The patch was deftly pasted on.

'Take the foot pump and blow her up,' said Hookey.

There was a long silence while Peter, lines of worry on his little puckered face, inspected the tube. Then he said. 'I can't find the valve.'

'Show it to me,' said Hookey.

He ungoggled himself, descended and surveyed the ailing member.

'Peter,' he said, 'you're a prize. The valve's gone and you put a patch on the hole it left behind it.'

The crowd around us was increasing and highly appreciative.

'Borrow a bicycle, Peter,' said Hookey, 'cycle to the town and ask John MacKenna for the loan of a tube.'

'To pass the time,' said my mother, 'we'll look at the sports.'

So we left Hookey to mind his car and, being practically gentry as compared with the rustic throng around us, we walked to the gateway that led into the sportsfield where my mother civilly enquired of two men, who stood behind a wooden table, the price of admission.

'Five shillings a skull missus, barring the cub,' said the younger of the two. 'And half a crown for the cub.'

'For the what?' said my mother.

'For the little boy, ma'am,' said the elder of the two.

'It seems expensive,' said my mother.

'I'd see them all in hell first – let alone in Tattysallagh,' my father said. 'One pound, twelve shillings and sixpence to look at six sally rods stuck in a field and four yahoos running round in rings in their sock soles.'

We took our places on the roadside with the few who, faithful to athletics and undistracted by the novelty of the machine, were still looking over the hedge. Four lean youths and one stout one in Sunday shirts and long trousers with the ends tucked into their socks were pushing high-framed bicycles round and round the field. My father recalled the occasion in Virginia, County Cavan, when Martin Murphy was to run at sports and his wife Maria stiffened his shirt so much with starch it wouldn't go inside his trousers, and when he protested she said, 'Martin, leave it outside and you will be able to fly.'

We saw two bicycle races and a tug-of-war.

'Hallions and clifts,' he said.

Those were two words he seldom used.

'Yobs and sons of yobs,' he said.

He led us back to the car. Peter soaked in perspiration had the new tube on and the wheel ready.

'Leave the jack in and swing her,' Hookey said. 'She's cold by now.'

There was a series of explosions that sent gulpins, yobs and yahoos reeling backwards in alarm. Peter screwed out the jack. We scrambled aboard, a few of the braver among the decent people, rushing into the line of fire to lend a hand to the ladies. Exploding, we departed, and when we were a safe distance away the watchers raised a dubious cheer.

'In God's name, Henry,' said my father, 'get close to the town before you blow us all up. I wouldn't want our neighbours to have to travel as far as Tattysallagh to pick up the bits. And the yobs and yahoos here don't know us well enough to be able to piece us together.'

Three miles further on Peter blushingly confessed that in the frantic haste of embarkation he had left the jack on the road.

'I'll buy you a new one, Henry,' my father said. 'Or perhaps Peter here could procure one on the side. By now at any rate, they're shoeing jackasses with it in Tattysallagh.

'A pity in a way,' he said, 'we didn't make as far as the stone fiddle. We might have heard good music. It's a curious thing that in the townlands around that place the people have always been famed for music and singing. The Tunneys of Castle Caldwell now are noted. It could be that the magic of the stone fiddle has something to do with it.'

'Some day,' he said, 'we'll head for Donegal. When the cars, Henry, are a bit improved.'

He told us about the long windings of Mulroy Bay. He explained exactly how and why and in what year the fourth Earl of Leitrim had been assassinated in Cratloe Wood. He spoke as rapidly and distinctly as he could in the lulls of the backfiring.

Then our town was below us in the hollow and the Gortin mountains, deep purple with evening, away behind it.

'Here we'll part company, Henry boy,' said my father. ''Tisn't that I doubt the ability of Peter and yourself to navigate the iron horse down the hill. But I won't have the town blaming me and my family for having hand, act or part in the waking of the dead in Drumragh graveyard.'

Sedately we walked down the slope into the town and talked with the neighbours we met and asked them had they heard Hookey and Peter passing and told them of the sports and of the heavenly day it had been out at the seven streams.

My father died in a seaside town in the County Donegal – forty miles from the town I was reared in. The road his funeral followed back to the home places led along the Erne shore by the stone fiddle and the glistening water, across the Boa Island where there are no longer crossroads dances. Every roadside house has a television aerial. It led by the meadowland saucer of the Minnieburns where the river still springs from seven magic sources. That brooding place is still much as it was but no longer did it seem to me to be as vast as Siberia. To the left was the low sullen outline of Cornavara and

Pigeon Top, the hurdle that our Bucephalus refused to take. To the right was Drumlish. The old schoolhouse was gone and in its place a white building, ten times as large, with drying rooms for wet coats, fine warm lunches for children and even a gymnasium. But the belt of trees that he and Paddy Hamish planted to break the wind and shelter the children is still there.

Somebody tells me, too, that the engine of Hookey Baxter's car is still with us, turning a circular saw for a farmer in the vicinity of Clanabogan.

As the Irish proverb says: It's a little thing doesn't last longer than a man.

# Homes on the Mountain

The year I was twelve my father, my mother, my brother and myself had our Christmas dinner in the house my godmother's husband had built high up on the side of Dooish Mountain, when he and she came home to Ireland from Philadelphia.

That was a great godmother. She had more half-crowns in her patch pockets than there were in the Bank of England and every time she encountered me which, strategically, I saw was pretty often, it rained half-crowns. Those silver showers made my friend Lanty and myself the most popular boy bravados in our town. A curious thing was, though, that while we stood bobby-dazzler caramels, hazelnut chocolate, ice cream, cigarettes and fish and chips by the ton to our sycophants, we ourselves bought nothing but song-books. Neither of us could sing a note.

We had a splendid, patriotic taste in song-books, principally because the nearest newsagent's shop, kept by an old spinster in Devlin Street, had a window occupied by a sleeping tomcat, two empty tin boxes, bundles of pamphlets yellowed by exposure to the light, and all members of a series called Irish Fireside Songs. The collective title appealed by its warm cosiness. The little books were classified into Sentimental, Patriot's Treasury, Humorous and Convivial, and Smiles and Tears. Erin, we knew from Tom Moore and from excruciating music lessons at school, went wandering around with a tear and a smile blended in her eye. Because even to ourselves our singing was painful, we read together, sitting in the sunshine on the steps that led up to my father's house, such gems of the Humorous and Convivial as: 'When I lived in Sweet Ballinacrazy, dear, the girls were all bright as a daisy, dear.' Or turning to the emerald-covered Patriot's Treasury we intoned: 'We've men from the Nore, from the Suir and the Shannon, let the tyrant come forth, we'll bring force against force.'

Perhaps, unknown to ourselves, we were affected with the nostalgia that had brought my godmother and her husband back from the comfort of Philadelphia to the bleak side of Dooish Mountain. It was a move that my mother, who was practical and who had never been far enough from Ireland to feel nostalgia, deplored.

'Returned Americans,' she would say, 'are lost people. They live between two worlds. Their heads are in the clouds. Even the scrawny, black-headed sheep – not comparing the human being and the brute beast – know by now that Dooish is no place to live.'

'And if you must go back to the land,' she said, 'let it be the land, not rocks, heather and grey fields no bigger than pocket handkerchiefs. There's Cantwell's fine place beside the town going up for auction. Seventy acres of land, a palace of a dwelling-house, outhouses would do credit to the royal family, every modern convenience and more besides.'

For reasons that had nothing to do with prudence or sense, Lanty and myself thought the Cantwell place an excellent idea. There were crabapple trees of the most amazing fertility scattered all along the hedgerows on the farm; a clear gravel stream twisted through it; there were flat pastures made for football and, behind the house, an orchard that not even the most daring buccaneer of our generation had ever succeeded in robbing.

But there were other reasons – again nostalgic reasons – why my godmother's husband, who was the living image of Will Rogers, would build nowhere in Ireland except on the rough, wet side of Dooish, and there, on the site of the old home where he had spent his boyhood, the house went up. There wasn't a building job like it since the building of the Tower of Babel.

'Get a good sensible contractor from the town,' said my mother, 'not drunken Dan Redmond from the mountain who couldn't build a dry closet.'

But my godmother's husband had gone to school with Dan Redmond. They had been barefooted boys together and that was that, and there was more spent, according to my mother, on malt whisky to entertain Dan, his tradesmen and labourers, than would have built half New York. To make matters worse it was a great season for returned Americans and every one of them seemed to have known my godmother and her husband in Philadelphia. They came in their legions to watch the building, to help pass the bottle and to proffer advice. The acknowledged queen of this gathering of souls fluttering between two worlds was my Aunt Brigid, my mother's eldest sister. She was tiny and neat, precise in her speech, silver-haired, glittering with rimless spectacles and jet-black beads. In the States she had acquired a mania for euchre, a passion for slivers of chicken jelled in grey-green soup, a phonograph with records that included a set of the favourite songs of Jimmy Walker, and the largest collection of snapshots ever carried by pack mule or public transport out of Atlantic City.

Then there was a born American – a rarity in our parts in those days – a young man and a distant relative.

Generous and jovial, he kissed every woman, young or old, calling them cousin or aunt; but it was suspected among wise observers that he never once in the course of his visit was able to see the Emerald Isle clearly. For the delegation, headed by my Aunt Brigid, that met him in Dublin set him straight away on the drink and when he arrived to view the building site – it was one of the few sunny days of that summer – he did so sitting on the dickey seat of a jaunting car and waving in each hand a bottle of whisky. The builder and his men and the hay-makers in June meadows left their work to welcome him, and Ireland, as the song says, was Ireland through joy and through tears.

Altogether it was a wet season: the whisky flowed like water, the mist was low over the rocks and heather of Dooish and the moors of Loughfresha and Cornavara, the mountain runnels were roaring torrents. But miracu-lously the building was done; the returned Americans with the exception of, Aunt Brigid, my godmother and her husband, went westwards again in the fall; and against all my mother's advice on the point of health, the couple from Philadelphia settled in for late November. The house-warming was fixed for Christmas Day.

'Dreamers,' my mother said. 'An American apartment on the ground-walls of an old cabin. Living in the past. Up where only a brave man would build a shooting lodge. For all they know or care there could be wolves still on the mountain. Magazines and gewgaws and chairs too low to sit on. With the rheumatism the mountain'll give them, they'll never bend their joints to sit down so low.'

Since the damp air had not yet brought its rheuma-tism we all sat down together in the house that was the answer to the exile's dream. Lamplight shone on good silver and Belfast linen. My godmother's man was proud to the point of tears.

'Sara Alice,' he said to my mother.

Content, glass in hand, he was more than ever like Will Rogers.

'Sara Alice,' he said. 'My mother, God rest her, would be proud to see this day.'

Practicality momentarily abandoned, my mother, moist-eyed and sipping sherry, agreed.

'Tommy,' he said to my father, 'listen to the sound of the spring outside.'

We could hear the wind, the voices of the runnels, the spring pouring clear and cool from a rainspout driven into a rock-face.

'As far as I recollect, that was the first sound my ears ever heard, and I heard it all my boyhood, and I could hear it still in Girard Avenue, Philadelphia. But the voices of children used to be part of the sound of the spring. Seven of us, and me to be the youngest and the last alive. When my mother died and my father took us all to the States we didn't know when we were going away whether to leave the door open or closed. We left it open in case a travelling man might pass, needing shelter. We knocked gaps in the hedges and stone walls so as to give the neighbours' cattle the benefit of commonage and the land the benefit of the cow dung. But we left the basic lines of the walls so that nobody could forget our name or our claim to this part of the mountain.'

'In Gartan, in Donegal,' said my father, 'there's a place called the Flagstone of Loneliness where Saint Colmcille slept the night before he left Ireland under sentence of banishment. The exiles in that part used to lie down there the day before they sailed and pray to the saint to be preserved from the pangs of homesickness.'

My Aunt Brigid piped in a birdlike voice a bit of an exile song that was among her treasured recordings: 'A strange sort of sigh seems to come from us all as the waves hide the last glimpse of old Donegal.'

'Our American wake was held in Aunt Sally O'Neill's across the glen,' said my godmother's husband. 'Red Owen Gormley lilted for the dancers when the fiddlers were tired. He was the best man of his time at the mouth music.'

'He was also,' said my father, 'the first and last man I knew who could make a serviceable knife, blade and haft out of a single piece of hardwood. I saw him do it, myself and wild Martin Murphy who was with me in the crowd of sappers who chained these mountains for the 1911 Ordnance Survey map. Like most of us, Martin drank every penny and on frosty days he would seal the cracks in his shoes with butter – a trick I never saw another man use. It worked too.'

'Aunt Sally's two sons were there at our American wake,' said my godmother's husband. 'Thady that was never quite right in the head and, you remember, Tommy, couldn't let a woman in the market or a salmon in the stream alone. John, the elder brother, was there with Bessy from Cornavara that he wooed for sixty years and never, I'd say, even kissed.'

The old people were silently laughing. My brother, older than myself, was on the fringe of the joke. As my godmother came and went I sniffed fine cooking. I listened to the mountain wind and the noise of the spring and turned the bright pages of an American gardening magazine. Here were rare blooms would never grow on Dooish Mountain.

'All dead now I suppose,' my father said to end the laughing.

'Bessy's dead now,' said my Aunt Brigid. 'Two years ago. As single as the day she was born. Like many another Irishman, John wasn't overgiven to matrimony. But in the village of Crooked Bridge below, the postman told me that John and Thady are still alive in the old house on Loughfresha. Like pigs in a sty, he said. Pigs in a sty. And eight thousand pounds each, according to all accounts, in the Munster and Leinster Bank in the town.'

'God help us,' said my mother. 'I recall that house as it was when Aunt Sally was alive. It was beautiful.'

My father was looking out of the window, down the lower grey slopes of Dooish and across the deep glen towards Loughfresha and Cornavara.

'It won't rain again before dark or dinner,' he said. 'I haven't walked these hills since I carried a chain for His Majesty's Ordnance Survey. Who'd ever have thought the King of England would be interested in the extent of Cornavara or Dooish Mountain.'

'Get up, you two boys,' he said, 'and we'll see if you can walk as well as your father before you.'

The overflow of the spring came with us as we descended the boreen. Winter rain had already rutted the new gravel laid by drunken Dan Redmond and his merry men. Below the bare apple-orchard the spring's overflow met with another runnel and with yet another where another boreen, overgrown with hawthorn and bramble, struggled upwards to an abandoned house.

'Some people,' said my father, 'didn't come back to face the mountain. Living in Philadelphia must give a man great courage.'

He walked between us with the regular easy step of an old soldier who, in days of half-forgotten wars, had footed it for ever across the African veldt.

'That was all we ever did,' he would say. 'Walk and walk. And the only shot I ever fired that I remember was at a black snake and I never knew whether I hit or missed. That was the Boer war for you.'

Conjoined, innumerable runnels swept under a bridge where the united boreens joined the road, plunged over rock in a ten-foot cataract, went elbowing madly between bare hazels down to the belly of the glen. White cabins, windows already lamp-lighted and candle-lighted for Christmas, showed below the shifting fringe of black grey mist.

'This house I knew well,' he said; 'this was Aunt Sally's. The Aunt was a title of honour and had nothing to do with blood relationship. She was stately, a widow, a great manager and aunt to the whole country. She had only the two sons.'

By the crossroads of the thirteen limekilns we swung right and descended the slope of the glen on what in a dry summer would have been a dust road. Now, wet sand shifted under our feet, loose stones rattled ahead of us, the growing stream growled below us in the bushes. To our left were the disused limekilns, lining the road-way like ancient monstrous idols with gaping toothless mouths, and as we descended the old man remembered the days when he and his comrades, veterans all, had walked and measured those hills; the limekilns in operation and the white dust on the grass and the roadside hedges; the queues of farm carts waiting for the loading. Fertilisers made in factories had ended all that. There was the place (he pointed across a field) where a tree, fallen on a mearing fence, had lain and rotted while the two farmers whose land the fence divided, swept away by the joy of legal conflict, had disputed in the court in the town the ownership of the timber. The case never reached settlement. Mountainy men loved law and had their hearts in twopence. And here was Loughfresha bridge. (The stream was a torrent now.) The gapped, stone parapet hadn't been mended since the days of the survey. And there was the wide pool where Thady O'Neill, always a slave to salmon, had waded in after a big fish imprisoned by low water, taken it with his bare hands after a mad struggle and, it was said, cured himself by shock treatment of premature arthritis.

Once across the bridge our ascent commenced. Black brooding roadside cattle looked at us with hostility. On a diagonal across a distant meadow a black hound dog ran silently, swiftly up towards the mist, running as if with definite purpose – but what, I wondered, could a dog be doing running upwards there alone on a Christmas Day. The thought absorbed me to the exclusion of all else until we came to the falling house of John and Thady O'Neill.

'Good God in heaven,' said my father.

For a full five minutes he stood looking at it, not speaking, before he led his two sons, with difficulty, as far as the door.

Once it must have been a fine, long, two-storeyed, thatched farmhouse, standing at an angle of forty-five degrees to the roadway and built backwards into the slope of the hill. But the roof and the upper storey had sagged and, topped by the growth of years of rank decayed grass, the remnants of the thatched roof looked, in the Christmas dusk, like a rubbish heap a maniacal mass-murderer might pick as a burial mound for his victims.

'They won't be expecting us for our Christmas dinner,' said my brother.

To reach the door we went ankle-deep, almost, through plashy ground and forded in the half-dark a sort of seasonal stream. One small uncurtained window showed faintly the yellow light of an oil-lamp.

Knock, knock, knock went my father on the sagging door.

No dogs barked. No calves or cocks made comforting farmhouse noises. The wind was raucous in the bare dripping hazels that overhung the wreck of a house from the slope behind. An evil wizard might live here.

Knock, knock, knock went my father.

'Is there anybody there said the traveller?' said my brother, who had a turn for poetry.

'John O'Neill and Thady,' called my father. 'I've walked over from the Yankee's new house at Dooish and brought my two sons with me to wish you a happy Christmas.'

He shouted out his own name.

In a low voice he said to us, 'Advance, friends, and be recognised.'

My brother and myself giggled and stopped giggling as chains rattled and slowly, with a thousand creaks of aged iron and timber in bitter pain and in conflict with each other, the door opened. Now, years after that Christmas, I can rely only on a boyhood memory of a brief visit to a badly lighted cavern. There was a hunched decrepit old man behind the opening door. Without extending his hand he shuffled backwards and away from us. His huge hobnailed boots were unlaced. They flapped around him like the feet of some strange bird or reptile. He was completely bald. His face was pear-shaped, running towards the point at the forehead. His eyes had the brightness and quickness of a rodent's eyes. When my father said, 'Thady, you remember me,' he agreed doubtfully, as if agreement or disagreement were equally futile. He looked sideways furtively at the kitchen table half-hidden in shadows near one damp-streaked yellow wall. For a tablecloth, that table had a battered raincoat and when our knock had interrupted him Thady had, it would seem, been heeling over onto the coat a pot of boiled potatoes. He finished the task while we stood uncertainly inside the doorway. Then, as if tucking in a child for sleep, he wrapped the tails of the coat around the pile of steaming tubers. A thunderous hearty voice spoke to us from the corner between the hearth and a huge four-poster bed. It was a rubicund confident voice. It invited us to sit down, and my father sat on a low chair close to the hearth-fire. My brother and myself stood uncomfortably behind him. There was, at any rate, nothing for us to sit on. The smoky oil-lamp burned low but the bracket that held it was on the wall above the owner of the voice. So it haloed with a yellow glow the head of John O'Neill, the dilatory lover of Bessie of Cornavara who had gone unwed to the place where none embrace. It was a broad, red-faced, white-haired head, too large and heavy, it seemed, for the old wasted body.

'It's years since we saw you, Tommy,' said John.

'It's years indeed.'

'And all the wild men that had been in the army.'

'All the wild men.'

'Times are changed, Tommy.'

'Times are changed indeed,' said my father.

He backed his chair a little away from the fire. Something unpleasantly odorous fried and sizzled in an unlidded pot-oven. The flagged floor, like the roof, had sagged. It sloped away from the hearth and into the shadows towards a pyramid of bags of flour and meal and feeding stuffs for cattle.

'But times are good,' said John. 'The land's good, and the crops and cattle.'

'And the money plentiful.'

'The money's plentiful.'

'I'm glad to hear you say it,' said my father.

'The Yankee came back, Tommy.'

'He came back.'

'And built a house, I hear. I don't go abroad much beyond my own land.'

'He built a fine house.'

'They like to come back, the Yankees. But they never settle.'

'It could be that the change proves too much for them,' said my father.

Then after a silence, disturbed only by the restless scratching of Thady's nailed soles on the floor, my father said, 'You never married, John.'

'No, Tommy. Bessy died. What with stock to look after and all, a man doesn't have much time for marrying.'

'Thady was more of a man for the ladies than you ever were,' said my father to John.

Behind us there was a shrill hysterical cackle and from John a roar of red laughter.

'He was that. God, Tommy, the memory you have.'

'Memory,' said my father.

Like a man in a trance he looked, not at John or Thady, but into the red heart of the turf fire.

'There was the day, Thady,' he said, 'when Martin Murphy and myself looked over a whin hedge at yourself and Molly Quigley from Crooked Bridge making love in a field. Between you, you ruined a half-acre of turnips.'

The red laughter and the cackle continued.

'Tommy, you have the memory,' said John. 'Wasn't it great the way you remembered the road up Loughfresha?'

'It was great,' said my father. 'Trust an old soldier to remember a road.'

The odour from the sizzling pot-oven was thickening.

'Well, we'll go now,' said my father. 'We wouldn't have butted in on you the day it is only for old time's sake.'

'You're always welcome, Tommy. Anytime you pass the road.'

'I don't pass this road often, John.'

'Well, when you do you're welcome. Those are your two sons.'

'My two sons.'

'Two fine clean young men,' said John.

He raised a hand to us. He didn't move out of the chair. The door closed slowly behind us and the chains rattled. We forded the seasonal stream, my brother going in over one ankle and filling a shoe with water.

We didn't talk until we had crossed the loud stream at Loughfresha Bridge. In the darkness I kept listening for the haunted howl of the black hound dog.

'Isn't it an awful way, Da,' I said, 'for two men to live, particularly if it's true they have money in the bank.'

'If you've money in the bank,' said my brother, who suffered from a sense of irony, 'it's said you can do anything you please.'

With a philosophy too heavy for my years I said, 'It's a big change from the house we're going to.'

'John and Thady,' said my brother, 'didn't have the benefit of forty-five years in Philadelphia.'

My father said nothing.

'What, I wonder,' I said, 'was cooking in the pot-oven?'

'Whatever it was,' said my brother, 'they'll eat it with relish and roll into that four-poster bed and sleep like heroes.'

The black brooding roadside cattle seemed as formidable as wild bison.

'Sixty years,' said my father to himself. 'Coming and going every Sunday, spending the long afternoons and evenings in her father's house, eating and drinking, and nothing in the nature of love transpiring.'

Like heroes I thought, and recalled from the song-books the heroic words: 'Side by side for the cause have our forefathers battled when our hills never echoed the tread of a slave; in many a field where the leaden hail rattled, through the red gap of glory they marched to their grave.'

Slowly, towards a lost lighted fragment of Philadelphia and our Christmas dinner, we ascended the wet boreen.

'Young love,' soliloquised the old man. 'Something happens to it on these hills. Sixty years and he never proposed nothing, good or bad.'

'In Carlow town,' said the song-books to me, 'there lived a maid more sweet than flowers at daybreak; their vows contending lovers paid, but none of marriage dared speak.'

'Sunday after Sunday to her house for sixty years,' said the old man. 'You wouldn't hear the like of it among the Kaffirs. It's the rain and the mist. And the lack of sunshine and wine. Poor Thady, too, was fond of salmon and women.'

'For I haven't a genius for work,' mocked the Humorous and Convivial, 'it was never a gift of the Bradies; but I'd make a most iligant Turk for I'm fond of tobacco and ladies.'

To the easy amusement of my brother and, finally, to the wry laughter of my father I sang that quatrain. Night was over the mountain. The falling water of the spring had the tinny sound of shrill, brittle thunder.

After dinner my godmother's husband said, 'Such a fine house as Aunt Sally O'Neill kept. Tables scrubbed as white as bone. Dances to the melodeon. I always think of corncrakes and the crowds gathered for the mowing of the meadows when I recall that house. And the churning. She had the best butter in the country. Faintly golden. Little beads of moisture showing on it.'

'We'll have a game of euchre,' said my Aunt Brigid.

'Play the phonograph,' said my godmother's husband. He loathed euchre.

So on the gramophone, high up on Dooish, we heard that boys and girls were singing on the sidewalks of New York.

I wondered where the hound dog could possibly have been running to. In a spooky story I had once read the Black Hound of Kildare turned out to be the devil.

My godmother asked me to sing.

'But I can't sing,' I said.

'Then what do Lanty and yourself do with all the song-books?'

'We read them.'

Laughter.

'Read us a song,' said my brother.

So, because I had my back to the wall and also because once when visiting a convent with my mother I had sung, by request, 'Let Erin Remember,' and received a box of chocolates from the Reverend Mother, I sang: 'Just a little bit of Heaven fell from out the sky one day, and when the angels saw it sure they said we'll let it stay; and they called it Ireland.'

That spring, following my heralding of the descent from Elysium of the Emerald Isle, there was a steady downpour of half-crowns.

# The Shortest Way Home

The first school I ever went or was sent to was full of girls and that wasn't the worst of it. We were taught by big black nuns who had no legs or feet but who moved about as if, like the antediluvian chest of drawers in my mother's bedroom, they went on concealed casters. They used to haunt my dreams, moving uncannily about in thousands, their courses criss-crossing like the navigational lines on the maps on the classroom walls, bouncing off each other and spinning around like bumper cars at a fancy fair, holding aloft white canes like witch's wands. They didn't teach us much. All I remember is making chains by tearing up and intertwining thin strips of coloured paper, and rolling plasticine, which we called plaster seed, into sticky balls. I can smell the turpentiny smell of it still.

At any rate the wells on my path to learning in that harem of a school were poisoned by the affair of the school-reader and by the blow Sister Enda caught me on the knuckles with her cane when I was absorbed drawing funny faces, with spittle and finger tip, on the glossy brown wooden desk.

'Wipe the desk clean this instant,' she said. 'You naughty little boy.' The offending funny faces – they were a first effort at recapturing the fine careless rapture observed, in a newspaper strip, on the faces of Mutt and Jeff – I wiped out or dried off with my handkerchief fastened with a safety pin to my white woollen gansey. That was a precautionary measure taken against loss of linen by my mother who for years preserved a snapshot of me pennant-come-nosebag flying, a surly freckled boy with uncontrollable hair who looked as if he had just murdered nine reverend mothers. In more select schools, I've heard tell, they had in those days an inhuman device by which gloves too were ensured against loss. An elastic string passed around the back of the young victim's neck and then down the insides of the sleeves and from each extremity of the string a glove depended: so that when not in use, the gloves retreated up the sleeves like mice into holes. Fortunately, we were never grand enough for gloves. The worst we had was this pinned-on wiper with which I extinguished Mutt and Jeff, and I looked for sympathy towards Big May, and hated Sister Enda, as the long Act of Charity said, with my whole heart and soul and above all things.

At that time Big May was the only woman I loved and, great-hearted queen that she was, it wasn't Big May betrayed to the nun that I already had at home a duplicate copy of the coloured school reader, the first book that I, a born collector of books, ever possessed. She was nine and a half, four years older than me, her protégé, and big even then so that she might, in the words of the poet, with her great shapely knees and the long flowing line, have walked to the altar through the holy images at Pallas Athene's side, or been fit spoil for a centaur drunk with the unmixed wine. She was big and wild and lovely and never could take the straight road to school nor the straight road home, so that to be in her company was always an unguessable adventure. She ran messages for my mother and undertook to chaperone me to school when my sister, who was thirteen and a half, was too busy and superior and too absorbed in her own companions to be pestered with the care-taking of a toddler of a brother. May was lithe, laughing-eyed and dark-headed and could box better than most boys and climb trees like a monkey. She was an adorable woman and a born mother, so with my knuckles smarting, I turned my moistening eyes towards her for sympathy.

But the morning that martinet, Sister Enda, tried to commandeer my second copy of the school reader, Low Babies Edition, I wasn't looking for any woman's sympathy. Sister Enda said precisely, 'Your sister tells me you have one of these at home.'

It was a lovely reading-book: sixteen pages of simple sentences, big print, coloured pictures. It told the most entrancing stories. This one, for instance: My dog Rags has a house. He has a little house of his own. See, his name is over the door.

Or this one: Mum has made buns for tea. She has made nice hot buns.

Or yet another: When the children went to the zoo they liked the elephant best of all. Here is the elephant with happy children on his back.

Or breaking into verse: When the old owl lived in the oak never a word at all he spoke.

To have one copy, which my mother had bought me, at home, and another copy, supplied by regulations, in school, gave that miracle of coloured picture and succinct narrative the added wonder of twins or of having two of anything. So when Sister Enda, soaring to the top of her flight in the realms of wit, said one reader should be enough for such a little boy, and when all the girls except May giggled, I saw red and grabbed, leaving Sister Enda momentarily quite speechless with shock and turning over and over in her hand a leaf that said on one side: Here comes the aeroplane, says Tom; and on the other: When the children came home from town they had much to tell Mum.

Gripping the rest of the reader I glared at the nun who was white in the face with something – fright or fury – at this abrupt confrontation with the male forces of violence and evil. She looked at me long and thoughtfully. Fortunately for me she was perambulating without benefit of cane. She said, 'You naughty boy. Now your poor mother will have to pay for the book you destroyed. Stand in the corner under the clock with your face to the wall until home-time.'

Which I did: tearless, my face feverish with victory, because that onset with Sister Enda had taught me things about women that some men never learn and, staring at the brown varnished wainscotting in the corner of the room, I made my resolve. On the homeward journey I told May all about it.

I said, 'As long as I live I'm not going back to that school. It's all women.'

'Not till tomorrow morning.'

'Never. Never, if I die.'

'Where will you go?'

'To the Brothers with the big boys.'

'You're too little.'

'I'll go all the same.'

'They mighn't take you.'

'They'll take me.'

'What will your mother say?'

'I don't care what she says.'

Which was true, because I knew if I could best Sister Enda I could best my mother. It was a man's world.

'You're a terrible boy,' May said. 'But I'll miss you.'

She believed me, I felt, and knew in her heart that that was our last day at school together, and she was proud of me. So with my hand in hers we went on the last detour of my career at the female academy, leaving Brook Street and Castle Street, our proper route, and wandering into the cosy smelly crowded world of the gridiron of lanes of one-storeyed whitewashed houses below and at the back of the towering double-spired Catholic Church; Fountain Lane, Brook Lane, The Gusset, St. Kevin's Lane, Potato Lane, and the narrowest of all, which was a cul-de-sac called the Rat's Pad. Previously we had prudently passed it by because even to May, the narrow roofed-over entry opening out into a small close that held only four houses was a little daunting. Besides, you could not go through it and come out the other end and, as May saw things, a place of that sort did not constitute a classical diversion.

It was a dog's walk, she said. You came back the way you went.

But on this day the Rat's Pad attracted us because a woman in one of its four houses was shouting her head off and outside her half-door a dozen or so people had gathered to find out what all the noise was about. Skilfully May worked her way in to a point of vantage, carrying me pick-a-back, both to save space and to give me enough altitude to study the domestic interior. The woman, in blouse and spotted apron, was gesticulating with a long knife. Of all the words or sentences only one remained with me, 'I'll cut the head off you, you lazy gazebo.'

The man saying nothing, his head bowed as if meekly to accept the blade, sat on a low stool by an open, old-fashioned grate. The fire burned brightly.

'May,' I whispered, 'will she really and truly cut the head off him?'

I wasn't sure whether I did or did not want to witness the spectacle.

'From what they say,' said May, 'she couldn't cut a slice of bread.'

So since there was nothing happening but shouting we rejoined our main route homewards and May bought for me, as a special treat to mark the ending of the first phase of my scholastic career, a toffee apple in Katy McElhatton's huckster shop in Castle Street. Those toffee apples were a noted home-made delicacy, and Katy was a woman, old as the Hag of Beare, who lived in the end to be one hundred and eight and died of a stomach disorder that came on her only when she mistook a bottle of Jeyes fluid for a bottle of stout she kept always on a shelf behind the counter. But her toffee apples were something to savour and remember, and the flavour of thick golden syrup toffee and roasted green apple was still in my mouth when I fell asleep that night to dream of a severed head held aloft by the hair in the hand of an irate wife. There was no blood neither from stump nor severed neck, nor any jagged dangling sinews. When, for purposes of demonstration, the vengeful spouse turned the head and neck around and around, the cross-section of the neck was solid and shiny like the corned beef when it had been subjected to the slicer in James Campbell's big shop. That was the way you were when your head was cut off. It was also true that husbands and wives could work themselves into such a state that they threatened each other with knives and decapitation. My last day at the school for girls had taught me a lot and I owed it all not to any organised institutional education but to my own assertion of manly independence and to the divagations of my Amazonian love and protectress, that queen among women, Big May. Henceforth I would be a man and would bear my expanding satchel into the world of the big boys. Farewell, farewell for ever to first love and all it had given me.

'The only Brother I'll go to,' I dictated to my mother, 'is the Wee Brother.'

Having won my battle against any return to the monstrous regiment of women I was advancing to invest new positions.

The six black Brothers of the Christian Schools emerged from their monastery every morning to kneel in the top pew, to the left of the nave and under the marble pulpit, at eight o'clock mass. A wide-eyed study of their movements, kneeling, sitting, standing, praying, yawning, genuflecting, reading missals, blowing noses, had for some time been for me a substitute for any form of worship: latria or dulia.

The Grey Brother, whose place was on the extreme right of their pew, was Brother Superior. His bush of grey hair was clipped and shaved in an exact straight line dead level with the tops of his ears. He had a fine Roman nose and a trumpet style of blowing it that never since have I seen or heard surpassed. His production of hand-kerchief from a slit in his black habit, his preliminary flourish of white linen, added up to a ritual fascinating to watch. He never produced the handkerchief with his right hand. He always flourished before he trumpeted and, when he blew, even the two old voteens, one man and one woman, who prayed out loud and talked over their affairs with God for all to hear, were momentarily startled out of the balance and rhythm of their recitative.

To the left of the Grey Brother stood or knelt or sat, according to the stage of the celebration, Brother Busto and Brother Lanko, for even then I knew them according to the nicknames the boys bestowed on them, and had to that extent my instruction in the lingua franca of the world of men. They had the same soothering Munster accents and the same surnames and were distinguished from each other only, as the nicknames so subtly indicated, by the robust girth of one and the handsome height of the other. The Beardy Brother was unusual because beards were rare among Brothers, but the phenomenon was satisfactorily explained by the boys saying that the Beardy Brother had been in China, and later in life it came as a shock to me to find that beards were comparatively as rare among Chinamen as among Brothers. The Red Brother, true to the colour of his hair and the close, disciplined army cut of it, was the terror of the school and the legend went so far as to say that on one of his punitive forays he had trapped the shoulders of a delinquent boy under a window sash and thumped him on the buttocks with a hurling stick. To my extreme relief he had withdrawn from the religious life, possibly to devote more time to hurling, before I had advanced as far as the grade he so robustly instructed.

But it would have been clear to me, even if the opinion of the grown-up people had not already been there to confirm my intuitive judgement that the Wee Brother was an angel descended from above. The children adored him. They ran messages for him, swept the schoolrooms and the schoolyard for him, and in the season, under his direction, shook the trees and picked up the fallen apples in the monastery orchard. They banded themselves at his behest into groups of all sorts, from paper and comb orchestras to football teams, or went walking with him in crowds in the country learning the names of birds and trees, and not too often wandering off in small foraging parties to rob orchards or egghouses. In spite of the vow of poverty he always clinked with small coins to reward them for their more meritorious efforts. He was good to the poor and his favourite pupil was Packy Noble, a shuffling albino boy too big for his grade and mentally incapable of advancing further or of mastering more than the alphabet. Grown men admired the Wee Brother because he had been a famous amateur horse jockey before religion claimed him, and – although this was something I did not then understand – the girls, looking at him, sighed heartbroken resignation to the inscrutable ways of the Lord who claimed such a paragon for the cloister.

It was his waving fair hair and the way the light reflected on his pince-nez that caused me first to worship him, and shining pince-nez seemed to me the clearest of all marks of the angelic nature manifesting itself in mortal shape. Even still I'm inclined to think that the world is the way it is because not half enough people wear pince-nez.

So I said to my mother, 'The only Brother I'll go to is the Wee Brother.'

It was autumn, and the schoolyard was the best place in our world for horse-chestnuts. The yard was triangular with the apex pointing up a slope towards the schoolhouse, an oblong cut-stone building of two storeys. Access to the second storey, because of the oversight of the builder who forgot the stairs originally planned for, was by an iron outside stairway. The long branches of the chestnut trees overhung the walls of the yard and with a little encouragement from sticks and stones readily dropped their thorny green fruit. Wonder was all around my mother and myself as we ascended towards the school. Ten million boys, it seemed to me, were playing conkers, swinging the seasoned chestnuts scientifically on lengths of string, slashing at and bashing their opponents' chestnuts. Fragments of the casualties of a myriad battles crackled under our feet like cinders. Surrounded by an excited crowd a tiny fellow called Tall Jimmy Clarke was bending down with his hands behind his back and picking ha'pence off the ground with his teeth. He did it for the price of the ha'pence he picked up and prospered by it because the fascination of what's difficult always proved overpowering, even for boys who had seen and paid for the trick a dozen times over. In a corner by the concrete lavatories and washrooms a crowd of hydromaniacs were having the time of their lives pumping the handles of the drinking fountains and covering each other and the ground around them with water. This was life, this was a battlefield, this was the wonderful world of school and, apart from my mother, there wasn't a petticoat to be seen.

Then a whistle blew and in shuffling hordes the boys ascended, to be swallowed up by the old stone building. The slamming of doors, the clatter of iron-tipped heels on the iron stairway were wonderful to hear; then we were alone, my mother and I. Dust still rose from the yard. It steamed in the sun on the damp patch left by the water-sprites. Beyond a row of chestnut trees the gardens kept by the Brothers were well-ordered and radiant. Variously regulated chants arose from various classrooms and we listened to them, my hand in hers, until the Grey Brother came to us from the monastery beside the schoolhouse and said, 'So this is the little man who doesn't like the girls.'

The Grey Brother I took to from the start for he was a fellowman and he saw my point.

'And what book shall we put him into,' he said. 'He's so far under the admittance age.'

Book, I thought, I have my own books. In the satchel on my back there was one jotter, slightly scribbled on, one pencil, two school readers even if one of them, due to the villainy of woman, was lacking a leaf. There was also my lunch of bread and butter sandwiches, a small bottle of milk, two biscuits and one piece of cake.

'He wants nobody but the Wee Brother,' my mother said.

'Then the Wee Brother it shall be.'

He waved his arm at a window on the second storey and on the landing of the stairway at the corner of the building the vision appeared, fair hair like a halo blowing around its head, the sunlight shining through the halo, the sun beaming out of its glass eyes, truly an angel descending to walk with us. He took me up the stairs again with him and that was how I came to meet the Four Horsemen of the Apocalypse who, after Big May and the Wee Brother, were the greatest teachers I ever had.

Sometimes the Wee Brother called them the Twelve Apostles because he said any one man of them was as good as three. Other times he called them simply the Four Just Men. But mostly, and I think merely because they ran most of his messages for him – carrying despatches all over the town, from errands of charity to admonitory notes to parents who weren't sending their boys to school – he called them the Four Horsemen of the Apocalypse. They sat, or knelt at prayer time, on the bench nearest to the door, making sure in winter that the door was securely closed against draughts, enjoying in summer a high green view of the neighbouring convent field where the nuns, for some symbolic devotional purpose, grazed a small black donkey; the happiest laziest donkey in the world, the Wee Brother said. That big bench by the door was the highest and oldest in the classroom.

Even by the standards of those days it was a museum piece. It had survived several changes of school furniture. It was battle-scarred with the names of boys now grown to be men. It towered over the other desks like a Spanish galleon over the dogged little ships of Elizabeth's gunners. It creaked with age every time one of its occupants moved. It had space, the Wee Brother said, for four and a quarter men, so he lifted me up, seated me at one end of it, my legs dangling, beside Packy Noble, told me I was the image of an artistic mantelpiece ornament in a modern house, and placed me thus under the Tutelage of the Four Horsemen; Packy himself, Tall Jimmy Clarke, Jinkins Creery and Tosh Mullan who later in life was to become a boxer and to acquire by a painful accident the pseudonym of Kluterbuck.

My two school readers opened before me, I studied the pictures and listened to the drone of learning all around me and sometime in the afternoon fell asleep. For no lullaby ever sung soothingly by loving peasant mother could equal the power of the simple addition table to induce slumber: One and one are two, one and two are three, one and three are four. Before my eyes radiant woolly balls rolled up and down hills and I slept and as I learned afterwards, was gently lifted by the snowheaded Packy and under the direction of the Wee Brother, laid to rest on the broad bottom shelf of a brown press used as a wardrobe on dry days for the scholars' coats and caps. Comfortably cushioned, I slumbered until it was time for the litany of the Blessed Virgin and the journey home and then, thumbing the sleep out of my eyes, I boarded the galleon again and balanced on my knees for a prayer so soothing that I would have fallen asleep again except that, just as the Wee Brother said Tower of Ivory and we sang out Pray for Us, the old desk gave up the ghost and collapsed with a crash, and the litany dissolved in the laughter of boys and when the Wee Brother saw that nobody was hurt he laughed too. That was a day's learning I'll remember when I've forgotten – as I have already – sines, cosines and declensions and the fine poem about the Latin prepositions that govern the accusative case.

The Four Horsemen, taking the place of Big May, conducted me home. Tall Jimmy Clarke, by stooping and lifting, acquired on the way four halfpennies and bought sweets and shared them out. Jinkins Creery held me up on the parapet of the bridge over the Strule and showed me where he had caught a river lamprey a mile long and promised to show me the seven baby lampreys he had in a glass jar at home. He explained to me how he had caught them by holding a tennis-ball in among a maze of them in a foot of water in the Killyclogher Burn and how the stupid, vicious creatures had clung on to it so tightly with the suckers they had instead of mouths that he was able to lift seven of them out of the water. Packy, who was Master of All, and Tosh Mullan put on, for my instruction, a display of the noble art of self-defence which was great fun because Packy was huge and white-headed and his battered boots were too big for him and his toes turned up and he could imitate a dancing bear he had once seen in John Duffy's travelling circus.

Packy's greatest weakness was that he could never be in time for school in the morning. His mother or, to be more charitable, his aunt, went by the strange name of Pola and was the proprietress of what we knew bluntly as a tramp lodging-house where, it was rumoured, the itinerant patrons cooked over candles and slept on their feet, elbows hooked on a common rope, so that inexorably they were all roused together when the rope was slackened at reveille. Cooking conditions may not have been so primitive nor sleeping conditions so arbitrary in Pola's caravanserai, but certain it was that the mixed clientele of sallow-faced oriental bagmen, pedlars, vagrant musicians, buskers and downright beggars who patronised it did not go to bed until the small hours and then only to the accompaniment of a pretty consistent bedlam. So, shuffling in late, morning after morning, Packy would wearily rub red eyes that had around them rims of sleep, like grey mud around a weeping flowering marsh; and the back of his white poll was never devoid of a tiny pillow-feather or two. Every morning the prolegomena to his day's study followed the same pattern.

'He who rises late must gallop all day. Do you know what that means, Packy?'

'Yes, sir.'

'What, Packy?'

'It's in the headline copy, sir.'

The headline copy with its incomprehensible maxims in stiff old-fashioned copperplate, in elegant lines and curves that no young inexperienced hands could ever imitate, was the master-work on which we were supposed to model our handwriting.

Packy, you're right. I suppose one way or another the sum total of wisdom is in the headline copy.'

'Yes, sir.'

'Packy, I must buy you an alarm clock.'

'Yes, sir.'

'Diluculo surgere saluberrimum est, Packy. To rise early is most healthful.'

Tenderly, with his finger-tips, the Wee Brother would pick the feathers of the night before from the close-cropped white head.

'Yes, sir,' said Packy.

'Early to bed and early to rise makes a man healthy, wealthy and wise, Packy.'

With those gentle finger-tips he would drum out on Packy's shoulder a rhythm to go with the words.

'That's in the headline copy too, Packy.'

'Yes, sir.'

The early bird catches the worm was also in the headline copy and it struck me as a brutal saying because the early worm was the head of a fool to be out at that hour. The only saying I liked at all in the headline copy was about violets: I would give you some violets but they withered when my father died. Not one of us, not even John MacBride, a clean boy who was clever and was taught by his musical mother to sing Moore's melodies at parochial concerts, knew what it meant or who said it or who died or who wanted to give violets to whom. But, regardless, we copied out the words painfully and with all the intensity of faith: slope lightly up, slope heavily down, curve at the top and curve at the bottom, Packy peering so closely at the page that his nose was as good as in the inkwell, the tip of Tall Jimmy Clarke's tongue peeping out like a moist pink rodent.

Packy, being as he was and doomed to an early grave, could only in some heavenly fields ever have discovered the coy beauty of the modest flower. Here on this earth his peering eyes discovered more about nettles than violets for Pola was a great believer in the health-giving powers of nettle tea, nettle soup or nettles as a vegetable and it was Packy's task to gather, in the spring, the soft succulent young nettles before age had soured them and forced them to show their stings. The other three horsemen went along to help and I went with them.

Because of the four oblong fields that belonged to Big James Campbell, the butcher, and the engine shed and Spyglass Hill and the grass wigwam and the cave at the spot where four hedgerows joined and the Ali Baba's treasure house of a town dump and the roaring bull in Mackenna's meadow, gathering the nettles was not as prosaic a business as you might readily imagine. Three of the fields were gently rising slopes and the fourth was a dome of a hill overlooking the bull's deep meadow, and the four of them lay just beyond the straggling fingers of houses at the edge of the town.

You crossed the town dump, a grey-black wasteland, smoking with an occasional volcano where discarded cinders had refused to die. There were always a few old people, sacks in hands, shoulders hunched and eyes on the ground, wandering slowly about, gathering the makings of a fire and hoping for treasures of scrap. Since the most extraordinary relics of careless housekeeping came to that island of lost ships the aged searchers were quite frequently rewarded and the curious schoolboy could find there, too, objects to delight the heart: shining biscuit tins, discarded motor wheels and tyres, bicycle frames that could be refurbished and made useful. Tosh Mullan, who was lucky at finding things, had once come upon a handsome point-twenty-two rifle that would do everything but shoot.

The best nettles were always found on the fringe of the dump just before you ascended the slope, climbed a fence and crossed the railway line to the turntable and the engine shed.

'Nettles for measles and pimples,' Packy would say. 'That's what my aunt Pola says.'

In the murk of the one-night lodging house for wandering men who had no parish of their own Pola managed to maintain a flawless olive complexion.

'Boil them in water, she says, and drink the tea. She says if you drink nettle tea you'll always have a clear skin.'

'Tosh could do with it,' said Tall Jimmy Clarke.

For Tosh, with a hanging lower lip and a squint and a recurring rash of pimples was not the most beautiful of boys. Yet even then he had in his social relations the tolerant mildness of the natural professional fighter who never, outside the ring, feels called upon to prove his prowess; and the pummellings with which he responded to Tall Jimmy's witticisms were perfectly good-natured.

One day – if I can distinguish one day from another over a period of years – Tosh flourished in his hand a full-grown dead lamprey that Jinkins had caught and given to him. He carried it as proudly as if it had been a policeman's truncheon, until the stench became too much. Waving it in his hand he pursued Jimmy with warlike whoops towards the railway line and the engine shed. Jinkins, carrying his fishing rod, ran after them and I ran after Jinkins because, bright ferret-eyes glistening in his turnip of a head, he had promised to show me how he caught fish and how, incidentally, he had acquired the nickname we called him by. I never knew his Christian name.

From the fence on top of the railway embankment we looked back at Packy the Herbalist on hands and knees among the rank green growth at the fringe of the wasteland. Even if he was never to know much about violets it could just be part of the irony of living that he knew more than any of us about the meaning of growing things. He was so close to them because, being half-blind, he had to kneel to see them, their shapes and colours, and when the rare flowering nettle showed its fragile white bloom through the red mist of his eyes it must have meant something miraculous to him. He was the herbalist gathering plants from the ground to make messes and potions to keep blood pure and a woman beautiful.

'Come on, Packy,' Tosh called. 'We have nettles enough to sink a battleship.'

Packy rose, clutching his herbs, and to excite our laughter, did his bear's gallop towards us.

'We'll cross over the engine shed and grease our boots.'

'We'll wait for the goods first. We always wait for the goods.'

Swinging on the wire fence we watched with a wonder that never lessened the variety of cargo on the interminable lumbering goods train. We counted the trucks. Cattle on their last sad journey looked out at us morosely. The wind blew towards us smells of dung and good timber, the sour smell of scrap metal, the wet milky smell of farm produce. The tick-tock of wheels over joints and fish-plates was delightfully soothing. We cheered the guard in his van at the end of the train as a crowd in a theatre might cheer the author. He waved his flag to us as he always did before the embankment and the round mouth of a bridge devoured him.

'Big Mick O'Neill, the railway porter, can turn the turntable with one hand and an engine and a coal-wagon on it.'

'He's farandaway the strongest man in this town.'

'He's the strongest man in Ireland.'

We had never, you see, heard of the bragging man who said: 'Give me a lever and I'll move the world.'

'There was a stronger man in Dublin once,' said Tall Jimmy Clarke. 'My father told me about him.'

Tall Jimmy's father, a roadworker, was admittedly a man of great knowledge as all makers and menders of roads come, by dint of their occupation, to be. All day long they watch the world, unaware of their observation, passing them by.

'He was a policeman. His name was Patrick Sheehan. He caught a mad bull by the horns once and when people asked him was he afraid he said he was only afraid the horns would break.'

In the middle of the railway track we stopped and listened, each one of us thinking that far away across the four fields we could hear our own private bull roaring in Mackenna's meadow.

'He went down a manhole once,' said Tall Jimmy, 'to rescue a workman was stuck in a pipe and he rescued the workman and he was smothered dead by the gas. He was so strong that was the only way he could be killed. My da says there's a monument to him in Dublin.'

'We'll grease our boots,' said Packy.

It was a thick yellow suet-like grease kept in little iron boxes on the sides of the freight trucks. It was meant to soothe and cool the friction of axles and wheels and not to be applied to any leather ever hammered out of an animal's hide. But in ritual fashion, like savages daubing on war paint, we greased our boots with it before we entered the four fields. Its one beneficial quality was that it could withstand moisture and, if the grass was wet, the beads of rain or dew danced like jewels on the dulled leather. Leather treated with that yellow grease could defy for ever all shine and polish and cause quarrels between mystified parents and indignant bootsellers about the quality of the material they put in footwear nowadays.

With our feet anointed we slipped through a well-worn hole in a high hawthorn hedge and trod the holy grass of the first field. Tall Jimmy was in the lead, dancing a dance that was halfway between his idea of an Indian war-dance and his slightly more accurate idea of a sailor's hornpipe. Packy came in the rear, beaming like a bride over his bouquet of nettles. Pola, who never had had a wedding, white or coloured, or a groom from whose arm she could dangle, was an assiduous spectator at every wedding in the parish church, and Packy could simper like any lace-clad virgin just as well as he could prance like a circus bear.

In the middle of a clump of rushes a tall unheeded wooden pole carried a notice saying trespassers would be prosecuted. We regarded it as the dissolute members of an aristocratic family would regard a family ghost who had become an old-fashioned bore. No longer even did we use it as a cockshot for cinders carried from the engine shed.

'Tony,' Tall Jimmy shouted, 'Tony.'

Running away from us he called back, 'Watch me. I'm Tom Mix.'

For the old horse grazed or wearily sucked the grass in the first field. Nothing less like the renowned Tony ever shuffled along on four shaky feet. He was an old saddle-backed bay left out there to die in peace. There were white spots of age on his hide like stabs of lichen on old stone. He was just about able and no more, to bear the featherweight of agile Jimmy and it was Jimmy's delight to straddle on the sunken back that seemed almost to creak like a worn iron bedstead, to hammer his heels as if they were spurred against the withered flagging flanks, to hang from the scraggy neck as if he was a Red Indian, to wind up the exhausted slack-springed body to a trot in which every leg seemed to limp away in a different direction.

'Look at him now. Hasn't he the lovely smile?'

He pulled the lips apart to show great green and yellow teeth lazily floating in saliva. They weren't bright or beautiful, yet the expression was more like a smile than it was like anything else.

He was an amiable old animal and to him and Tall
Jimmy I owe it that I was never afraid of the long heads
of horses, and that, later in life, I was able to find myself
in agreement with the Tipperary trainer who at the
Curragh of Kildare races smacked the tight-skirted titled
lady on her prancing buttocks and cried out for all to
hear, 'Women, the best things God made – after horses.'

Tall Jimmy on horseback leading us, we went in
procession through the gapped hedge and up the slope
to the grass wigwam on Spyglass Hill. From the Wee
Brother's public readings we knew about Long John
Silver, Jim Hawkins and the fifteen men on a dead
man's chest so, although the dome-shaped hill that
was the highest of the four fields offered no view of
the blue Pacific, that was still the only name we could
give it. From the wigwam that Tosh and Tall Jimmy had
lovingly plaited from branches, rushes and long grass
you could see the traffic on the road to Clanabogan, the
long scimitar-shaped meadow where our bull fed, Pigeon
Top Mountain where the sportsmen went for grouse, the
town's three steeples, the deep Drumragh River where
Jinkins fished and the clanking metal structure called
the Lynn Bridge which carried the railway over the river.
So we called the place Spyglass Hill. The wigwam was
a magic restful place. Green light filtered down into it.
The air was sweet with the smell of warm grass. The
particoloured branches, peeled in strips by Tosh who had
a clasp-knife as long as a sabre, seemed, if you lay flat on
your back and looked up at them long enough, to move
and writhe like serpents. Although that big man James
Campbell who owned the fields went to the trouble of
putting up notices banning trespassers, neither he nor his
foreman nor working men ever tampered with the grass
wigwam and, when Tosh had built around it a circular

palisade of strong sticks to protect it from the curiosity of cows, it lasted for a whole summer.

All together we lay in the green light and Tall Jimmy's exhausted discarded mount lay thinking the thoughts of age on the grass outside the palisade. From the tired horse to the roaring bull was no distance at all because the wigwam was our halfway house to the cave that wasn't a cave. It was a sort of unfinished tunnel that cattle seeking shade from the sun had made under branches at the meeting place of four hedgerows. Smaller than the cattle we could penetrate further into gloom and then, parting a few branches, peer down into the meadow where the big red bull grazed. The game was to roar at him until he roared back. He never failed to oblige us. He would delight us still further by rooting at the ground with his horned head and sometimes even drive us into sheer ecstasy by racing around in circles and kicking his hind legs in the air as a horse would. He was a fine performer. He was our own menagerie: a giant red bull alone like a king in his private park.

'They'll kill him some day,' Jimmy said sadly. 'They'll kill him and make Bovril out of him. That's what they do with bulls.'

Our roaring done – Packy, who could dance like a bear, was also the best of us to roar like a bull – we wandered aimlessly across the grass thinking sadly of all the noble roaring bulls, black and red, who had gone down to the doom of being melted to fill small bottles with meat extract. To brighten our mood Tall Jimmy seized one of a pair of pitchforks, left stuck in a hedge by some of Campbell's men, and shouted, 'We'll play "Ninety-Eight".'

It wasn't a card game. It was a by-product of the Wee Brother's fervent lecturing on the long sad history of Irish

Rebellion. The pitchforks, one in the hands of Packy and one in the hands of Tall Jimmy, became the pikes the boys of Wexford carried in 1798. Before their glistening points hordes of redcoats fell back at Camolin, Enniscorthy, Tubberneering; and Tosh with the dead lamprey was beating an invisible big drum and Jinkins with his fishing rod was a galloping lancer, and the high town of New Ross and Three Bullet Gate were about to be stormed and taken, when Big James and his foreman appeared through a gap in a hedge and roared at us and we ran.

'They'll prosecute us, sure as God,' said Jinkins who had a natural horror of the law.

So we ran faster and the two men for the hell of it ran after us. For my age and the length of my legs I could run well but the Four Horsemen were bigger and better athletes and I was losing ground badly: confused, too, with the awesome thought that I was a trespasser, one of a group referred to specifically in the Lord's Prayer. Staggering under the weight of that thought I stumbled and fell and was resigning myself to prosecution and prison when I was picked up by Packy and carried through a narrow gap between two trees to the covert of a terraced whindotted slope above the river. Concealed by green thorn and yellow blossom we sat whispering for half an hour and looking at, and listening to, the water. It came rattling down over the shallows, curved and spread out to make a deep pool that went on under the railway and the girders of the Lynn Bridge.

'That's where I catch my fish,' Jinkins said.

'Where you catch the jinkins you should throw back,' said Tall Jimmy. 'Some day Robert McCaslan, the water bailiff, will get you.'

On our river the salmon fry and the tiny trout were called jinkins and our friend, the great hunter, had earned his name from his passion for catching, cooking and eating them against all the laws ever made for the conserving of game fish.

Packy held his nose. He said, 'Jinkins always stinks like a fish.'

'No. It's this,' said Tosh.

He dangled the hideous, headless, mouthless lamprey under Packy's nose.

'Come and watch me catch them,' Jinkins said to me.

So when we thought the coast was clear and our pursuers gone Jinkins mounted his rod and readied his dry flies and in single file we marched out from the shelter of the whins, to be greeted with gales of friendly laughter from Big James and his foreman. They waved at us through our escape gap between the two trees.

'They were only fooling all the time,' said Packy.

'They're funny men,' said Tall Jimmy with scorn.

'Don't kill all the fish in the river,' the foreman shouted.

And when Tall Jimmy, never at a loss for an answer, cried back that we'd cut them up and use them for bait they laughed even louder and went back laughing towards Spyglass Hill.

Far away our lonely doomed bull roared on his own demesne.

With a light breeze at his back Jinkins let the long line float out easily. Packy, on his bended knees peering at the earth, might have been the image of the ancient herbalist half-blind from searching the fields and from concocting in his magic cellar, but Jinkins by the river bank was for sure the natural hunter. The stiff hair stood up on him like the bristles on a hedgehog. His ferret eyes pierced the water for the first white flash of soft under-belly. The small hook struck with deadly accuracy and

Jinkins chuckled to himself as he unhooked the tiny, silvery, fluttering bodies and strung them through the gills on a looped, peeled ash-twig. It was methodical massacre; and if the salmon are not in that water as they were of old then the cause of their absence, under God and new land-drainage systems, is the Herod-complex that impelled Jinkins Creery to his slaughter of the innocents. As Tall Jimmy taught me never to fear horses, so the sight of Jinkins at work taught me to pity fish: fish on the hook, fish in aquariums gazing sadly through the frustrating glass, pinkeens imprisoned in jam jars, fish sacrificed on slabs in shops and doomed to the fire and the knife and fork.

When the killing was all done we walked the railway line to the middle of the Lynn Bridge, opened a metal trap door between the rails and descended a ladder to a plank walk that workmen used when inspecting or painting the girders. The deep water was quite still below us. Packy held me by the shoulders but, in spite of his protection, I had, that night, my first falling nightmare.

'Long Alex Nixon,' Tosh said, 'drowned himself in that pool.'

'He didn't drown himself,' said Packy. 'He just sank.'

'He couldn't sink.'

'He wasn't cork, was he?'

'I saw them dragging the river for his body,' Tall Jimmy said. 'There was a man diving all the time from a boat looking for him.'

'We all saw that,' Jinkins said. 'They were at it for days.'

'He was the best swimmer in the world,' Tosh said. 'He just held his nose and sank and drowned himself. He was always fighting with his wife.'

'That doesn't prove he drowned himself,' Packy said. 'You couldn't drown yourself just by holding your nose.'

He released my shoulder and holding his nose with his left hand, did on the swaying plank a few steps of his bear's shuffle. But our laughter between the unanswering black water and the metal girders was hollow. Awed by the sound of it we climbed back up the ladder and gratefully closed the clanking door on the mystery of Long Alec Nixon.

The possibility or otherwise of drowning by holding the nose was a topic that kept us talking all the way back along the rusted branch-line to the town's auxiliary goods station, where the coal-wagons were lined up with the supplies for the lunatic asylum, and halfway up the town's main street where shops were closed and the tea-time hush had descended. Thought and remembrance came with the hush and we heard the agonised voice of Packy, 'Mother of God, I've lost my nettles.'

Red and blue shop-blinds carefully drawn made the town look like a place of the dead. Not a nettle grew on the cruel pavement. With guilt I remembered that I had seen Packy's nettles fall to the grass when he redeemed me, the trespasser. With the folly of youth I said, 'We'll go back for more.'

'We wouldn't have time. We're late already. She'll murder me.'

Generously Jinkins the hunter said, 'Give her a couple of fish.'

'She never eats fish. She says they're greasy.'

'Give her my ampor eel,' said Tosh.

Ampor eel was our mispronunciation for lamprey.

But sick to the soul, we all knew that this was no joke for Pola put great faith in nettles.

Then as we stood sadly thinking, the angel came to our rescue. She came, tall, wild-haired and ragged. She came as she always came, from a side street of shabby, brown-and-yellow brick houses. She bore in her arms a jungle profusion of wild nettles and, bending her ear to the sorrowful tale, she said simply to Packy, 'One of the women I work for is mad about nettles. But take half of mine. I have enough to physic the town let alone one old woman.'

She patted my head. She said, 'How do you like the big boys?'

She took the lead as if she was the biggest boy of all and we followed her up the street for fifty yards until, being Big May, she left us to make her own detour along another side street.

The day the Wee Brother would no longer close me in the press to slumber my way to learning on the piled coats and caps I knew sorrowfully that life had begun. What happened was that one of the scholars, for reasons known only to himself and which he was never sufficiently articulate to explain, had a pocket of his coat full of broken glass. Turning over in my slumber I lacerated my left hand – still have a faint scar. I emerged, when awakened, dripping blood. The Wee Brother looked as if he and the class were guilty of murder. He staunched the flow, sent Jinkins to buy me a bag of hard sweets, then sent me home in the company of shambling Packy. It wasn't a serious wound but it was the beginning of the end. Thereafter there was nothing for me but the common lot, the hard reality of wooden desks and, as I mentioned – Life; and Life remorselessly was to take me away from Big May and the Wee Brother and the Four Horsemen, my six favourite teachers.

The Wee Brother is with the Saints and Packy is more than likely his favourite pupil still, for Packy died young. Short of dancing like a bear and roaring like a bull, being late for school and being kind to me, and gathering nettles to preserve Pola from pimples, he never accomplished much in life that I ever heard of. But he had a splendid funeral paid for by the subscriptions of the Wee Brother's numerous clients and led by Pola and the Wee Brother as chief mourners.

Tosh took to boxing and retained his professional amiability except for one unfortunate moment when he was engaged in conflict with a fighter who had the provoking name of Kluterbuck. Every just man loses his composure at least once and Tosh struck Kluterbuck very much and very severely below the belt, lost the fight and gained a new name. Never afterwards was he known as Tosh. The change of name may have altered his character. He gave up boxing. He left the town and never came back. He was last heard of just before the war, working in a bicycle factory in Coventry. In occasional dreams I see him grown larger but otherwise unchanged, swinging a bicycle tyre around his head as once he swung the dead and odorous ampor eel.

Jinkins had a mental breakdown and went for treatment to the asylum whose coal supply we walked past the day Packy lost the nettles. He remained there as a trusted patient, working around the grounds and fishing in the river that flows just outside the walls.

Tall Jimmy Clarke became a jockey but took to drink, put on weight, descended to truck-driving and became a wealthy owner of trucks. No longer as supple or as close to the ground as he was that day under the chestnut branches he makes no money by picking ha'pence up with his teeth. But then, as he told me himself, he now has other ways of earning his living.

Big May went off to London and, if you could believe on their Bible oaths the people in the town I came from, went on thinking the longest way round was the shortest way home. Her thick dark hair, the outline of her strong jawbone is still visible to me. She holds me pick-a-back. Together we peer at the flashing knife and the raving woman and the slave of a man in the dim kitchen, and May says, 'From what they say she couldn't cut a slice of bread.'

By the tone of her voice then, she never put much weight on what people said. She gave generously. What violets she had she shared them with Packy.

# A Room in Linden

One day in the dark maze of the yew-hedges Sister Lua, who has arthritis, looks up at him from her wheelchair which he's pushing, and says: Tell me the truth. Don't be modest about it. Are you Nanky Poo?

Since he is a bookish young man it is an exciting thing for him to have history living along the corridor. The poet he's reading just before he leaves his room writes that there's a wind blowing, cold through the corridor, a death-wind, the flapping of defeated wings from meadows damned to eternal April. The poet has never seen it, but he could have been writing about this corridor. On its dull green walls, a mockery of the grass and green leaves of life, the sun never shines. All day and all night the big windows at the ends of the corridor, one at the east wing of the house and one at the west, are wide open, and from whichever airt the wind does blow it always blows cold. The rooms on the north side of the corridor are, as one might expect, colder and darker than the rooms on the south side, or would be if their light and heat depended totally on the sun.

Before the nuns got here and turned the place into a convalescent home it was lived in by a family famous for generations for a special brand of pipe tobacco. The old soldier who is reluctantly, vociferously fading away in a room on the north side of the corridor, says: This house was built on smoke. Just think of that. Smoke.

The old soldier himself belongs to some branch of the family that emigrated to South Africa and made even more money out of burgundy than the people who stayed at home made out of smoke, and there was always as much soldiering as smoke in the family; and big-game hunting, too, to judge by the fearful snarling mounted heads left behind and surviving, undisturbed by nuns or convalescents, in the entrance hall.

—You'll be nice to the old man, won't you, Mother Polycarp had said to him. He'll bore you to death. But he needs somebody to listen to him. He hasn't much longer to talk, in this world at any rate.

So he talks to the old soldier in the evenings and, in the afternoons, to the old priest and historian, dying as methodically and academically as he has lived, checking references, adding footnotes, in a room on the south side of the corridor. At other times he reads in his own room, or has visitors, or wheels Sister Lua's wheelchair in the ample bosky grounds, or leaves the grounds on his own and goes through quiet suburban roads to walk slowly, tapping his stick, in the public park that overlooks, across two walls and a railway, the flat sand and the bay. It is not an exciting life, but it's not meant to be.

He wheels Sister Lua round and round the dark cloisters of the yew-hedge maze from the corner where Jesus is condemned to death to the central circle where he is laid in the tomb. He tells her that he is not Nanky Poo.

—Well, I heard you had poems in that magazine. And I didn't see your name. And there is this poet called Nanky Poo. And he's very good. About the missions.

—Not me, alas, sister. I was never on the missions.

—Know you weren't. A university student.

Although she is always sitting down and being wheeled she is also always breathless and never quite begins or finishes a sentence, and it is necessary to fill in her words and meanings as she goes along. Bird-like, he knows, isn't much of a description, but she is bird-like, little hands like claws because of the arthritis, of course, a little nose like a beak peeking out from under the nun's pucog. To the left corner of her pale unvarnished little mouth, so often twisted with patience in pain, there's a mole with two hairs. She loves the dark green maze that grew up, like the house, out of smoke and was used by the nuns as a setting for a via dolorosa with life-size figures; and backgrounds of good stone columns and arches robbed from the wreckage of some eighteenth-century mansion. His first faux pas with the old historian had to do with those stations of the cross. One dull evening when the talk wasn't going so well he had, just to make chat, said: Don't they have a big day here once a year? People coming in hundreds to do the stations of the cross. What day does that happen on?

The old man pulls the rug more tightly around his long legs. His feet are always cold. In large bodies, Edmund Burke held, circulation is slower at the extremities, but the coldness of the old man's feet is just the beginning of death. He snuffs black snuff expertly from the hollow between thumb and forefinger, he sneezes, he says with crushing deliberation: Good Friday, my good young man. Even the younger generation should be aware that the Lord was crucified on Good Friday.

He's a carnaptious old bastard and even for the sake of Mother Polycarp, the kindly reverend mother, who is always thanking God for everything, it's sort of hard to suffer him at times. But he has both made and written history, and poems, too, of a learned sort, and collected folksong, and the best people have written about him and discovered an old-world courtesy and all the rest of that rot behind his rude exterior: the old-world courtesy of a Scandinavian sea-rover putting the full of a monastery of shaven-pated monks to the gory hatchet. By comparison the old soldier who has actually killed his man in far-away wars, is a gentleman. But then the old soldier is simply fading away, all battles fought and won, all comrades gone before him, all trumpets sounding from the other side. The old priest, still trying to work, has his last days aggravated by a mind that remembers everything and by the pain of a stomach cancer.

He leaves Sister Lua in the charge of a big red-headed nurse and walks down the main avenue towards suburbia and the park by the sea. The old white-haired vaudeville entertainer who has some sort of shaking paralysis, which he says is an occupational disease, waves to him from his seat by the grotto under the obelisk and gives him three letters to post at the postbox outside the gate. They are, he notices, all addressed to well-known celebrities of screen, stage and television: one in Dublin, one in London, one in New York. Out there is the world of healthy living people.

Life and playing children are, of course, all around him in the park by the sea but it isn't quite the same thing. There isn't enough of life there to help him to stop thinking of old men dying. He is very much on his own either because of his sullenness, or because he thinks that while he may be of interest to himself he couldn't possibly be of interest to anybody else. Nothing humble about that, though. In that park he's really a visitor from a special sort of world, from a cold green corridor damned to eternal December: sort of exclusive, though, a rich old soldier, a famous old historian, the artist who is still in touch with the best people; and only the best die in that corridor.

One old man who sits on a green wooden seat, close to the play-hall where the children run when it rains, talks to him as if he would gladly talk longer. He discourages that old man with abrupt sentences for he has, at the moment, enough of old men. He walks on beyond him and along by the tennis courts. A stout bespectacled girl with strong tanned legs plays awkwardly with a tall blond handsome fellow who wins every set and enjoys his superiority, while she seems to enjoy being beaten. A stranger from a strange land, he enjoys, as he passes or rests for a while on a seat and watches, the leaping of her legs. So everybody is happy and the park is beautiful. The blond boy isn't even good at the game and he, the stranger, knows that if it wasn't for the stiff hip, still slowly recovering, he could challenge him and beat him easily. But then the stout girl, legs excepted, isn't really interesting.

He himself is blond and doesn't take too well to the sun. So his favourite seat is in a shady corner under dark horse-chestnuts whose white candles are fading. He likes the place also because nobody else sits there. Strollers seem to accelerate as they walk past. Once in a while children run shouting, hooting through the dark tunnel, from one shire of sunshine into another. Through a fence of mournful laurels and copper beeches he sees the glitter of the sun on the lake. Out of the corner of his left eye he sees a well-built girl in white shorts flat on her back on the sunny grass. Sometimes she reads. Sometimes she raises her legs and, furiously with flashing thighs, pedals an invisible bicycle, faster and faster until it seems as if she has seven or seventeen legs, until the flash of her thighs takes the shape of a white circle. Her belly muscles must be jingling like springs. The joints in her hips, unlike his own, must be in perfect lubricated condition.

She is at the moment one of the five women in his life: Polycarp thanking God for the rain and the sunshine, for the hail and the snow; Lua, twisted in her chair; she who, nameless, cycles on her back on the grass; the strong-legged tennis player whose name, he has heard the blond fellow shout, is Phyllis; and A. N. Other.

To the rear of his shady corner there is a privet hedge and a high wooden fence and a gate with a notice that says no admission except on business. That's exactly the way he feels. Adam in Eden must have had just such a corner where he kept his tools and experimented with slips and seeds. But then before Adam and Eve made a pig's ass out of a good arrangement the garden must have looked after itself and needed none of that sweat-of-the-brow stuff. What would old Thor the thunderer, brooding in his room, biting on his cancer, think of that?

Belloc, says the old priest, was a big man who looked as if all his life he had eaten too much and drunk too much. The best way to learn French is to read cowboy and injun stories. They hold the interest better than Racine.

Aware of his own inanity, he says: translations.

Before that face, oblong, seemingly about twelve feet long, like a head cut out of the side of some crazy American mountain, he is perpetually nonplussed into saying stupidities.

—Cowboys and injuns, my good young man, are not indigenous to the soil of France.

—There's a city called Macon in Georgia, U.S.A.

—There's a city called everything somewhere in the States. Naturally they mispronounce the names.

So it goes on. You can't win with the old bastard.

—Darlington, he says, used to call on Hopkins to take him out for walks. Hopkins was for ever and always complaining of headaches. What else can you expect, Darlington would say to him, immured up there in your room writing rubbish. I'm not so sure that Darlington wasn't right.

He is at that time just entering his Hopkins phase and if he wasn't afraid of that granite face, eyes sunken and black and burning, jawbones out rigid like a forked bush struck by lightning, he would defend the poet, quoting his sonnet about the windhover which, with some difficulty, he has just memorised. Yet it still is something to hear those names tossed about by a man who knew the men, and was a name himself. He feels grateful to Mother Polycarp who, as a friend of his family, has invited him to this place for a while, after his year in orthopaedic, so that he can read his books and learn to walk at his ease. In all that green cold corridor, which is really a place for old men, he is the only person who is going to live. He searches for something neutral to say: Wasn't Hopkins always very scrupulous about marking students' papers?

—He was a neurotic Englishman, my good fellow. They never could make up their minds between imperialism and humanitarianism. That's what has them the way they are. Darlington was English, too, of course, the other sort, the complacent Englishman, thinking that only what is good can happen to him, and that all his works are good. Then a young upstart called Joyce put him in a book. That should have been a lesson to Darlington, if they have books in heaven or wherever he went to.

He should, as Mother Polycarp says, be taking notes, thank God, except he feels that if he did so, secretly even in his room, the old lion might read his mind and take offence. The old man laughs seldom, but he's laughing now, perhaps at some memory of two English Jesuits marooned in Ireland, or at some other memory surfacing for a second in the dark crowded pool behind his square forehead. He has kept his hair, a dirty grey, standing up and out as if it had never encountered a comb. The long bony hands tighten the rug about his knees. The cold is creeping upwards.

In the green corridor he kneels for a while at the prie-dieu before the shrine, not praying, just thinking about age and death, and looking up at the bearded face of St. Joseph, pure and gentle, guardian of the saviour child. With a lily in his hand. Another old man and, by all accounts, very patient about it. What in hell is St. Joseph, like Oscar Wilde or somebody, always doing with a lily in his hand? An awkward class of a thing for a carpenter to be carrying.

Before his hip betrayed him he has had a half-notion of being a priest, but a year in orthopaedic, bright nurses hopping all around him, has cured him by showing him that there are things that priests, in the ordinary course of duty, are not supposed to have.

—You're too young, the old soldier says, to be in this boneyard.

He's a small man with a red boozy face, a red dressing-gown, a whisky bottle and a glass always to his right hand. The whisky keeps him alive, thank God, Mother Polycarp says. He is, like St. Joseph, gentle but not so pure, rambling on about dirty doings in far-away places, Mombasa and Delhi are much mentioned, about Kaffir women, and about blokes who got knocked off in the most comical fashion. He laughs a lot. He doesn't need a considered answer or a balanced conversation, just a word now and then to show he's not alone. He shares the whisky generously. He has bags of money and, when he dies, he'll leave the perishing lot to the nuns.

—They do good, you know. Keep perky about it, too. Who else would look after the likes of me? Ruddy bone-yard, though. Elephants' graveyard. Get out of here and get a woman. Make sons. Before it's too late. Would get out myself only nobody would have me any more, and I couldn't have them. Only whisky left. But I had my day. When I was your age I laid them as quick as my batman could pull them out from under me. Three women shot under me at the battle of Balaclava and all that. Fit only for the boneyard now and the nuns. They don't want it and I can't give it. But there's always whisky, thank God, as the mother says. A field behind the barracks where old wind-broken cavalry mounts went on grass with the shoes off until they died. At least we didn't eat them like the bloody Belgians. Smell of slow death around this place.

He sniffs the whisky and laughs and then coughs. By night the coughing is constant. Lying awake and listening, the young man has a nightmarish feeling that they are all in prison cells, all dying, which is true, all the living are dying, and after one night the sun will never rise again on the park, and every time the cycling girl spins her legs she's another circle nearer to the grave. His own healthy youth has already collapsed in illness. Life is one collapse after another. The coughing goes on and on. To be a brave soldier and to end up coughing in a lonely room. Let me outa here. No, Sister Lua, I am not Nanky Poo.

—But every day that passes, Mother Polycarp tells him, brings you a day nearer to getting back to your stud-ies, thank God. You made a great recovery in orthopaedic.

She is a tall woman with a long flat-footed step and more rattlings of keys and rosary beads than seem natu-ral even in a nun. When he tells her that, she laughs and says, of course, that she has the keys of the kingdom, thank God. She has a good-humoured wrinkled mannish face, and she is famous everywhere for her kindness and her ability to gather money and build hospitals.

Does she say to the old men: Every day that passes brings you a day nearer heaven, thank God?

She naturally wouldn't mention death as the gate of heaven.

He has a feeling that none of them want to go any farther forward, they look backward to see heaven: on the day a new book was published or a new woman mounted or a new show went well. Heaven, like most things, doesn't last, or could only be an endless repetition of remembered happiness, and would in the end be, like dying, a bloody bore.

In her chair as he wheels her, Sister Lua, chirping like the little robin that she is, prays a bit and chats a bit and, because of her breathlessness and the way she beheads her sentences and docks the tails off them, he has to listen carefully to know whether she is chatting or praying. The life-size figures in the maze of dark yews – fourteen Christs in various postures, with attendant characters from jesting Pilate to the soldiers by the tomb – have acquired a sombre existence of their own. Do they relax at night, yawn, stretch stiff limbs, mutter a curse, light a cigarette, say to hell with show business? He must try that one out on the vaudeville man, shaking his way to the grave, on the seat by the grotto under the obelisk.

—Weep not for me, Sister Lua prays, but for yourselves and for your children.

The lord is talking to the weeping women of Jerusalem and not doing a lot to cheer them up. Some anti-semitical Irish parish priest must have written the prayers that Lua reels off. He didn't think much either of the kind of recruitment that got into the Roman army: These barbarians fastened him with nails and then, securing the cross, allowed him to die in anguish on this ignominious gibbet.

From the prayer book she has learned, by heart, not only the prayers but the instructions that go with them. She says, as the book instructs: Pause a while.

He pauses. The yew-hedges are a dark wall to either hand. Twenty paces ahead, the lord, in an arbour, is being lowered from the cross. The dying has been done.

—Nanky Poo. Nanky Poo.

—Sister, I am not Nanky Poo.

—But I call you Nanky Poo. Such a lovely name.

—So is Pooh Bah.

—Pooh Bah is horrible. Somebody making mean faces. Nanky Poo, you must write a poem for Mother Polycarp's feast-day. So easy for you. Just a parody. Round Linden when the sun was low, Mother Polycarp the Good did go.

—There's a future in that style.

—You'll do it, Nanky Poo?

—At my ease, sister. Whatever Nanky Poo can do, I can do better.

By the laying of the lord in the tomb they encounter A. N. Other. She tries to escape by hiding behind the eighteenth-century cut-stone robbed from the old house, but Sister Lua's bird's-eye is too quick and too sharp for her.

—Nurse Donovan, Nurse Donovan, the French texts have arrived.

—Yes, Sister Lua.

—When can you begin, Nanky Poo?

—Any time, sister.

—So useful to you, Nurse Donovan, French, when you're a secretary.

She is a small well-rounded brunette who has nursed in the orthopaedic hospital until something happened to her health. He is in love with her, has been for some time. Nothing is to come of it. He is never to see her again after he leaves the convalescent home. The trouble is that Sister Lua has decided that the girl must be a secretary and that Nanky Poo must teach her French, and it is quite clear from the subdued light in the girl's downcast dark eyes that she doesn't give a fiddler's fart about learning anything, even French, out of a book. Worse still: on the few occasions on which he has been able to corner the girl on her own he hasn't been able to think of a damn thing to talk about except books. How can he ever get through to her that pedagogy is the last thing in his mind?

She wheels Sister Lua away from him to the part of the house where the nuns live. Between the girl and himself Sister Lua has thrown a barbed-wire entanglement of irregular verbs. No great love has ever been so ludicrously frustrated.

A white blossom that he cannot identify grows copiously in this suburb. Thanks be to God for the thunder and lightning, thanks be to God for all things that grow.

No, Sister Lua, I am not Nanky Poo, am a disembodied spirit, homeless in suburbia, watching with envy a young couple coming, white and dancing, out of a house and driving away to play tennis, am a lost soul blown on the blast between a green cold corridor of age and death, and the children running and squealing by the lake in the park.

Beyond the two walls and the railway line the sea is flat and purple all the way to Liverpool. He envies the young footballers in the playing fields close to where the cycling girl lies flat on her back and rides to the moon on her imaginary bicycle. He envies particularly a red-headed boy with a superb left foot, who centres the ball, repeating the movement again and again, a conscious artist, as careless as God of what happens to the ball next, just so that he drops it in the goalmouth where he feels it should go. The footballer is on talking terms with the cycling girl. He jokes and laughs with her when the ball bounces that way. She stops her cycling to answer him. From his shadowy corner under the chestnuts Nanky Poo watches and thinks about his latest talk with the vaudeville man on his seat by the grotto under the obelisk.

The obelisk has also been built on smoke to celebrate the twenty-first birthday of a son of the house who would have been the great-granduncle of the old soldier.

—Vanished somewhere in India, the poor fellow. There was a rumour to the effect that he was eaten by wild beasts. A damn hard thing to prove unless you see it happen. Anyway he did for a good few of them before they got him. Half of the heads in the hallway below are his.

The obelisk stands up on a base of a flowering rockery, and into the cave or grotto underneath the rockery the nuns have, naturally, inserted a miniature Lourdes: the virgin with arms extended and enhaloed by burning candles, Bernadette kneeling by a fountain of holy water that is blessed by the chaplain at its source in a copper tank.

—The candles, says the vaudeville man, keep my back warm.

He wears a faded brown overcoat with a velvet collar. His white hair is high and bushy and possibly not as well trimmed as it used to be. The skin of his shrunken face and bony Roman nose has little purple blotches and, to conceal the shake in his hands, he grips the knob of his bamboo walking-cane very tightly. When he walks his feet rise jerkily from the ground as if they did so of their own accord and might easily decide never to settle down again. The handwriting on the envelopes is thin and wavery as if the pen now and again took off on its own.

—You know all the best people.

—I used to.

He is never gloomy, yet never hilarious. Somewhere in between he has settled for an irony that is never quite bitter.

—You still write to them.

—Begging letters, you know. Reminders of the good old days. They almost always work with show people. I never quite made it, you know, not even when I had the health. But I was popular with my own kind. This one now.

He points to a notable name on one envelope.

—We met one night in a boozer in London when I wasn't working. He stood me a large Jameson straight away, then another, then another. He asked me to dine with him. We talked about this and that. When we parted I found a tenner in the inside breast pocket of my overcoat. While we were dining he had slipped into the cloakroom. No note, no message, just a simple tenner to speak for itself. He wasn't rich then, mark you, although as the world knows he did well afterwards. But he remembers me. He promises to come to see me. Do you know, now that I think of it, this was the very overcoat.

The cycling girl has stopped cycling and is talking to the red-headed footballer. He stands above her, casually bouncing the ball on that accurate left foot. Whatever he's saying the girl laughs so loudly that Nanky Poo can hear her where he sits in gloom and broods on beggary. She has a good human throaty sort of a laugh.

The night there is no coughing, but only one loud single cry, from the next room, he knows that the old soldier has awakened for a moment to die. He rises, puts on slippers and dressing-gown, and heads down the corridor to find the night nurse. But Mother Polycarp is there already, coming stoop-shouldered, beads and keys rattling, out of the old man's room.

—Thank God, she says, he died peacefully and he had the blessed sacrament yesterday morning. He wandered a lot in his time but he came home in the end.

He walks down the stairway to the shadowy main hall. Do the animals in the half-darkness grin with satisfaction at the death of a man whose relative was eaten by one or more of their relatives? The front door is open for the coming of the doctor and the priest. Above the dark maze of yew-hedge the obelisk is silhouetted against the lights of the suburb. The place is so quiet that he can hear even the slight noise of the sea over the flat sand. This is the first time he has been out of doors at night since he went to orthopaedic. Enjoying the freedom, the quiet, the coolness, he walks round and round in the maze until his eyes grow used to the blackness and he is able to pick out the men and women who stand along the via dolorosa. They are just as motionless as they are during the day. When he comes back Mother Polycarp is waiting for him in the hallway.

—Now you're bold, she says. You could catch a chill. But every day that passes brings you nearer to freedom, thank God, and you can walk very well now.

She crosses herself as she passes the shrine in the corridor. She says: One thing that you could do now that you are up, is talk to himself. Or listen to him. He's awake and out of bed and lonely for somebody to talk to.

He is out of bed but not fully dressed; and, in a red dressing-gown that must have been presented to him by Mother Polycarp, he doesn't seem half as formidable as in his black religious habit. There is an open book on the rug that, as usual, covers and beats down the creeping cold from his thighs and knees. He is not reading. His spectacles are in their case on the table to his right hand. Above the light from the shaded reading-lamp his head and shoulders are in shadow. For once, since he is red and not black and half-invisible, Nanky Poo feels almost at ease with him.

From the shadows his voice says: Credit where credit is due, young man. The first Chichester to come to Ireland was certainly one of the most capable and successful robbers who ever lived. He stole most of the north of Ireland not only from its owners but even from the robbers who stole it from its owners. Twice he robbed his royal master, James Stuart, the fourth of Scotland and the first of England. The man who did that had to rise early in the morning. For although King James was a fool about most things he was no fool about robbery: it was he who got the Scots the name for parsimony. Chichester stole the entire fisheries of Lough Neagh, the largest lake in the British Isles, and nobody found out about it until after he died. *Age quod agis,* as the maxim says. Do what you do. At his own craft he was a master. I dealt with him in a book.

—I read it.

—Did you indeed? A mark in your favour, young man.

—As a matter of fact, sir, the copy of it I read had your name on the flyleaf. Father Charles from your monastery loaned it to me when I was in orthopaedic.

As soon as the words are out he knows he has dropped the biggest brick of his career, and prays to Jesus that he may live long and die happy and never drop a bigger one. He has never known silence to last so long and be so deafening. Even the bulb in the reading-lamp makes a sound like a big wind far away. Blood in the ears?

—They're not expecting me back, so.

—What do you mean, sir?

—You know damned well what I mean. In a monastery when they know you're dead and not coming back they empty your room. There's another man in it now. They were kind and never told me. That room was all I had, and my books. They have sent me to the death-house as they so elegantly say in the United Sates. This here is the death-house. What do you do here, young man?

He is asking himself that question. So far no easy answer has offered itself.

—Books you build around you, more than a house and wife and family for a layman, part of yourself, flesh of your flesh, more than furniture for a monk's cell, a shell for his soul, the only thing in spite of the rule of poverty I couldn't strip myself of, and my talents allowed me a way around the rule, but man goeth forth naked as he came, stripped of everything, death bursts among them like a shell and strews them over half the town, and yet there are men who can leave their books as memorials to great libraries…

Sacred Heart of Jesus, he thinks, up there in the shadows there may be tears on that granite face.

—I'm sorry, sir.

—You didn't know, young man. How could you know?

—You will be remembered, sir.

—Thank you. The old must be grateful. Go to bed now. You have reason to rest. You have a life to live.

In his room he reads for what's left of the night. He has a life to live.

Through a drowsy weary morning he feels he wants to leave the place right away. Never again will he see the old soldier. Never again can he face the old scholar.

—Nanky Poo, Nanky Poo, you won't see your old friend again.

—No, sister. He died last night.

—Not him. Your old friend on the seat by the grotto.

Flying from French, A. N. Other cuts across their path through the maze. But she's moving so fast that not even Lua can hail her. Somewhere in the maze and as quietly as a cat she is stealing away from him for ever. Dulled with lack of sleep his brain is less than usually able to keep up with the chirpings of Lua.

—Is he dead too?

Let them all die. Let me outa here. I am not Nanky Poo.

—A stroke, not fatal yet, but, alas, the final one.

—I'll go to see him.

But Mother Polycarp tells him there's no point in that: all connection between brain and tongue and eyes is gone.

—He wouldn't know whether you were there or not.

—Couldn't he see me?

—We don't know. The doctor says, God bless us, that he's a vegetable.

—I wondered had he any letters to send out. I used to post them for him.

—He can't write any more.

A silence. So he can't even beg.

—It's a blow to you, she says. You were his friend. He used to enjoy his talks with you. But it'll soon be over, thank God. Pray for him that he may pray for us. For some of us death isn't the worst thing and, as far as we can tell, he's content.

A vegetable has little choice. Refusing to lie down and rest in that green place of death he walks dumbly through the suburb. The white blossoms blind him. When he leaves this place he will do so with the sense of escape he might have if he was running on a smooth hillside on a sunny windy day. But later he knows that the place will be with him for ever: the cry in the night, the begging letters sent to the stars, the pitiful anger of an old man finding another man living in his room. Crucified god, there's life for you, and there's a lot more of it that he hasn't yet encountered. He expects little, but he will sit no longer expecting it alone in any dark corner.

He would like to be able to tell the cycling girl a really good lie about how he injured his hip. The scrum fell on me on the line in a rather dirty game, just as I was sneaking away and over: that's how it happens, you know.

Or: An accident on a rockface in Snowdonia, a bit of bad judgment, my own fault actually.

Or: You've heard of the parachute club that ex-air force chap has started out near Celbridge.

He would prefer if he had crutches, or even one crutch, instead of a stick which he doesn't even need. A crutch could win a girl's confidence for no harm could come to her from a fellow hopping on a crutch unless he could move as fast as, and throw the crutch with the accuracy of, Long John Silver.

There he goes, thinking about books again. He'd better watch that.

The red-headed footballer is far-away and absorbed in the virtues of his own left foot. For the first time Nanky Poo notices the colour of her hair, mousy, and the colour of her sweater, which today is mauve, because when she lay flat on the grass and he watched from a distance, she was mostly white shorts and bare circling thighs.

He sits down, stiffly, on the grass beside her. She seems not in the least surprised. She has a freckled face and spectacles. That surprises him.

He says: I envy the way your hips work.

If he doesn't say something wild like that he'll begin talking about books and his cause is lost.

—Why so?

—I was laid up for a year with a tubercular hip. I'm in the convalescent over there.

—Oh I know who you are. Sister Lua told me. You're Nanky Poo. You write poetry.

He is cold all over.

—You know Sister Lua?

—She's my aunt. I write poetry too. Nobody has ever printed it though. Yet. Sister Lua said that some day she'd ask you to read some of it.

—I'd be delighted to.

—I watched you sitting over there for a long time. But I didn't like to approach you. Sister Lua said you were standoffish and intellectual.

She walks back with him as far as the obelisk and the grotto. They will meet again on the following day and take a bus into a teashop in the city. They may even go to a show if Mother Polycarp allows him – as she will – to stay out late.

He suspects that all this will come to nothing except to the reading of her poetry which as likely as not will be diabolical. He wonders if some day she will, like her aunt, be arthritic, for arthritis, they say, like a stick leg, runs in the blood. But with one of his three friends dead, one estranged and one a vegetable, it is something to have somebody to talk to as you stumble through suburbia. He has a life to live. Every day that passes brings him a day nearer to somewhere else.

So thanks be to God for the rain and the sunshine, thanks be to God for the hail and the snow, thanks be to God for the thunder and lightning, thanks be to God that all things are so.

# Maiden's Leap

The civic guard, or policeman, on the doorstep was big, middle-aged, awkward, affable. Behind him was green sunlit lawn sloping down to a white horse-fence and a line of low shrubs. Beyond that the highway, not much travelled. Beyond the highway, the jetty, the moored boats, the restless lake-water reflecting the sunshine.

The civic guard was so affable that he took off his cap. He was bald, completely bald. Robert St. Blaise Macmahon thought that by taking off his cap the civic guard had made himself a walking, or standing, comic comment on the comic rural constable, in the Thomas Hardy story, who wouldn't leave his house without his truncheon: because without his truncheon his going forth would not be official.

Robert St. Blaise Macmahon felt like telling all that to the civic guard and imploring him, for the sake of the dignity of his office, to restore his cap to its legal place and so to protect his bald head from the sunshine which, for Ireland, was quite bright and direct. Almost like the sun of that autumn he had spent in the Grand Atlas, far from the tourists. Or the sun of that spring when he had submitted to the natural curiosity of a novelist, who was also a wealthy man and could afford such silly journeys, and gone all the way to the United States, not to see those sprawling vulgar cities, Good God sir no, nor all those chromium-plated barbarians who had made an industry out of writing boring books about those colossal bores, Yeats and Joyce, but to go to Georgia to see the Okefenokee Swamp which interested him because of those sacred drooping melancholy birds, the white ibises, and because of the alligators. Any day in the year give him, in preference to Americans, alligators. It could be that he made the journey so as to be able at intervals to say that.

But if he talked like this to the bald guard on the ancestral doorstep the poor devil would simply gawk or smirk or both and say: Yes, Mr. Macmahon. Of course, Mr. Macmahon.

Very respectful, he would seem to be. For the Macmahons counted for something in the town. His father's father had as good as owned it. The fellow's bald head was nastily ridiculously perspiring. Robert St. Blaise Macmahon marked down that detail for his notebook. Henry James had so wisely said: Try to be one of those on whom nothing is lost.

Henry James had known it all. What a pity that he had to be born in the United States. But then, like the gentleman he was, he had had the good wit to run away from it all.

The bald perspiring cap-in-hand guard said: Excuse me, Mr. Macmahon. Sorry to disturb you on such a heavenly morning and all. But I've come about the body, sir.

Robert St. Blaise Macmahon was fond of saying in certain circles in Dublin that he liked civic guards if they were young, fresh from the country, and pink-cheeked; and that he liked Christian Brothers in a comparable state of development. In fact, he would argue, you came to a time of life when civic guards and Christian Brothers were, apart from the uniforms, indistinguishable. This he said merely to hear himself say it. He was much too fastidious for any fleshly contact with anybody, male or female. So, lightly, briefly, flittingly, trippingly, he now amused himself with looking ahead to what he would say on his next visit to town: Well if they had to send a guard they could have sent a young handsome one to enquire about the ...

What the guard had just said now registered and with a considerable shock. The guard repeated: About the body, sir. I'm sorry, Mr. Macmahon, to disturb you.

—What body? Whose body? What in heaven's name can you mean?

—I know it's a fright, sir. Not what you would expect at all. The body in the bed, sir. Dead in the bed.

—There is no body in my bed. Dead or alive. At least not while I'm up and about. I live here alone, with my housekeeper, Miss Hynes.

—Yes, Mr. Macmahon, sir. We know Miss Hynes well. Very highly respected lady, sir. She's below in the barracks at the moment in a terrible state of nervous prostration. The doctor's giving her a pill or an injection or something to soothe her. Then he'll be here directly.

—Below in the barracks? But she went out to do the shopping.

—Indeed yes, sir. But she slipped in to tell us, in passing, like, sir. Oh it's not serious or anything. Foul play is not suspected.

—Foul what? Tell you what?

—Well, sir.

—Tell me, my good man.

—She says, sir, there's a man dead in her bed.

—A dead man?

—The very thing, Mr. Macmahon.

—In the bed of Miss Hynes, my housekeeper.

—So she says, sir. Her very words.

—What in the name of God is he doing there?

—Hard to say, Mr. Macmahon, what a dead man would be doing in a bed, I mean like in somebody else's bed.

With a huge white linen handkerchief that he dragged, elongated, out of a pants pocket, and then spread before him like an enveloping cloud, the guard patiently mopped his perspiration: Damned hot today, sir. The hottest summer, the paper says, in forty years.

The high Georgian-Floridian sun shone straight down on wine-coloured swamp-water laving (it was archaic but yet the only word) the grotesque knobbly knees of giant cypress trees. The white sacred crook-billed birds perched gravely, high on grey curved branches above trailing Spanish moss, oh far away, so far away from this mean sniggering town and its rattling tongues. It was obvious, it was regrettably obvious, that the guard was close to laughter.

—A dead man, guard, in the bed of Miss Hynes, my housekeeper, and housekeeper to my father and mother before me, and a distant relative of my own.

—So she tells us, sir.

—Scarcely a laughing matter, guard.

—No, sir. Everything but, sir. It's just the heat, sir. Overcome by the heat. Hottest summer, the forecast says, in forty years.

That hottest summer in forty years followed them, panting, across the black and red flagstones of the wide hallway. A fine mahogany staircase went up in easy spirals. Robert St. Blaise Macmahon led the way around it, keeping to the ground floor. The guard placed his cap, open end up, on the hall stand, as reverently as if he were laying cruets on an altar, excusing himself, as he did so, as if the ample mahogany hall stand, mirrored and antlered, were also a

Macmahon watching, or reflecting, him with disapproval. It was the first time he or his like ever had had opportunity or occasion to enter this house.

In the big kitchen, old-fashioned as to size, modern as to fittings, the hottest summer was a little assuaged. The flagstones were replaced by light tiles, green and white, cool to the sight and the touch. She had always held on to that bedroom on the ground floor, beyond the kitchen, although upstairs the large house was more than half-empty. She said she loved it because it had French windows that opened out to the garden. They did, too. They would also give easy access for visitors to the bedroom: a thought that had never occurred to him, not once over all these years.

Earlier that morning she had called to him from the kitchen to say that she was going shopping, and had made her discreet escape by way of those windows. They still lay wide open to the garden. She was a good gardener as she was a good housekeeper. She had, of course, help with the heavy work in both cases: girls from the town for the kitchen, a healthy young man for the garden. All three, or any, of them were due to arrive, embarrassingly, within the next hour. Could it be the young man for the garden, there, dead in the bed? No, at least, thank God, it wasn't her assistant gardener, a scape-grace of a fellow that might readily tempt a middle-aged woman. She hadn't stooped to the servants. She had that much Macmahon blood in her veins. This man was, or had been, a stranger, an older man by far than the young gardener. He was now as old as he would ever be. The hottest summer was heavy and odorous in the garden, and flower odours and insect sounds came to them in the room. The birds were silent. There was also the other odour: stale sweat, or dead passion, or just death? The guard sniffed. He said: He died sweating. He's well tucked in.

Only the head was visible: sparse grey hair, a few sad pimples on the scalp, a long purple nose, a comic Cyrano nose. Mouth and eyes were open. He had good teeth and brown eyes. He looked, simply, surprised, not yet accustomed to wherever he happened to find himself.

—Feel his heart, guard.

—Oh dead as mutton, Mr. Macmahon. Miss Hynes told no lie. Still, he couldn't die in a better place. In a bed, I mean.

—Unhouselled, unappointed, unannealed.

—Yes, sir, the guard said, every bit of it.

—I mean he died without the priest.

With something amounting almost to wit – you encountered it in the most unexpected places – the guard said that taking into account the circumstances in which the deceased, God be merciful to him, had passed over, he could hardly have counted on the company of a resident chaplain. That remark could be adopted as one's own, improved upon, and employed on suitable occasions and in the right places, far from this town and its petty people.

—Death, said the guard, is an odd fellow. There's no being up to him, Mr. Macmahon. He can catch you unawares in the oddest places.

This fellow, by heaven, was a philosopher. He was, for sure, one for the notebook.

—Quite true, guard. There was a very embarrassing case involving a president of the great French Republic. Found dead in his office. He had his hands in the young lady's hair. They had to cut the hair to set her free.

—Do you tell me so, sir? A French president? 'Twouldn't be the present fellow, de Gaulle, with the long nose would be caught at capers like that.

—There was a Hemingway story on a somewhat similar theme.

—Of course, sir. You'd know about that, Mr. Macmahon. I don't read much myself. But my eldest daughter that works for the public libraries tells me about your books.

—And Dutch Schultz, the renowned American gangster, you know that he was shot dead while he was sitting, well in fact while he was sitting on the toilet.

—A painful experience, Mr. Macmahon. He must have been surprised beyond measure.

Far away, from the highway, came the sound of an automobile.

—That, said the guard, could be the doctor or the ambulance.

They waited in silence in the warm odorous room. The sound passed on and away: neither the doctor nor the ambulance.

—But that fellow in the bed, Mr. Macmahon, I could tell you things about him, God rest him.

—Do you mean to say you know him?

—Of course, sir. It's my business to know people.

—Try to be one of those on whom nothing is lost.

—Quite so, sir, and odd that you should mention it. For that fellow in the bed, sir, do you know that once upon a time he lost two hundred hens?

—Two hundred hens?

—Chickens.

—Well, even chickens. That was a lot of birds. Even sparrows. Or skylarks. He must have been the only man in Europe who ever did that.

—In the world, I'd say, sir. And it happened so simple.

—It's stuffy in here, Robert said.

He led the way out to the garden. The sound of another automobile on the highway was not yet the doctor nor the ambulance. They walked along a red-sanded walk. She had had that mulch red sand brought all the way from Mullachdearg Strand in County Donegal. She loved the varied strands of Donegal: red, golden or snow-white. To right and left her roses flourished. She had a good way with roses, and with sweetpea, and even with sunflowers, those lusty brazen-faced giants.

—He was up in Dublin one day in a pub, and beside him at the counter the mournfullest man you ever saw. So the man that's gone, he was always a cheery type, said to the mournful fellow: Brighten up, the sun's shining, life's not all that bad. The mournful one says: If you were a poultry farmer with two hundred hens that wouldn't lay an egg, you'd hardly be singing songs.

—The plot, said Robert St. Blaise Macmahon, thickens.

—So, says your man that's inside there, and at peace we may charitably hope, how much would you take for those hens? A shilling a hen. Done, says he, and out with two hundred shillings and buys the hens. Then he hires a van and a boy to drive it, and off with him to transport the hens. You see, he knows a man here in this very town that will give him half-a-crown a hen, a profit of fifteen pounds sterling less the hire of the van. But the journey is long and the stops plentiful at the wayside pubs, he always had a notorious drouth, and whatever happened nobody ever found out, but when he got to this town at two in the morning, the back doors of the van were swinging open.

—The birds had flown.

—Only an odd feather to be seen. And he had to pay the boy fifteen shillings to clean out the back of the van. They were never heard of again, the hens I mean. He will long be remembered for that.

—If not for anything else.

—His poor brother, too, sir. That was a sad case. Some families are, you might say, addicted to sudden death.

—Did he die in a bed?

—Worse, far worse, sir. He died on a lawnmower.

—Guard, said Robert, would you have a cup of tea? You should be writing books, instead of me.

—I was never much given to tea, sir.

—But in all the best detective stories the man from Scotland Yard always drinks a cup o' tea.

—As I told you, sir, I don't read much. But if you had the tiniest drop of whisky to spare, I'd be grateful. It's a hot day and this uniform is a crucifixion.

They left the garden by a wicket-gate that opened through a beech-hedge on to the front lawn. The sun's reflections shot up like lightning from the lake-water around the dancing boats. Three automobiles passed, but no doctor, no ambulance, appeared. Avoiding the silent odorous room they re-entered the house by the front door. In the dining-room Robert St. Blaise Macmahon poured the whisky for the guard, and for himself: he needed it.

—Ice, guard?

—No thank you sir. Although they say the Americans are hell for it. In everything, in tea, whisky, and so on.

Two more automobiles passed. They listened and waited.

—You'd feel, sir, he was listening to us, like for a laugh, long nose and all. His brother was the champion gardener of all time. Better even than Miss Hynes herself, although her garden's a sight to see and a scent to smell.

—He died on a lawnmower?

—On his own lawn, sir. On one of those motor mowers. It blew up under him. He was burned to death. And you could easily say, sir, he couldn't have been at a more harmless occupation, or in a safer place.

—You could indeed, guard. Why haven't I met you before this?

—That's life, sir. Our paths never crossed. Only now for that poor fellow inside I wouldn't be here today at all.

This time it had to be the doctor and the ambulance. The wheels came, scattering gravel, up the driveway.

—He was luckier than his brother, sir. He died in more comfort, in a bed. And in action, it seems. That's more than will be said for most of us.

The doorbell chimed: three slow cathedral tones. That chime had been bought in Bruges where they knew about bells. The guard threw back what was left of his whisky. He said: You'll excuse me, Mr. Macmahon. I'll go and put on my cap. We have work to do.

When the guard, the doctor, the ambulance, the ambulance attendants, and the corpse had, all together, taken their departure, he sprayed the bedroom with Flit, sworn foe to the housefly. It was all he could think of. It certainly changed the odour. It drifted out even into the garden, and lingered there among the roses. The assistant gardener and the kitchen girls had not yet arrived. That meant that the news was out, and that they were delaying in the town to talk about it. What sort of insufferable idiot was that woman to put him in this way into the position of being talked about, even, in the local papers, written about, and then laughed at, by clods he had always regarded with a detached and humorous, yet godlike, eye?

He sat, for the sake of the experience, on the edge of the rumpled bed from which the long-nosed corpse had just been removed. But he felt nothing of any importance. He remembered that another of those American dons had written a book, which he had slashingly reviewed, about love and death in the American novel. To his right, beyond the open windows, was her bureau desk and bookcase: old black oak, as if in stubborn isolated contradiction to the prevalent mahogany. She had never lost the stiff pride that a poor relation wears as a mask when he or she can ride high above the more common servility. She was a high-rider. It was simply incomprehensible that she, who had always so rigidly kept herself to herself, should have had a weakness for a long-nosed man who seemed to have been little better than a figure of fun. Two hundred hens, indeed!

The drawers of the bureau-bookcase were sagging open, and in disorder, as if in panic she had been rooting through them for something that nobody could find. He had seldom seen the inside of her room but, from the little he had seen and from everything he knew of her, she was no woman for untidiness or unlocked drawers. Yet in spite of her panic she had not called for aid to him, her cousin-once-removed, her employer, her benefactor. She had always stiffly, and for twenty-five years, kept him at a distance. Twenty-five years ago, in this room. She would have been eighteen, not six months escaped from the mountain valley she had been reared in, from which his parents had rescued her. He closes his eyes and, as best he can, his nose. He remembers. It is a Sunday afternoon and the house is empty except for the two of them.

He is alone in his room reading. He is reading about how Lucius Apuleius watches the servant-maid, Fotis, bending over the fire: Mincing of meats and making pottage for her master and mistresse, the Cupboard was all set with wines and I thought I smelled the savour of some dainty meats. Shee had about her middle a white and clean apron, and shee was girdled about her body under the paps with a swathell of red silk, and shee stirred the pot and turned the meat with her faire and white hands, in such sort that with stirring and turning the same, her loynes and hips did likewise move and shake, which was in my mind a comely sight to see.

Robert St. Blaise Macmahon who, at sixteen, had never tasted wine except to nibble secretively at the altar-wine when he was an acolyte in the parish church, repeats over and over again the lovely luscious Elizabethan words of Adlington's translation from the silver Latin: We did renew our venery by drinking of wine.

For at sixteen he is wax, and crazy with curiosity.

Then he looks down into the garden and there she is bending down over a bed of flowers. She is tall, rather sallow-faced, a Spanish face in an oval of close, crisp, curling dark hair. He has already noticed the determination of her long lithe stride, the sway of her hips, the pendulum swish and swing of her bright tartan pleated skirt. For a girl from the back of the mountains she has a sense of style.

She has come to this house from the Gothic grandeur of a remote valley called Glenade. Flat-topped mountains, so steep that the highest few hundred feet are sheer rock-cliffs corrugated by torrents, surround it. One such cliff, fissured in some primeval cataclysm, falls away into a curved chasm, rises again into one cold pinnacle of rock. The place is known as the Maiden's Leap, and the story is that some woman out of myth – Goddess, female devil, what's the difference? – pursued by a savage and unwanted lover, ran along the ridge of the mountain, and when faced by the chasm leaped madly to save her virtue, and did. But she didn't leap far enough to save her beautiful frail body which was shattered on the rocks below. From which her pursuer may have derived a certain perverse satisfaction.

All through her girlhood her bedroom window has made a frame for that extraordinary view. Now, her parents dead, herself adopted into the house of rich relatives as a sort of servant-maid, assistant to the aged housekeeper and in due course to succeed her, she bends over a flowerbed as Fotis had bent over the fire: O Fotis how trimly you can stir the pot, and how finely, with shaking your buttocks, you can make pottage.

Now she is standing tall and straight snipping blossoms from a fence of sweetpea. Her body is clearly outlined against the multi-coloured fence. He watches. He thinks of Fotis. He says again: We did renew our venery with drinking of wine.

When he confronts her in this very room, and makes an awkward grab at her, her arms are laden with sweetpea. So he is able to plant one kiss on cold unresponding lips. The coldness, the lack of response in a bondswoman, surprises him. She bears not the slightest resemblance to Fotis. It was the done thing, wasn't it: the young master and the servant-maid? In the decent old days in Czarist Russia the great ladies in the landed houses used to give the maids to their sons to practise on.

The sweetpea blossoms, purple, red, pink, blue, flow rather than fall to the floor. Then she hits him with her open hand, one calm, deliberate, country clout that staggers him and leaves his ear red, swollen and singing for hours. She clearly does not understand the special duties of a young female servant. In wild Glenade they didn't read Turgenev or Saltykov-Shchedrin. He is humiliatingly reminded that he is an unathletic young man, a pampered only child, and that she is a strong girl from a wild mountain valley. She says: Mind your manners, wee boy. Pick up those sweetpea or I'll tell your father and mother how they came to be on the floor.

He picks up the flowers. She is older than he is. She is also taller, and she has a hand like rock. He knows that she has already noticed that he is afraid of his father.

This room was not then a bedroom. It was a pantry with one whole wall of it shelved for storing apples. He could still smell those apples, and the sweetpea. The conjoined smell of flower and fruit was stronger even than the smell of the insect-killing spray with which he had tried to banish the odour of death.

That stinging clout was her great leap, her defiance, her declaration of independence but, as in the case of the Maiden of Glenade, it had only carried her halfways. To a cousin once-removed, who never anyway had cared enough to make a second attempt, she had demonstrated that she was no chattel. But she remained a dependant, a poor relation, a housekeeper doing the bidding of his parents until they died and, after their death, continuing to mind the house, grow the roses, the sweetpea and the sunflowers. The sense of style, the long lithe swinging stride, went for nothing, just because she hadn't jumped far enough to o'erleap the meandering withering enduring ways of a small provincial town. No man in the place could publicly be her equal. She was part Macmahon. So she had no man of her own, no place of her own. She had become part of the furniture of this house. She had no life of her own. Or so he had lightly thought.

He came and went and wrote his books, and heard her and spoke to her, but seldom really saw her except to notice that wrinkles, very faint and fine, had appeared on that Spanish face, on the strong-boned, glossy forehead, around the corners of the eyes. The crisp dark hair had touches of grey that she had simply not bothered to do anything about. She was a cypher, and a symbol in a frustrating land that had more than its share of ageing hopeless virgins. He closed his eyes and saw her as such when, in his writing, he touched satirically on that aspect of life in his pathetic country. Not that he did so any more often than he could help. For a London illustrated magazine he had once written about the country's low and late marriage rate, an article that had astounded all by its hard practicality. But as a general rule he preferred to think and to write about Stockholm or Paris or Naples or Athens, or African mountains, remote from everything. His travel books were more than travel books, and his novels really did show that travel broadened the mind. Or to think and write about the brightest gem in an America that man was doing so much to lay waste: the swamp that was no swamp but a wonderland out of a fantasy by George MacDonald, a Scottish writer whom nobody read any more, a fantasy about awaking some morning in your own bedroom, which is no longer a bedroom but the heart of the forest where every tree has its living spirit, genial or evil, evil or genial.

At that moment in his reverie the telephone rang. To the devil with it, he thought, let it ring. The enchanted swamp was all around him, the wine-coloured water just perceptibly moving, the rugged knees of the cypress trees, the white priestly birds curved brooding on high bare branches, the silence. Let it ring. It did, too. It rang and rang and refused to stop. So he walked ill-tempered to the table in the hallway where the telephone was, picked it up, silenced the ringing, heard the voice of the civic guard, and then noticed for the first conscious time the black book that he carried in his right hand.

The guard said: She's resting now. The sergeant's wife is looking after her.

—Good. That's very good.

It was a ledger-type book, eight inches by four, the pages ruled in blue, the margins in red. He must, unthinkingly, have picked it up out of the disorder in which her morning panic had left the bureau-bookcase. For the first time that panic seemed to him as comic: it wasn't every morning a maiden lady found a long-nosed lover, or something, cold between the covers. It was matter for a short story, or an episode in a novel: if it just hadn't damned well happened in his own house. What would Henry James have made of it? The art of fiction is in telling not what happened, but what should have happened. Or what should have happened somewhere else.

The guard was still talking into his left ear, telling him that the doctor said it was a clear case of heart failure. Oh, indeed it was: for the heart was a rare and undependable instrument. With his right hand he flicked at random through the black book, then, his eye caught by some words that seemed to mean something, he held the book flat, focused on those words until they were steady, and read. The hand-writing was thick-nibbed, black as coal, dogged, almost printing, deliberate as if the nib had bitten into the paper. He read: Here he comes down the stairs in the morning, his double jowl red and purple from the razor, his selfish mouth pursed as tight as Mick Clinton, the miser of Glenade, used to keep the woollen sock he stored his money in when he went to the market and the horsefair of Manorhamilton. Here he comes, the heavy tread of him in his good, brown hand-made shoes, would shake the house if it wasn't as solid on its foundations as the Rock of Cashel. Old John Macmahon used to boast that his people built for eternity. Thud, thud, thud, the weight of his big flat feet. Here he comes, Gorgeous Gussie, with his white linen shirt, he should have frills on his underpants, and his blue eyeshade to show to the world, as if there was anybody to bother looking at him except myself and the domestic help, that he's a writer. A writer, God help us. About what? Who reads him? It's just as well he has old John's plunder to live on.

The black letters stood out like basalt from the white, blue-and-red lined paper. Just one paragraph she wrote to just one page and, if the paragraph didn't fully fill the page, she made, above and below the paragraph, whorls and doodles and curlicues in inks of various colours, blue, red, green, violet. She was a lonely self-delighting artist. She was, she had been, for how long, oh merciful heavens, an observer, a writer.

The guard was saying: She said to the sergeant's wife that she's too shy to face you for the present.

—Shy, he said.

He looked at the black words. They were as distinct as that long-ago clout on the side of the head: the calloused hard hand of the mountainy girl reducing the pretensions of a shy, sensitive, effeminate youth.

He said: She has good reason to be shy. It is, perhaps, a good thing that she should, at least, be shy before her employer and distant relation.

—It might be that, sir, she might mean not shy, but ashamed.

—She has also good reason for being ashamed.

—She says, Mr. Macmahon, sir, that she might go away somewhere for a while.

—Shouldn't she wait for the inquest and the funeral? At any rate, she has her duties here in this house. She is, she must realise, paid in advance.

So she would run, would she, and leave him to be the single object of the laughter of the mean people of this town? In a sweating panic he gripped the telephone as if he would crush it. There was an empty hungry feeling,

by turns hot, by turns cold, just above his navel. He was
betraying himself to that garrulous guard who would report
to the town every word he said. It was almost as if the
guard could read, if he could read, those damnable black
words. He gripped the phone, slippy and sweaty as it was,
gulped and steadied himself, breathed carefully, in out,
in out, and was once again Robert St. Blaise Macmahon,
a cultivated man whose education had commenced at
the famous Benedictine school at Glenstal. After all, the
Jesuits no longer were what once they had been, and
James Joyce had passed that way to the discredit both of
himself and the Jesuits.

—Let her rest then, he said. I'll think over what she
should do. I'll be busy all day, guard, so don't call me
unless it's absolutely essential.

He put down the telephone, wiped his sweating hand
with a white linen handkerchief, monogrammed and
ornamented with the form of a feather embroidered in
red silk. It was meant to represent a quill pen and also
to be a symbol of the soaring creative mind. That fancy
handkerchief was, he considered, his one flamboyance.
He wore, working, a blue eye-shade because there were
times when lamplight, and even overbright daylight,
strained his eyes. Any gentleman worthy of the name
did, didn't he, wear hand-made shoes?

On the first page of the book she had pasted a square of
bright yellow paper and on it printed in red ink: Paragraphs.

In smaller letters, in Indian black ink, and in an elegant
italic script, she had written: Reflections on Robert the
Riter.

Then finally, in green ink, she had printed: By his
Kaptivated Kuntry Kusin!!!

He was aghast at her frivolity. Nor did she need those
three exclamation marks to underline her bitchiness, a

withdrawn and secretive bitchiness, malevolent among
the roses and the pots and pans, overflowing like bile, in
black venomous ink. She couldn't have been long at this
secret writing. The book was by no means full. She had
skipped, and left empty pages here and there, at random
as if she dipped her pen and viciously wrote wherever
the book happened to open. There was no time sequence
that he could discern. He read: He says he went all the
way to the States to see a swamp. Just like him. Would he
go all the way to Paris to see the sewers?

—But the base perfidy of that.

He spoke aloud, not to himself but to her.

—You always pretended to be interested when I
talked about the swamp. The shy wild deer that would
come to the table to take the bit out of your fingers
when you breakfasted in the open air, the racoon with
the rings round its eyes, the alligators, the wine-coloured
waters, the white birds, the white sand on the bed of the
Suwannee River. You would sit, woman, wouldn't you,
brown Spanish face inscrutable, listening, agreeing, with
me, oh yes, agreeing with me in words, but, meanly, all
the time, thinking like this.

Those brief words about that small portion of his
dreamworld had wounded him. But bravely he read
more. The malice of this woman of the long-nosed
chicken-losing lover must be fully explored. She was also,
by heaven, a literary critic. She wrote: Does any novelist,
nowadays, top-dress his chapters with quotations from
other authors? There is one, but he writes thrillers and
that's different. Flat-footed Robert the Riter, with his
good tweeds and his brass-buttoned yellow waistcoat,
has a hopelessly old-fashioned mind. His novels, with
all those sophisticated nonentities going nowhere, read
as if he was twisting life to suit his reading. But then

what does Robert know about life? Mamma's boy, Little Lord Fauntleroy, always dressed in the best. He doesn't know one rose from another. But a novelist should know everything. He doesn't know the town he lives in. Nor the people in it. Quotations. Balderdash.

He found to his extreme humiliation that he was flushed with fury. The simplest thing to do would be to let her go away and stay away, and then find himself a housekeeper who wasn't a literary critic, a secret carping critic, a secret lover too, a Psyche, by Hercules, welcoming by night an invisible lover to her bed. Then death stops him, and daylight reveals him, makes him visible as a comic character with a long nose, and with a comic reputation, only, for mislaying two hundred hens, and with a brother, a great gardener, who had the absurd misfortune to be burned alive on his own lawn. Could comic people belong to a family addicted to sudden death? Somewhere in all this, there might be some time the germ of a story.

But couldn't she realise what those skilfully chosen quotations meant?

—Look now, he said, what they did for George MacDonald. A procession of ideas, names, great presences, marching around the room you write in: Fletcher and Shelley, Novalis and Beddoes, Goethe and Coleridge, Sir John Suckling and Shakespeare, Lyly and Schiller, Heine and Schleiermacher and Cowley and Spenser and the Book of Judges and Jean Paul Richter and Cyril Tourneur and Sir Philip Sidney and Dekker and Chaucer and the Kabala.

But, oh Mother Lilith, what was the use of debating thus with the shadow of a secretive woman who was now resting in the tender care of the sergeant's wife who was, twenty to one, relaying the uproarious news to every other wife in the town: Glory be, did you hear the fantasticality that happened up in Mr. Robert St. Blaise Macmahon's big house? Declare to God they'll never again be able to show their faces in public.

Even if she were with him, walking in this garden as he now was, and if he was foolish enough thus to argue with her, she would smile her sallow wrinkled smile, look sideways out of those dark-brown eyes and then go off alone to write in her black book: He forgot to mention the Twelve Apostles, the Clancy Brothers, and the Royal Inniskilling Fusiliers.

All her life she had resisted his efforts to make something out of her. Nor had she ever had the determination to rise and leap again, to leave him and the house and go away and make something out of herself.

He read: He's like the stuck-up high-falutin' women in that funny story by Somerville and Ross, he never leaves the house except to go to Paris. He doesn't see the life that's going on under his nose. He says there are no brothels in Dublin. But if Dublin had the best brothels in the long history of sin …

Do you know, now, that was not badly put. She has a certain felicity of phrase. But then she has some Macmahon blood in her, and the educational advantages that over the years this house has afforded her.

… long history of sin, he'd be afraid of his breeches to enter any of them. He says there are no chic women in Dublin. What would he do with a chic woman if I gave him one, wrapped in cellophane, for Valentine's Day? He says he doesn't know if the people he sees are ugly because they don't make love, or that they don't make love because they're ugly. He's the world's greatest living authority, isn't he, either on love or good looks?

On another page: To think, dear God, of that flat-footed bachelor who doesn't know one end of a woman from the other, daring to write an article attacking the mountainy farmers on their twenty pitiful acres of rocks, rushes, bogpools and dunghills, for not marrying young and raising large families. Not only does he not see the people around him, he doesn't even see himself. Himself and a crazy priest in America lamenting about late marriages and the vanishing Irish. A fine pair to run in harness. The safe, sworn celibate and the fraidy-cat bachelor.

And on yet another page: That time long ago, I clouted him when he made the pass, the only time, to my knowledge, he ever tried to prove himself a man. And he never came back for more. I couldn't very well tell him that the clout was not for what he was trying to do but for the stupid way he was trying to do it. A born bungler.

The doodles, whorls and curlicues wriggled like a snakepit, black, blue, green, red, violet, before his angry eyes. That was enough. He would bring that black book down to the barracks, and throw it at her, and tell her never to darken his door again. His ears boomed with blood. He went into the dining-room, poured himself a double whisky, drank it slowly, breathing heavily, thinking. But no, there was a better way. Go down to the barracks, bring her back, lavish kindness on her, in silence suffer her to write in her book, then copy what she writes, reshape it, reproduce it, so that some day she would see it in print and be confounded for the jade and jezebel that she is.

With deliberate speed, majestic instancy, he walked from the dining-room to her bedroom, tossed the book on to her bed where she would see it on her return and know he had read it, and that her nastiness was uncovered. He had read enough of it, too much of it: because the diabolical effect of his reading was that he paused, with tingling irritation, to examine his tendency to think in quotations. Never again, thanks to her malice, would he do so, easily, automatically, and, so to speak, unthinkingly.

Coming back across the kitchen he found himself looking at his own feet, in fine hand-made shoes, his feet rising, moving forwards, settling again on the floor, fine flat feet. It was little benefit to see ourselves as others see us. That was, merciful God, another quotation. That mean woman would drive him mad. He needed a change: Dublin, Paris, Boppard on the Rhine – a little town that he loved in the off-season when it wasn't ravished by boat-loads of American women doing the Grand Tour. First, though, to get the Spanish maiden of wild Glenade back to her proper place among the roses and the pots and pans.

The guard answered the telephone. He said: She's still resting, Mr. Macmahon, sir.

—It's imperative that I speak to her. She can't just take this lying down.

That, he immediately knew, was a stupid thing to say. On the wall before him, strong black letters formed, commenting on his stupidity.

There was a long silence. Then she spoke, almost whispered: Yes, Robert.

—Hadn't you better get back to your place here?

—Yes, Robert. But what is my place there?

—You know what I mean. We must face this together. After all, you are half a Macmahon.

—Half a Macmahon, she said, is better than no bread.

He was shocked to fury: This is nothing to be flippant about.

—No, Robert.

—Who was this man?

—A friend of mine.

—Do you tell me so? Do you invite all your friends to my house?

—He was the only one.

—Why didn't you marry him?

—He had a wife and five children in Sudbury in England. Separated.

—That does, I believe, constitute an impediment. But who or what was he?

—It would be just like you, Robert, not even to know who he was. He lived in this town. It's a little town.

—Should I have known him?

—Shouldn't a novelist know everybody and everything?

—I'm not an authority on roses.

—You've been reading my book.

She was too sharp for him. He tried another tack: Why didn't you tell me you were having a love affair? After all, I am civilised.

—Of course you're civilised. The world knows that. But there didn't seem any necessity for telling you.

—There must be so many things that you don't feel it is necessary to tell me.

—You were never an easy person to talk to.

—All your secret thoughts. Who could understand a devious woman? Far and from the farthest coasts …

—There you go again. Quotations. The two-footed gramophone. What good would it do you if you did understand?

—Two-footed, he said. Flat-footed.

He was very angry: You could have written it all out for me if you couldn't say it. All the thoughts hidden behind your brooding face. All the things you thought when you said nothing, or said something else.

—You really have been reading my book. Prying.

The silence could have lasted all of three minutes. He searched around for something that would hurt.

—Isn't it odd that a comic figure should belong to a family addicted to sudden death?

—What on earth do you mean?

Her voice was higher. Anger? Indignation?

—That nose, he said. Cyrano. Toto the Clown. And I heard about the flight of the two hundred hens.

Silence.

—And about the brother who was burned.

—They were kindly men, she said. And good to talk to. They had green fingers.

It would have gratified him if he could have heard a sob.

—I'll drive down to collect you in an hour's time.

—He loved me, she said. I suppose I loved him. He was something, in a place like this.

Silence.

—You're a cruel little boy, she said. But just to amuse you, I'll give you another comic story. Once he worked in a dog kennels in Kent in England. The people who owned the kennels had an advertisement in the local paper. One sentence read like this: Bitches in heat will be personally conducted from the railway station by Mr. Dominic Byrne.

—Dominic Byrne, she said. That was his name. He treasured that clipping. He loved to laugh at himself. He died for love. That's more than most will ever do. There you are. Make what you can out of that story, you flat-footed bore.

She replaced the telephone so quietly that for a few moments he listened, waiting for more, thinking of something suitable to say.

On good days, light, reflected from the lake, seemed to brighten every nook and corner of the little town. At the end of some old narrow winding cobbled laneway there would be a vision of lake-water bright as a polished mirror. It was a graceful greystone town, elegantly laid-out by some Frenchman hired by an eighteenth-century earl. The crystal river that fed the lake flowed through the town and gave space and scope for a tree-lined mall. But grace and dancing light could do little to mollify his irritation. This time, by the heavenly father, he would have it out with her, he would put her in her place, revenge himself for a long-ago affront and humiliation. Body in the bed, indeed. Two hundred hens, indeed. Swamps and sewers, indeed. Bitches in heat, indeed. She did not have a leg to stand on. Rutting, and on his time, with a long-nosed yahoo.

The Byzantine church, with which the parish priest had recently done his damnedest to disfigure the town, struck his eyes with concentrated insult. Ignorant bloody peasants. The slick architects could sell them anything: Gothic, Byzantine, Romanesque, Igloo, Kraal, Modern Cubist. The faithful paid, and the pastor made the choice.

Who would ever have thought that a lawnmower could be a Viking funeral pyre?

The barracks, a square, grey house, made ugly by barred windows and notice-boards, was beside the church. The guard, capless, the neck of his uniform jacket open, his hands in his trouser pockets, stood in the doorway. He was still perspiring. The man would melt. There was a drop to his nose: snot or sweat or a subtle blend of both. Robert St. Blaise Macmahon would never again make jokes about civic guards. He said: I've come for Miss Hynes.

—Too late, Mr. Macmahon, sir. The bird has flown.

—She has what?

—Gone, sir. Eloped. Stampeded. On the Dublin train. Ten minutes ago. I heard her whistle.

—Whistle?

—The train, sir.

—But the funeral? The inquest?

—Oh, his wife and children will bury him. We phoned them.

—But the inquest?

—Her affidavit will do the job. We'll just say he dropped while visiting your house to look at the roses.

—That's almost the truth.

—The whole truth and nothing but the truth is often a bitter dose, sir.

—As I said, guard, you are a philosopher.

He remembered too late that he hadn't said that, he had just thought it.

—Thank you kindly, sir. Would you chance a cup of tea, sir? Nothing better to cool one on a hot day. Not that I like tea myself. But in this weather, you know. The hottest day, the forecast says.

Well, why not? He needed cooling. The bird had flown, sailing away from him, over the chasm, laughing triumphant eldritch laughter.

In the austere dayroom they sat on hard chairs and sipped tea.

—Nothing decent or drinkable here, sir, except a half-bottle of Sandeman's port.

—No thank you, guard. No port. The tea will suffice.

—Those are gallant shoes, sir, if you'll excuse me being so pass-remarkable. Hand-made jobs.

—Yes, hand-made.

—Costly, I'd say. But then they'd last for ever.

—Quite true, guard.

—He's coffined by now. The heat, you know.

—Don't remind me.

—Sorry, sir. But the facts of life are the facts of life. Making love one minute. In a coffin the next.

—The facts of death, guard. Alone withouten any company.

—True as you say, sir. He was a droll divil, poor Byrne, and he died droll.

—Among the roses, guard.

—It could happen to anyone, God help us. Neither the day nor the hour do we know. The oddest thing, now, happened once to the sergeant's brother that's a journalist in Dublin. This particular day he's due to travel to Limerick City to report on a flower show. But he misses the train. So he sends a telegram to ask a reporter from another newspaper to keep him a carbon. Then he adjourns to pass the day in the upstairs lounge bar of the Ulster House. Along comes the Holy Hour as they call it for jokes, when the pubs of Dublin close for a while in the early afternoon. To break up the morning boozing parties, you understand. There's nobody in the lounge except the sergeant's brother and a strange man. So the manager locks them in there to drink in peace and goes off to his lunch. And exactly halfways through the Holy Hour the stranger drops down dead. Angina. And there's me man that should be at a flower show in Limerick locked in on a licensed premises, the Ulster House, during an off or illegal hour, with a dead man that he doesn't know from Adam.

—An interesting legal situation, guard.

—Oh it was squared, of course. The full truth about that couldn't be allowed out. It would be a black mark on the licence. The manager might lose his job.

—People might even criticise the quality of the drink.

—They might, sir. Some people can't be satisfied. Not that there was ever a bad drop sold in the Ulster House. Another cup, Mr. Macmahon, sir.

—Thank you, guard.

—She'll come back, Mr. Macmahon. Blood they say is thicker than water.

—They do say that, do they? Yet somehow, in spite of what they say, I don't think she'll be back.

On she went, leaping, flying, describing jaunty parabolas. He would, of course, have to send her money. She was entitled to something legally and he could well afford to be generous beyond what the law demanded.

—So the long-nosed lover died, guard, looking at the roses.

—In a manner of speaking, sir.

—Possibly the only man, guard, who ever had the privilege. Look thy last on all things lovely.

But the guard was not aware of De La Mare.

—That's what we'll say, sir. It would be best for all. His wife and all. And no scandal.

—Days of wine and roses, guard.

—Yes, sir. Alas, that we have nothing here but that half-bottle of Sandeman's port. She was a great lady to grow roses, sir. That's how they met in the beginning, she told me. Over roses.

# The Weavers at the Mill

Baxbakualanuxsiwae, she said to herself as she walked by the sea, was one of the odd gods of the Kwakiutl Indians, and had the privilege of eating human flesh. That pale-faced woman with the strained polite accent would devour me if her teeth were sharp enough. She even calls me, intending it as an insult, Miss Vancouver, although she knows damned well in her heart and mind, if she has a heart, that I don't come from Vancouver.

She loved the vast flat strand, the distant sea, the wraithlike outline of rocky islands that looked as if they were sailing in the sky, the abruptness with which a brook cradled by flat green fields became a wide glassy sheet of water spreading out over the sand.

A thatched cottage, gable end to the inshore gales, was palisaded against the sea by trunks of trees driven deep into the sand. On the seafront road that curved around the shanty village, wind and water had tossed seaweed over the wall so regularly that it looked like nets spread out to dry. All the young men she met on the road wore beards they had grown for the night's pageant: not the melancholy, wishy-washy, desiccated-coconut pennants of artistic integrity but solid square-cut beards or shaggy beards that birds could nest in. To walk among them was a bit like stepping back into some old picture of the time of Charles Stewart Parnell: stern men marching home to beleagured cabins from a meeting of the Land League.

That woman would say: They are all so handsome.

She was long-faced, pale and languid, the sort of woman who would swoon with craven delight at the rub of a beard. Yet she could never persuade the old man to abandon his daily careful ritual with cut-throat razor, wooden soap bowl, the strop worn to a waist in the middle, the fragments of newspaper splattered with blobs of spent lather and grey stubble.

—Eamonn, she would say to her husband, if you'd only grow a beard you'd look like Garibaldi with his goats on the island of Caprera.

—I have no knowledge of goats. I'm not on my own island any more.

To the girl she would say: If your bags are packed I'll run you at any time to the station.

—My bags are always packed. There's only one of them. A duffle-bag, she'd answer. But if it doesn't inconvenience you too much I'd like to stay another day. There are a few details I want to fill in.

It needed nerve to talk to a woman like that in her own house. But what could the girl do when the old man was plaintively urging her not to go, not to go, pay no heed to her, stay another day.

They had breakfast in bed every day and lunch in their own rooms, and all the time until four in the afternoon free. It was in some ways the most relaxed life the girl had ever known. She had been there for a week since she had come from London across England, Wales, the Irish Sea and a part of Ireland, to write one more article in the magazine series that kept her eating. It was a series about little-known heroes of our time.

The woman had met her at the train. She drove a station-wagon piled high in the back with hanks of coloured wool. They drove round the village, foam glimmering in the dusk to their right hand, then across a humped five-arched stone bridge and up a narrow, sunken, winding roadway to the old Mill House in the middle of gaunt, grey, eyeless ruins where – above the river foaming down a narrow valley – two hundred men had worked in days of a simple local economy. Four grass-grown water-wheels rusted and rested for ever.

—Only my weavers work here now, she said. That's what the wool's for. Aran sweaters and belts – criosanna, they call them here – and scarves and cardigans. We sell them in the States where you come from.

She sounded as friendly as her over-refined, Henley-on-Thames voice could allow her to sound.

—Canada, the girl said. British Columbia. My father worked among the Kwakiutl Indians.

—Can't say I ever heard of them. What do they do?

—They were cannibals once. For religious reasons. But not any longer. They catch salmon. They sing songs. They carve totem poles. They weave good woollens, too. With simplified totem designs.

—How interesting.

The car went under a stone archway topped by a shapeless mass that she was to discover had once represented a re-arising phoenix – until rain and salt gales had disfigured it to a death deeper than ashes. They were in a cobbled courtyard and then in a garage that had once been part of a stables.

—You want to write about my husband's lifeboat exploits when he was an islandman.

—The famous one. I was asked to write about it. Or ordered. I read it up in the newspaper files. It was heroic.

She slung the duffle-bag over her shoulder and they walked towards the seven-windowed face of the old stone house. From the loft above the garage the clacking of looms kept mocking time to their steps. The woman said: Do you always dress so informally?

—I travel a lot and light. Leather jacket and corduroy slacks. You need them in my business. A protection against pinchers and pawsey men.

—You're safe here, said the woman. The men are quiet. All the young ones have just grown lovely beards for a parish masque or a pageant or something. You mustn't tire him too much. Sometimes he can get unbearably excited when he remembers his youth.

His youth, the girl reckoned, was a long time ago.

She spread out her few belongings between the old creaking mahogany wardrobe and the marble-topped dressing-table, and tidied herself for dinner, and remembered that she had left her typewriter, smothered in wool, in the station-wagon. The newspaper that had told her about the rescue had been fifty years old; and Eamonn, the brave coxswain and the leader of the heroic crew, had been then a well-developed man of thirty. The newsprint picture had faded, but not so badly that she couldn't see the big man, a head taller than any of his companions, laughing under his sou'wester with all the easy mirth of a man who had never yet been afraid.

From her bedroom window she could look down into the courtyard and see girls in blue overalls carrying armfuls of wool from the wagon up an outside wooden stairway to the weaving shed. The thatched roofs of the village were, from her height, like a flock of yellow birds nestling by the edge of the sea and, far across the water, the outlines of the islands of Eamonn's origin faded into the darkness, as distant and lost for ever as his daring youth and manhood. Yet she knew so little, or had reflected so little, on the transfiguring power of time that she was ill-prepared for the gaunt, impressive wreck of a man who came slowly into a dining-room that was elaborately made up to look like a Glocca Morra farmhouse kitchen. He sat down on a low chair by the open hearth and silently accepted a bowl of lentil soup with fragments of bread softening in it. He didn't even glance at the low unstained oak table where the girl sat most painfully, on a traditional three-legged wooden chair. Dressed in black, her black hair piled on her head, her oblong face, by lamplight, longer and whiter than ever, the woman sat aloof at the head of the table. Two girls, daytime weavers magically transformed by the touch of the creeping dusk into night-time waitresses, blue overalls exchanged for dark dresses, white aprons, white collars, served the table; and a third stood like a nurse behind the old man's chair. He slopped with a spoon, irritably rejecting the handmaiden's effort to aid him. He recited to himself what was to the girl an unintelligible sing-song.

—Merely counting, the woman said. In Gaelic. One, two, three, and so on. He says it soothes him and helps his memory. I told him what you want. He'll talk when he's ready.

Suddenly he said: She cracked right across the middle, that merchant vessel, and she stuffed as full as a fat pig with the costliest bales of goods and furniture and God knows what. I can tell you there are houses on this coast but not out on the islands where the people are honest and no wreckers, and those houses are furnished well to this day on account of what the waves brought in that night.

The voice came out like a bell, defying and belying time, loud and melodious as when he must have roared over the billows to his comrades the time the ship cracked. Then he handed the empty soup bowl to the nervous weaver-handmaiden, sat up high in his chair, bade the girl welcome in Gaelic, and said to the woman: She's not one of the French people from the hotel.

—From London, said the woman.

—There's a fear on the people in the village below that there won't be a duck or a hen or any class of a domestic fowl left alive to them with the shooting of these French people. The very sparrows in the hedges and God's red robins have no guarantee of life while they're about. They came over in the beginning for the sea-angling and, when they saw all the birds we have, nothing would satisfy them but to go home to France for their guns. They say they have all the birds in France shot. And the women with them are worse than the men.

—Les femmes de la chasse, said the woman.

—Patsy Glynn the postman tells me there's one six feet high with hair like brass and legs on her like Diana and wading boots up to her crotch. God, Pats said to me, and I agreed, the pity Eamonn, you're not seventy again, or that the Capall himself is dead and in the grave. He'd manipulate her, long legs and boots and all.

—Our visitor, said the woman, is not here to write about the Capall.

—Then, girl from London, 'tis little knowledge you have of writing. For there have been books written about men that weren't a patch on the Capall's breeches. A horse of a man and a stallion outright for the women. That was why we called him the Capall.

With a raised right hand and cracking fingers the woman had dismissed the three girls. This was no talk for servants to hear.

—That John's Eve on the island, the night of the bonfires and midsummer, and every man's blood warm with poteen and porter in Dinny O'Brien's pub. Dinny, the old miser that he was, serving short measure and gloating over the ha'pennies. But, by God, the joke was on him and didn't we know it. For wasn't the Capall in the barn-loft at the back of the house with Dinny's young wife that married him for money, for that was all Dinny had to offer. She had to lie down for two days in bed, drinking nothing but milk, after the capers of the Capall and herself in the loft. He walked in the back door of the bar, his shirt open to the navel, no coat on him and the sweat on him like oil. Two pints he drank and saw for the first time the new barmaid, a niece of Dinny, that had come all the way from Cork City, and the fat dancing on her and her dress thin. So he lifted the third pint and said: Dhia! Is trua nach bhfuil dara bud ag duine.

Feeling that she did understand, and close to coarse laughter, the girl said that she didn't understand. Coldly and precisely the woman said: To put it politely, he regretted that he was merely one man, not two.

—But he saved my life did the Capall. For the gale swept us, and the eight men we took off the broken vessel, eastwards before it to a port in Wales. There was no turning back in the teeth of it. There we were trying to moor the boat by the mole in another country when, with weariness and the tossing of the water, didn't I slip and go down between the wall and the boat, to be crushed, sure as God, if the Capall hadn't hooked his elbow in mine and thrown me back into the boat the way a prize wrestler would. Remember that bit, girl, when you write the story, and thank God you never met the Capall on a lonely road. He came from a place called the Field of the Strangers that was the wildest place on the whole island. From the hill above it you could see the wide ocean all the way to Africa, and the spray came spitting in over the roofs of the little houses, and the salt burned the grass in the fields. There was no strand in it, no break-water, no harbour or slip for boats. Nothing man ever built could stand against that ocean. You held the currach steady and leaped into it from a flat rock as you shot out to sea. But there were men of strength and valour reared there who could conquer valleys before them and throw sledge-hammers over high houses. Dried sea bream we ate, boiled or roasted over hot sods, the strongest sweet-est food in the world. And rock birds taken in nets where they'd nest in the clefts of the cliffs. Bread and tea for a treat, and potatoes boiled or brusselled in the griosach.

The woman explained: Roasted in the hot peat ashes.

—Then a cow might break a leg in a split in the rocks and have to be destroyed. A black disaster in one way. But in another way a feast of fresh meat and liver with the blood running out of it, food for men. All out of tins nowadays, and nobody has his own teeth.

The woman said: You were, Eamonn, talking about the lifeboat.

—Good for its own purpose the lifeboat, he said. But you couldn't feel the heart of the sea beating in it as you could in the canvas currach. We had one fel-low with us that night who always had ill luck with currachs. Three of them he lost, and once he nearly lost his life. So we put him in the crew of the lifeboat to break his ill-fortune, and the trick worked. It could be that the sea didn't recognise him in his new yellow oilskins. Three days in that Welsh town we sweated in kneeboots and oilskins, having nothing else to wear, and the gales blowing in against us all the time. But the welcome we got. Didn't a deputation of ladies come to us with a white sheet of cloth to draw our names on, so that they could embroider our names for ever on the flag of the town's football team. Didn't the Capall write himself down as Martin McIntyre the Horse. There was the laughing, I can tell you, when the ladies wanted us to tell them why we put the title of the horse on Martin. They made heroes out of us. It was a sea-going town and there wasn't a woman in it hadn't a son or a husband or a lover on the salt water.

The attendant girls had come back silently. His great head, shaggy with uncombed white hair, sank down. With a napkin one of the girls mopped a splatter of soup from the green leather zipper jacket and, startlingly, with the yeeow of a shout a young fellow would give at a country dance, he came awake and slapped her buttocks before she could leap, laughing and blushing, and seemingly well used to the horseplay, out of his reach. The woman looked at the servant and then at her food. She said: Don't tire yourself.

—Never saw the tired day, he said, that the smell of a young girl wouldn't put life into me.

—Tell me more, said the girl, about the sea.

—What would you want to know about the sea and you from the smoky heart of London?

—I'm not from London.

—From Canada, said the woman. Her girlhood companions were cannibalistic Indians.

—On an island, the girl said.

He was wide awake, and interested, and upright. How tall he was when he sat up straight.

—Tell me, he said, about your wild Indians and your island.

Because he had hard blue eyes with a compelling icy light in them, and because for her benefit he had so carefully dredged his memory, she wanted to tell him. She wanted to tell him even more because as soon as he showed interest she had sensed the first stirrings of antagonism in the woman.

—Eamonn, the woman said, our guest may be tired.

—Tell me a little, he said. It's lucky to begin a story by lamplight.

—Nothing much to tell, she said. Don't think of me as sitting in the middle of a pack of noble savages, chewing on a hunk of Tyee salmon while they ate long pig. I didn't grow up with drums and war chants throbbing around me. I was some miles distant, on the other side of the hill. Of course I had plenty of contact with the confused no-man's-land Indian that the white man has made. Studied their history and sociology at college. But when I was a little girl the closest I got to them was to run to the top of the hill and peep down through cedar branches at the noble Indians pulling the guts out of salmon. Sounds bitter I know. But beauty and nobility had left them for a long while. And in our village the groups were so divided that not even the minds of the children could meet. When I was a girl I remember trying to get a little Indian girl to tell me some of her words. She stayed sullen and very silent. Then finally she and her little friend giggled and spat out one word. Matsooie – that was what it sounded like. I found out later that she had simply been saying: what's the matter with you? It was a rebuff.

—It's sad, he said, when people don't understand you, no matter what you do or try to do. We'll talk more tomorrow, girl, when you've rested after your journey.

—I've talked too much, she said. I came to listen to you.

He rose alertly when she passed him and shook her hand in a solemn old-fashioned way. He belonged to a time when men shook hands elaborately at every meeting and parting.

Later – very much later – she thought drowsily that she heard his slow tread on the old creaking stairs, his coughing in the next room as he lay down on his bed; and far away the faint sound of the sea along the shore and around the islands.

She carried two notebooks always in the right-hand pocket of her leather jacket.

All women, said the hopeful man she had met on the Irish Mail, are lascivious.

One of the notebooks was paper-backed, spined with spiral wire, and with tear-out leaves. It was for ephemera and temporalities – in other words, her work. The other book was stiff-backed, with stable, ruled leaves for the recording of the experiences she would use when the day would come and she'd sit down really to write. The stiff-backed book had another quality: it kept the weaker member straight in her jacket pocket, for she found nothing more maddening than note-taking on a page that was bent like a crescent.

The people she met she divided into two classes: tear-outs or stiff-backs.

This wonderful old man, an aged hero recalling islands, immured here by a female dragon, was as notable a stiff-back as she had ever encountered.

When the clacking of looms awoke her in the morning, she sat up in bed and reached for ball-point and stiff-back where she had left them in readiness on the bedside table. Or was it the looms had awakened her, or the purring of the motor-car engine in the cobbled yard, or the morning coughing of the old giant in the next room? For an ancient stone house, she thought, the walls were thin. But then she studied the slant of the ceiling, and realised that her room was only half a room and that the sound of coughing came to her, not through old stone, but through a wooden partition. She went to the window and looked out at three of the blue weaving girls walking in single file from the station-wagon to the weaving-shed and carrying hanks of coloured wool: obedient African kraal girls with burdens on their heads and disciplined by some wrinkled Zulu queen. Then the woman drove away under the faceless phoenix. When the girl was settled back in bed again, he spoke to her through the wall: I can hear you're awake. Has she driven off to do the shopping?

—Good morning, she said. She's driven off somewhere.

—Good morning to you, girl. Did you sleep well?

Her answer was lost in a fit of his coughing, and when his throat had cleared again, he said: No more rising with the lark for me. Nor the seagull itself. I'm old and lazy now. But I mind my father, the oldest day he was, walking barefoot in the dawn, the old greasy sailor's cap on his head, to the flagstone at the corner of the house, to look at the sea and the surf on the white strand, to sniff the wind and to tell the weather for the day to come. He had his own teeth to the age of ninety. If he was inland and far from the sea, he could tell by the smell of the wind whether the tide was ebbing or flowing. But it wasn't often he went inland, and he was never happy in an offshore wind.

This was the most wonderful way in the world to conduct an interview. The metallic voice came muted, but clear, through the timber. The looms, the sea, and the river made their noises. The wind muttered around grey stone. She could sit snug in bed, both notebooks open, and make notes at her ease without embarrassing her subject.

—Tell me more, she said.

He said: Tell me about your wild Indians.

So to entice him to talk, she talked about Quathiaski Cove at the mouth of the river, and about the wits among the Scots and Irish settlers who nicknamed it Quart of Whisky Cove, about the great argonauts of salmon homing up the Campbell River, about people of many nations, Scots, Swedes, Irish, Indians, Chinese, Japanese, living in one way or another on the rich red body of the salmon.

—The very air in that place smells of salmon. When my mother first took me to visit Vancouver I thought there was something wrong with the place, something missing. Finally she told me I felt that way because I could no longer smell the salmon.

—Like myself, he said, when I came here with her. This far inland you can't sniff the salt properly.

—And tell me about their songs, he said. In my days on the island there were sweet singers and old men who could tell stories to last the night.

So, for his sake, she remembered that when she had been a little girl she had sneaked out one night to listen to the singing of the Indians. One song particularly stayed in her memory. Years afterwards, when she and her people had long left the place, she went north by boat with her father to revisit the haunts of her childhood. To one old noble chieftain she spoke of the songs – and of that special song. He answered her about all the forms of songs: morning songs, harvest songs, giving songs to be chanted at the potlatch when a man gave all he had to his neighbours, gambling songs, lullabies. And song after song he sang until she stopped him and said: That's it. That's the song I loved when I was a little girl.

Then, with tears in his eyes, the old chieftain said: That's my gambling song, written for me by my own songwriter.

Her story faded into coughing that rattled the partition between them. Later he said in a hoarse carrying whisper: Don't go away soon, girl. Stay as long as you can whether she wants you to or not.

It wasn't easy to think of any response.

—She doesn't like strangers about the place. She's cold, God help her, and has no *fáilte* in her. Even when I was married to my first wife, and herself only a stranger visiting the islands, she was always jealous to find me in the middle of a crowd.

—You were married before?

—To a woman of my own people. And year after year herself came as a tourist until my wife died. Then I went away with her and we were married in London. A watery class of a wedding they give you in cities. It wasn't love, as they call it. She was too grand for that. But she was there always – and willing. The islands do something to visiting women. And with creams and perfumes and the best clothes out of the London shops she was different from any woman I'd ever smelled or seen. You know how it is with a strong imaginative young fellow, and he only a few months married.

—I can guess, she said. Some minor poet said something about white arms beckoning all around him.

—Minor or major he was poet enough to know what he was talking about. We haven't slept heads on one pillow for twenty years now, but in secret corners in those old days we'd play hide and seek in our pelt on the bare rocks – when it was a sin moreover. And look at me now, here, wrapped in coloured wool, and broken in health, and surrounded by stupid women, weaving.

Propped by pillows, and taking notes, she squatted like a tailor, and made up her mind. She would stay a week if she could, just to please the old man and – her blood warming to the conflict – to spite that cold dried fish of a woman. In his youth, to judge by his talk, the old man had eaten better.

When he heard the station-wagon returning he said: I'll doze for a while now. She wouldn't like to hear us talking through the wall. She was hinting last night she'd run you to the station for the late train. But don't go, don't go, stay as long as you can.

They had a week of mornings together talking through the wall. Reading her notes afterwards she found that morning mingled with morning. One morning, though, was distinct because it had been a morning of gale and rain. The coy red-and-purple blossoms were being whipped off the tormented fuchsia bushes, and when she stepped out for her daily walk – the sea was too tossed for a swim – the sand and salt were in her eyebrows and gritting between her teeth. Bloated by a night of rain the brown mad river bellowed around the dead millwheels and, for once, the clack, the mocking one-two-three of the looms couldn't be heard.

Through the wall and the frequent fits of coughing he had said to her: I've grown younger since you came. A gift to me from the god of the sea himself, a beautiful young girl from a far island.

As a clergyman's daughter, the object of as many jokes as an Aberdonian, she was calmly aware of her looks: neither better nor worse than they were. She laughed. She said: I've a nose like a pack saddle, and a square face and freckles, although they tell me I've honest eyes.

—But you're young, he said.

After a silence she heard his dry choking laughter: There's a lump on my own nose still where I had it

Benedict Kiely

broken and I no more than a boy. The way it happened
is a story will tickle you. There was this free and easy
girl, a rare thing on the islands I can tell you – with the
close way we lived. She wasn't an island girl, whatever.
She came from the mainland in the tourist season and,
as the song says, her stockings were white and you'd love
to be tickling her garter, even if she was no better than
a servant-maid in a lodging-house. This evening weren't
we lined up to see her, like penitents going to confession, at the bottom of the orchard behind the house she
worked in, and when Pat's Jameseen stepped out of his
fair place in the line to go ahead of me, I fought him and,
although he cracked my nose, hammered him back.

The dry laughter went on, choking now not with
phlegm but with remembered devilment.

—That was the way with me when I was young. A
chieftain among my own people, like your fine Indian,
and respected by all. Then when my first woman died
I never wanted to see the islands again. The English
woman had it easy to carry me to the smoke of London,
where, as God is my judge, I came near to choking. The
islands pulled at me again, even though I got only this
far and no farther. Old as I am, I think at times I'll take a
boat and return. But they don't want me any more since
I married a stranger, and grew grand, and left.

—It would be fun, said the girl, if we could go to an
island I know in Spain. Life is simple and gentle there,
and the food good, cooked over an open fire. Some
rough wine, wild and coarse, but with a kind flavour. A
little music and reading and story-telling by lamplight,
and water all around.

—That would be a holiday to remember, he said.

With the gale that morning they didn't hear the station-wagon returning, and it was the woman opening

170

the door of the old man's room that interrupted them. Afterwards, while the old man slept, she said, over black coffee, to the girl: Any time you're ready I'll run you to the station.

A conflict like this was, in some ways, worse than blows or eye-scratching. As steadily as she could the girl said: If it doesn't upset your arrangements too much I'd love to see the pageant. It would add colour to the story.

—Colour, the woman said. Well, the beards, yes. Please yourself. But don't talk to the girls so much. It holds them up at their work. They lose. I lose. They're paid by piece-work.

Walking out into the gale the girl, for the sake of peace and the old man, avoided the weaving-shed where, she had been glad to think, the sullen faces of the underpaid weavers brightened when she entered. She loved the soft coloured wool, the intricacies of warping mills and heddles, the careful spacing of the threads. When you looked at the process you were as much part of it as the woolwinder and the sound of the looms was comforting, not mocking.

In the hotel bar the French hunters, driven in by the tempest that had also driven the birds to shelter, clustered around Diana who wore tight red pants and sneakers. Through a red beard like a burning bush the barman told her how five years ago the old man had run amok: Terrified the bloody country for a week. Wandering around with a loaded shotgun. Shooting and spearing salmon in the pool below the old mill. Then pleurisy laid him low and he was never the same again. Out on the islands they're savages. Half-crazy with inbreeding.

The raised wind-driven sea was sucking around the tree trunks that palisaded the white cottage. She walked, fighting the gale, along the thin line of sand the water had not devoured.

Baxbakualanuxsiwae, she recalled, shared his house with his wife, Qominoqa, a frightful female who cooked his ghoulish meals. A female slave, Kinqalalala, rounded up victims and collected corpses, well-hung meat in the house of the gods.

The thunder of the waves made her want to run and shout. One Sunday morning the small, deep-toned drums of the potlatch had set the whole village vibrating, until her father was forced to abandon his pulpit and say with a good humour more than Christian: Let us marvel at the force of tradition which is also one of the works of the Lord.

Once, in one of the books in her father's library, she had read that the Dinka people of the southern Sudan had a special sort of priest known as Masters of the Fishing Spear. These men, if they had great names as heroes, could be honourably killed when old and failing, by being buried alive at their own request and before all their assembled kin.

The islands, lost in spume and low-running clouds, were not to be seen.

In the dusk the bearded young men came in twos and threes under the featureless phoenix, across the courtyard, out by another gateway at the back of the weaving-shed, and up the hill to the mounded rath that was to be the open-air, torch-lit stage for their pageant. They wore white shirts and saffron kilts, cowskin pampooties made on the islands and dyed all colours, and thick woollen stockings cross-gartered to the knees. Most of them carried long wooden spears with silvered cardboard heads, and cardboard shields bright with brassy tacks. Some of them carried and some of them even played the bagpipes.

The blue weaving girls gathered on the landing out-side the door of the shed, and cat-called, and addressed the bearded heroes by their ordinary everyday names and nicknames. They asked with irony if the men were going to the wars or to stick flounder on the flat sands with the flowing tide. When one bandy-legged, hairy-kneed veteran tottered past carrying a huge harp, and preceded by the curate who was directing the pageant, the blue girls held each other up, embracing in parox-ysms and pantomimes of suppressed mirth.

—Never yet, the old man said, did I hear tell of one of these pageants that wasn't a holy laugh in the end. The Orangemen in the North, they say, had a pageant about the landing of King Billy in Carrickfergus harbour. But the sea was choppy that day and the boat tilted and didn't his majesty land on his arse in the water. And in Straide in Mayo they had a pageant about the eviction of the family of Michael Davitt who founded the Land League. But they built the mock cabin so strong that all the guns of Germany, let alone the battering rams of the boys who were pretending to be the bailiff's men, couldn't knock it down. Still and all, for the laugh, we'll go up to the rath and drink porter and eat pork sausages with the rest. It'll be a fine night with a full moon.

—At your age, Eamonn, that's the worst thing you could do.

—At my age?

He tossed aside the blackthorn he leaned on and, on the flat flag at the door of the house, hopped, but stiffly, from one foot to the other.

—These days I'm a two-year-old. The Indian maiden here will lead me up the slope. Minnehaha.

The woman's eyelids came down – it seemed one after the other, and very deliberately – to hide her eyes.

—Please yourself, then. Those girls have wasted enough time. I'll go up later with coffee and sandwiches.

His arm was around the girl's shoulders as they walked up a twisting boreen towards bonfires reddening in the dusk.

—Kings lived on this high hill, he said. All gone now, and dead and buried, generations of ancient kings, but the mounds and the ramparts are as solid as the day they were raised.

For one night, she thought, the kings had returned. She sat beside him on a rug on the mound. They were sheltered by a blossoming whitethorn from the light seawind. She held his hand. A huge round moon was motionless in a cloudless sky. Under its influence, and in the glow of a dozen bonfires, the bearded, cross-gartered country boys, the one decrepit harper, were no longer comic.

It was a masque, not a pageant. In a hut in a forest a dozen old broken men, remnants of a beaten clan, waited sadly and with little hope for the fulfilment of a prophecy that told of the coming of a young hero to lead them back to victory.

—This, said the oldest of them, is the last day of the year of our foretold salvation, and the last hour of the last day, yet the prophecy still stands even if it was made by one of the faery women who make game of men.

Her own old man moved closer to her on the rug.

The blue girls were just ending the long day's weaving. The coffee and sandwiches, and the woman with them, were still a good hour away; and also the thought that her duffle-bag and typewriter had been stored, for simpler departure, in the hotel with the red-bearded barman. She felt a brute, but she had a job to do – such as it was – and an old man's dream couldn't go on for ever, nor could she any longer defy a woman who didn't want her about the place.

When he pressed her hand she returned the pressure. She felt the great bones from which the flesh had melted away. She could have wept.

—The pity, he said, I didn't meet you when I was a young blade.

—I wasn't born then.

—We'd have found our own island and lived on it.

—There was a Japanese poet, she said, who was born in 1911, the year after Halley's Comet. He reckoned with a sad heart that he'd never see the comet since it wouldn't come again until 1986. That it was the same case with human encounters. His true friend would appear after his death. His sweetheart had died before he was born.

—A fine young man there, he said.

For who should arrive at that moment but the red barman himself, striding from darkness into the glare of the fires. Spear on shoulder. With the firelight glinting in his bush of a beard, he could only be the hero who was promised. The crowds, seated on the slopes of the rath, cheered him. He was a popular man. For the broken old men he brought venison from the forest, cakes impaled on spears, and rolling barrels of ale from an enemy fortress he had that day captured single-handed. Also a sackful of golden goblets, made out of cardboard, and all the tokens, including a severed head in a sack, to prove he was the man of destiny. The exigencies of the drama did not, mercifully, call for the production of the severed head.

Then the harper harped on his harp and, far away in the shadows, the pipers played, slowly advancing towards the circle of fires to show that they were an army of young men following their unique leader. The watching crowds broke up into groups to eat sausages and pigs' feet and to drink porter. The dancing began on the rough dry grass. Led by two of the pipers, the dancers moved to find a better surface between the weaving-shed and the millhouse. Then the woman was there, and the curate with her helping her to carry cups and sandwiches and the coffee pot.

—Not pigs' feet, Eamonn. Not all that greasy fat.

—'Tisn't often now I have a night out under the moon.

—A midsummer night, she said. Madness.

—I could leap through bonfires, woman. I feel like twenty. Pour milk on the ground for the good people who lived here before kings were heard tell of. It's not lucky to let them go hungry.

—What silly waste, the woman said.

Slowly the girl tilted her cup and let the coffee drain down to the grass. She said: They might fancy coffee.

His great hand was in the bowl of brown sugar and the fistful he took he tossed into the air, scattering it over the crowd. Faces, some laughing, some curious, turned towards them in the firelight.

—The world knows, he said, that the good people have a sweet tooth. Halley's Comet, Minnehaha, will come again.

They laughed loudly together. She noticed that they were again hand in hand. The curate, pretending to answer a call from one of the bearded men, moved away. The woman poured more coffee. By the farthest fire the girl saw the red man standing and beckoning. He probably had notions above his state in life, but he could give her a lift to the nearest town, and her leather jacket was stout enough to resist even the paws and the pinches of a man mentioned in prophecy. When the barman moved off down the slope towards the mill-house, she excused herself.

—Come back soon, Minnehaha, the old man called after her. Don't delay. It's a fine night for seeing comets.

—Eamonn, isn't it time you went in out of the night air?

Like in movies about Italy, the girl thought, everything ends with a carnival. She walked down the slope, taking his second youth with her, towing the sailing islands behind her. She was the sea receding for ever from a stranded master of the sea.

By torchlight in the cobbled courtyard blue weaving girls danced with bearded warriors who had cast aside their spears.

She walked on under the stone phoenix that could never arise again because it had merely decayed, never been purified by fire and burned to ashes.

With car, duffle-bag and typewriter, the red barman was waiting. She sat beside him and was driven off to find her next little-known hero.

# There are Meadows in Lanark

The schoolmaster in Bomacatall or McKattle's Hut was gloved and masked and at his beehives when his diminutive brother, the schoolmaster from Knockatatawn, came down the dusty road on his high bicycle. It was an Irish-made bicycle. The schoolmaster from Knockatatawn was a patriot. He could have bought the best English-made Raleigh for half the price, but instead he imported this edifice from the Twenty-six into the Six Counties and paid a mountain of duty on it. The bike, and more of its kind, was made in Wexford by a firm that made the sort of mowing-machine that it took two horses to pull. They built the bikes on the same solid principle. Willian Bulfin from the Argentine who long ago wrote a book about rambling in Erin had cycled round the island on one of them and died not long afterwards, almost certainly from over-exertion. There was a great view from the saddle. Hugh, who was the son of the schoolmaster from Bomacatall, once, on the quiet, borrowed the bike and rode into the side of a motorcar that was coming slowly out of a hedgy hidden boreen. He was tossed sideways into the hedgerow and had a lacework of scratches on his face. The enamel on the car was chipped and the driver's window broken. The bike was unperturbed.

The little man mounted the monster by holding the grips on the handlebars, placing his left foot on

the extended spud or hub of the back wheel and then
giving an electrified leap. This sunny evening he dis-
mounted by stepping on to the top rail of the garden
fence at Bomacatall. He sat there like a gigantic rook,
the King Rook that you hear chanting base barreltone
in the rookery chorus. He wore a pinstriped dark suit
and a black wide-brimmed hat. He paid no attention
to the buzzing and swarming of the bees. The herba-
ceous borders, the diamond-shaped beds at Bomacatall
would blind you. There was a twisting trout stream a
field away from the far end of the garden. To his brother
who was six feet and more the little man said: I have a
scheme in mind.

From behind the mask the big man said: Was there
ever a day that God sent that you didn't have a scheme
in mind?

—It would benefit the boy Hugh. *Cé an aois é anois?*

That meant: What age is he now?

—Nine, God bless him.

—Time he saw a bit of the world. Bracing breezes, silvery
sands, booming breakers, lovely lands: Come to Bundoran.

That was an advertisement in the local newspaper.

—You could sing that if you had a tune to it, said the
man behind the mask.

—The holiday would do him good, the King Rook said,
and for three weeks there'd be one mouth less to feed.

That was a forceful argument. The master from
Knockatatawn, or the Hill of the Conflagrations, was a
bachelor. Hugh was midways in a household of seven,
not counting the father and mother.

The bees settled. The bee-keeper doffed the mask and
wiped the sweat off a broad humorous face. He said:
James, like St Paul you're getting on. You want another
to guide you and lead you where thou would'st not.

—John, said the man on the fence, in defiance of Shakespeare, I maintain that there are only three stages in a man's life: young, getting-on, and not so bad-considering. I've a sad feeling that I've got to the third.

The nine-year-old, as he told me a long time afterwards, was all for the idea of Bundoran except that, young as he was, he knew there was a hook attached. This was it. At home on the Hill of the Conflagrations there wasn't a soberer man than the wee schoolmaster, none more precise in his way of life and his teaching methods, more just and exact in the administering of punishments or rewards. But Bundoran was for him another world and he, when he was there, was another man. He met a lot of all sorts of people. He talked his head off, behaved as if he had never heard of algebra or a headline copy-book, and drank whisky as if he liked it and as if the world's stock of whisky was going to run dry on the following morning. Yet, always an exact man, he knew that his powers of navigation, when he was in the whisky, were failing, that – as Myles na Gopaleen said about a man coming home from a night at a boat-club dance in Islandbridge – he knew where he was coming from and going to, but he had no control over his lesser movements. He needed a pilot, he needed a tug, or both combined in one: his nephew. There was, also, this to be said for the wee man: he was never irascible or difficult in drink, he went where the pilot guided him and the tug tugged him. He was inclined to sing, but then he was musical and in the school in Knockatatawn he had a choir that was the terror of Féis Doire Cholmcille, the great musical festival held in Derry in memory of St Colmcille. He even won prizes in Derry against the competition of the Derry choirs – and that was a real achievement.

So for one, two, three, four years the nephew-and-uncle navigational co-operation worked well. The nephew had his days on the sand and in the sea. He even faced up to it with the expert swimmers at Roguey Rocks and the Horse Pool. By night while he waited until his uncle was ready to be steered back to the doss he drank gallons of lemonade and the like, and saw a lot of life. With the natural result that by the time the fifth summer came around, that summer when the winds were so contrary and the sea so treacherous that the priest was drowned in the Horse Pool, the nephew was developing new interests: he was looking around for the girls. At any rate, Bundoran or no Bundoran, he was growing up. Now this was a special problem because the schoolmaster from Knockatatawn had little time for girls, for himself or anybody else and, least of all, for his nephew who, in the fifth summer, had just passed thirteen.

One of the wonders of the day on which they helped the schoolmaster from Knockatatawn to the hotel and happed him safely into bed by four o'clock in the afternoon was that Hugh saw a woman, one of the Scotchies, swimming at her ease in the pool where the priest had been drowned. She was a white and crimson tropical fish, more blinding than the handsomest perch in the lake at Corcreevy or the Branchy Wood: white for arms, shoulders, midriff and legs; crimson for cap and scanty costume. Women were not supposed to be in the Horse Pool on any account but so soon after the drowning, the usual people were shunning it, and that woman either didn't know or didn't care. The Scotchies who came to the seaside to Bundoran in the summer had a great name for being wild.

In the hotel bedroom the sun came in as muted slanted shafts through the cane blinds. The shafts were all dancing dust. Carpet-sweepers weren't much in use in that hotel. They helped the wee man out of his grey sober clothes and into a brutal pair of blue-and-white striped pyjamas. He was a fierce hairy wee fellow. Arms long like an ape and a famous fiddler when he was sober. The big purple-faced schoolmaster from Lurganboy said: Begod, you're like a striped earthenware jar of something good.

The little man waved his arms and tried to sing and once slipped off the edge of the bed and sat on the floor and recited word-perfect:

A Chieftain to the Highlands bound
Cries: Boatman, do not tarry,
And I'll give thee a silver crown
To row me o'er the ferry.

The lot of it, every verse, all about how the waters wild swept o'er his child and how Lord Ullin's daughter and her lover were drowned. The drowning of the priest must have put it into his mind. The purple-faced man from Lurganboy, rocking a little, listened with great gravity, his head to one side, his black bushy eyes glistening, his thick smiling lips bedewed with malt. He said: In the training college he was renowned for his photographic memory. And for the fiddle.

Hugh said nothing. He was sick with delight. His uncle was a blue-and-white earthenware jar of Scotch whisky, as full as it could hold. He always drank Scotch in Bundoran, out of courtesy, he said, to the hundreds of Scotchies who came there every year on their holidays and spent good money in the country. The music of hurdy-gurdies and hobby-horses and the like came drifting to them from the strand, over the houses on the far side of the town's long street. This blessed day the blue-and-white jar could hold no more. He would sleep until tomorrow's dawn and Hugh was a free man, almost fourteen, and the world before him.

—He'll rest now, said the red-faced master from Lurganboy.

They tiptoed out of the room and down the stairs.

—What'll you do now, boy?

—Go for a walk.

—Do that. It's healthy for the young.

He gave Hugh a pound, taken all crumpled out of a trouser pocket. Then nimbly, for such a heavy man, he sidestepped into a raucous bar and the swinging doors, glass, brass and mahogany, closed behind him. It was an abrupt farewell yet Hugh was all for him, and not only because of the crumpled pound, but because in him, man to man and glass for glass, the schoolmaster from the Hill of the Conflagrations had for once taken on more than his match. Several times as they helped the little man towards his bed the unshakeable savant from Lurganboy had said to Hugh: Young man, you are looking at one who in his cups and in his declining years can keep his steps, sir, like a grenadier guard.

He had the map of his day already worked out in his head. The Scotchy girl wouldn't be sitting on the high windowsill until seven o'clock. She was there most evenings about that time. She and God knew how many other Scotchies, male and female, lived in a three-storeyed yellow boarding-house at the east end of the town. There was a garden in front of it, a sloping lawn but no fence or hedge, and the two oval flower-beds were rimmed with great stones, smoothed and shaped by the sea, tossed up on the beach at Tullaghan to the west, gathered and painted and used as ornaments by the local people. This

Scotchy girl was one that liked attention. The way she went after it was to clamber out of a bedroom window on the third floor and to sit there for an hour or more in the evening kicking her heels, singing, laughing, pretending to fall, blowing kisses, and shouting things in unintelligible Scottish at the people in the street below, throwing or dropping things, flowers, chocolates, little fluttering handkerchiefs and once, he had heard, a pair of knickers. He had seen her only once at those capers when one evening he navigated past, tug before steamship, with his uncle in tow. But a fella he knew slightly told him she was to be seen there at that time most evenings. She sure as God was there to be seen. It wouldn't have been half the fun if she'd worn a bathing-suit, but a skirt with nothing underneath was something to tell the fellas about when he got back to Bomacatall. Not that they'd believe him, but still.

Behind her in the room there must have been 30 girls. They squealed like a piggery. That was a hell of a house. A randyboo, the wee master called it. Bomacatall, Knockatatawn and Corcreevy all combined never heard the equal of the noise that came out of that house. On the ground floor the piano always going, and a gramophone often at the same time, and a melodeon and pipes, and boozy male voices singing Bonny Doon and Bonny Charlie's noo awa' and Over the Sea to Skye and Loch Lomond and The Blue Bells of Scotland and Bonny Strathyre and Bonny Mary of Argyle and, all the time and in and out between everything else:

> For I'm no awa tae bide awa,
> For I'm no awa tae leave ye,
> For I'm no awa tae bide awa,
> I'll come back an' see ye.

—They work hard all year, the wee master said. In the big factories and shipyards of Glasgow. Then they play hard. They're entitled to it. The Scots are a sensitive generous people and very musical.

This was the map that was in Hugh's mind when the red- or purple-faced master from Lurganboy left him outside the swinging doors of the saloon bar. That Lurganboy man was a wonder to see at the drink. When he moved, Hugh thought, he should make a sound like the ocean surf itself with the weight of liquid inside him. He had also said something remarkable and given Hugh a phrase to remember. For as they'd steered the Knockatatawn man round a windy corner from the promenade to the main street, a crowd, ten or eleven, of Scotchy girls had overtaken them, singing and shouting, waving towels and skimpy bathing-suits, wearing slacks and sandals, bright blouses, short skirts, sweaters with sleeves knotted round their waists and hanging over rumps like britchens on horses.

—This town, said the master from Lurganboy, is hoaching with women.

That was the northern word you'd use to describe the way fingerlings wriggle over and around each other at the shallow fringes of pools on blinding June days.

—Hoaching. Hoaching with women, Hugh said to himself as he set out to follow the map he had drawn in his mind that would bring him back at seven o'clock to the place where the daft girl kicked her heels and more besides on the windowsill.

From the house of glass to the Nuns' Pool by way of the harbour where the fishing boats are. It isn't really a house of glass. This shopkeeper has a fanciful sort of mind and has pebbledashed the front wall of his place with fragments of broken glass. The shop faces east, catching the morning sun, the whole wall then lives and dances like little coloured tropical fish frisking, hoaching, in a giant aquarium. Hugh can look down on it from his window which is right on top of the hotel across the street. Some people say the wall is beautiful. Some people say the man is crazy. The seer from Knockatatawn says that's the way with people.

Westward the course towards the Nuns' Pool. Passing the place where the sea crashes right into the side of the street, no houses here, and only a high strong wall keeps it from splattering the traffic. Here in the mornings when the tide is ebbed and the water quiet a daft old lady in a long dress walks out along rocks and sand, out and out until she's up to her neck in the water, dress and all, and only her head and wide-brimmed straw hat to be seen. Then she comes calmly out again and walks home dripping. Nobody worries or bothers about her. The bay is her bath tub. She lives here winter and summer.

This day the harbour is empty, a few white sails far out on the bay, pleasure boats. He sits on the tip of the mole for a while and looks down into the deep translucent water. On the gravelly bottom there are a few dead discarded fish, a sodden cardboard box, and fragments of lobster claws turned white. If he could clamber around that sharp rock headland and around two or three more of the same he could peep into the Nuns' Pool and see what they're up to. Do they plunge in, clothes and all, like the mad woman in the morning? It's hard to imagine nuns stripping like the Scotchy in the pool where the priest was drowned. Surely the priests and the nuns should share the one pool and leave Roguey Rocks and the Horse Pool to the men and the wild Scotchies. The

strand and the surf are for children and after five sum-
mers he knows he's no longer a child.

But he's also alone and he knows it. Tugging and
steering his mighty atom of an uncle has taken up all his
time and cut him off from his kind. On the clifftop path
by the Nuns' Pool there are laughing girls by the dozen,
and couples walking, his arm as tightly around her as if
she had just fainted and he is holding her up. In corners
behind sod fences there are couples asprawl on rugs or
on the naked grass, grappled like wrestlers but motionless and in deep silence. Nobody pays the least attention
to him. Fair enough, he seems to be the youngest person
present. Anyone younger is on the sand or in the surf.
Or going for rides on donkeys. He is discovering that,
unless you're the tiniest bit kinky, love is not a satisfac-
tory spectator sport.

Steep steps cut in rock go down to the Nuns' Pool.
Was it called after one nun or gaggles of nuns, season
after season? It must have been one horse. But what
was a horse ever doing out there on rocks and seaweed
and salt water? He sees as he walks a giant nun, a giant
horse. The steep steps turn a corner and vanish behind a
wall of rock as big as Ben Bulben mountain. Only God
or a man in a helicopter could see what goes on in there.
Do they swim in holy silence, praying perhaps, making
aspirations to Mary the Star of the Sea? He listens for
the sort of shouts and music and screaming laughs that
come from the house where the girl sits on the windowsill. He hears nothing but the wash of the sea, the wind
in the cliffside grass, the crying of the gulls. What would
you expect? It is ten minutes to five o'clock.

He has time to walk on to the place where the Drowes
river splits into two and goes to the sea over the ranked,
sea-shaped stones of Tullaghan, to walk back to the hotel

by the main road, feast on the customary cold ham and tomatoes and tea, bread and butter, wash his hands and face and sleek his hair with Brylcreem and part it up the middle, and still be on good time and in a good place for the seven o'clock show. He does all this. He is flat-footed from walking and a little dispirited. On the stony strand of Tullaghan there isn't even a girl to be seen. If there was he could draw her attention to the wonderful way the sea forms and places the stones, rank on rank, the biggest ones by the water line and matted with seaweed, the smallest and daintiest right up by the sand and the whistling bent-grass. They are variously coloured. The tide has ebbed. Far out the water growls over immovable stones.

He rests for a while by the two bridges over the Drowes river. If there was a girl there he could tell her how the river flows down from Lough Melvin, and how the trout in the lake and the trout in the river have the gizzards of chickens and how, to account for that oddity, there's a miracle story about an ancient Irish saint. There is no girl there. A passing car blinds him with dust. Has the evening become more chilly or is that just the effect of hunger? He accelerates. He knows that while a Scotchy girl might show some interest in stones shaped and coloured into mantelpiece or dressing-room ornaments, she would be unlikely to care much about trout or ancient miracles. In the hotel the master is sound asleep in blue-and-white bars, the bed-clothes on the floor. He doesn't snore. Hugh eats four helpings of ham and tomatoes, two for himself, two for the recumbent fiddler from the Hill of the Conflagrations.

The evening is still ahead of him and the fleshpots delectably steaming. There is no glitter from the house of glass. The hot tea and ham, the thought of the kicking girl on the high windowsill have done him a lot of good.

In the evening most of the children will be gone from the strand, the Palais de Danse warming up, the hoaching at its best.

He wasn't the only one watching for the vision to appear, and right in the middle, like a gigantic rugby-football forward holding together a monumental scrum, was the purple-faced man from Lurganboy. The Assyrian, Hugh thought, came down like a wolf on the fold and his cohorts were gleaming in purple and gold. He wasn't his uncle's nephew for nothing, even if he wasn't quite sure what a cohort meant. As he told me long afterwards in the Branchy Wood, or Corcreevy, if his literary education had then advanced as far as *Romeo and Juliet* he would have been able, inevitably, to say: But soft what light through yonder window etc. The man with the face as purple as cohorts saw it differently. To the men that ringed him round he said: Lads, I declare to me Jasus, 'tis like Lourdes or Fatima waiting for the lady to appear. All we lack is hymns and candles.

—We have the hymns, one voice said, she has the candles.

—*Ave ave,* said another voice.

The laughter wasn't all that pleasant to listen to. They were a scruffy enough crowd, Hugh thought, to be in the company of a schoolmaster that had the benefit of education and the best of training; the master from Bomacatall, kind as he was, would have crossed the street if he'd seen them coming. Shiny pointy toes, wide grey flannels, tight jackets, oiled hair; the man from Lurganboy must, at last, like the stag at eve, have drunk his fill or he wouldn't, surely to God, be in the middle of them. Hugh dodged. There was a fine fat flowering bush, white blossoms, bursting with sparrows when the place was quiet, right in the middle of the sloping lawn. He put it between himself and the waiting watching crowd. His back was to the bush. He was very close to the high yellow house. The din was delightful, voices male and female, a gramophone playing a military march, somebody singing that there are meadows in Lanark and mountains in Skye – and he was thinking what a wonderful people the Scots were and what a hell and all of a house that must be to live in, when the high window went up with a bang and there she was, quick as a sparrow on a branch, but brighter, much brighter.

He had heard of a bird of paradise but never had he, nor has he up to the present moment, seen one. But if such a bird exists then its plumage would really have to be something to surpass in splendour what Hugh, in the dying western evening, saw roosting and swinging on the windowsill. Far and beyond Roguey Rocks the sun would be sinking in crimson. The light came over the roofs of the houses across the street, dazzled the windows, set the girl on fire. Long red hair, red dress, pink stockings, red shoes with wooden soles. She was so high up, the angle was so awkward, the late sunlight so dazzling, that he could find out little about her face except that it was laughing. The scrum around the Lurganboy man cheered and whistled. He knew she was laughing, too, because he could hear her. She was shouting down to the Lurganboy contingent, the *caballeros,* but because of the noise from the house and the street he couldn't pick out any words and, anyway, she would be talking Scottish. Nor could he be certain that he had been correctly informed as to what, if anything, she wore underneath the red dress, although when he got home to his peers in McKattle's Hut or Bomacatall he sure as God wouldn't spoil a good story by unreasonable doubts.

All told it was an imperfect experience. She twisted and tacked so rapidly, agile as a monkey, that a man could see nothing except crimson. He couldn't even have known that her red shoes had wooden soles if it hadn't been that, with the dink of kicking, one of them came unstuck, and landed as surely as a cricket-ball in his cupped palms where he stood in hiding behind the bush. It was in the pocket of his jacket before he knew what he was doing. Cinderella lost her slipper. He was off through the crowd in a second and nobody but the girl saw him go. The eyes of Lurganboy and his men were on the vision. She screamed high and long. From the far end of the crowd he glanced back and saw her pointing towards him. But nobody bothered to look the way she was pointing. The map of his evening was as clear in his mind as the strand before him, as sure as the shoe in his pocket, and hunt-the-slipper was a game at which anything might happen.

The people in this place have, like the tides, their own peculiar movement. Evening, as he expected, draws most of the children away from the strand to a thousand boarding-house bedrooms. The promise of the moon draws the loving couples, the laughing and shouting groups away from the westward walk by the Nuns' Pool to dry sheltered nooks between strand and dunes, to the hollows in the grassy tops of the high cliffs above Roguey, to the place where later the drums will begin to feel their way in the Palais de Danse. Every night, including Sunday, in the palais there is not only a dance but a few brawls and a talent competition.

No moon yet. No drums yet. The last red rays are drowned in the ocean. The light is grey. The strand is pretty empty and a little chilly, the sea is far out. But as he runs, ankle deep in churned sand, down the slope from the now silent motionless hobby-horses and hurdy-gurdies, he sees a slow, silent procession of people coming towards him around the jagged black corner of Roguey Rocks. The sea washes up almost around their feet. They step cautiously across a shelf of rock, then more rapidly and boldly along the slapping wet sand by the water's edge. Four men in the lead are carrying something. He runs towards them, all girls forgotten. Whatever chance, anyway, he had of meeting a girl during the day he can only have less now in this half-desolate place. The red shoe will be his only souvenir, yet still something to show to the heathens in Bomacatall. Halfways across the strand a distraught woman in shirt and cardigan, hair blowing wild stops him. She says: Wee boy, see if it's a wee boy with fair hair. He's missing for an hour and I'm distracted. Jesus, Mary and Joseph protect him. I'm afraid to look myself.

But it isn't a wee boy with fair hair. It isn't even the crimson-and-white Scotchy girl who had been swimming in the Horse Pool and whom the sea might have punished for sacrilege, for surely a dead drowned priest must make some difference to the nature of the water.

What he sees is nothing that you could exactly put a name to. The four men carry it on a door taken off its hinges. It's very large and sodden. There's nothing in particular where the face should be – except that it's very black. A woman looks at it and gasps. Somebody says: Cover that up, for God's sake.

A tall red-headed man throws a plastic raincoat over the black nothing in particular. Hugh walks back to the woman in the skirt and cardigan. He tells her that it isn't a wee boy with fair hair. She thanks God.

—It's a big person that must have been a long time in the water.

But she has moved away and isn't listening. He falls
in at the tail of the procession. People leave it and join it,
join it and leave it. It's a class of a funeral. An ambulance
comes screaming down the slope from the long town
and parks beside the stabled silent hobby-horses. Two
civic guards come running, a third on a bicycle. Behind
on the strand one single man in a long black coat walks,
fearing no ghosts, towards Roguey Rocks. No couples
or laughing groups are to be seen, even on the grassy
clifftops. He fingers the shoe in his pocket to remind him
of girls. A drum booms, a horn blares from the Palais de
Danse which is halfways up the slope towards the town.
He gets in, and for free, simply by saying that he's singing in Irish in the talent competition.

The hall was already crowded because the evening had
turned chilly and the threat of rain was in the air. He
found a seat in a corner near the ladies where he could
watch the procession coming and going. They came and
went in scores and for all the attention any of them paid
to him he might have been invisible. He was grateful for
the anonymity. He was too weary to carry on with the
hopeless chase and that grim vision on the beach had
given him other things to think about. It was still fun
to sit and watch the women, all shapes and sizes and
colours, and moods. They went in demure and came out
giggling. That was because most of them, he had heard,
kept noggins of gin and vodka concealed in the cloakroom. It was a great world and all before him. The band
was thunderous, the floor more and more crowded until
somebody thumped a gong and everybody who could
find a chair sat down: girls who couldn't sitting reck-
lessly on the knees of strangers, nobody on his. So he
stood up and gave his chair to a girl who didn't even say

thanks. The band vanished. A woman sat at the piano, a man with a fiddle and a young fellow with a guitar stood beside her. This was the talent competition.

A grown man long afterwards in the Branchy Wood, or Corcreevy, he couldn't remember much of it. The time was after eleven, he had been on foot all day, his eyes were closing with sleep. A man with long brown hair and long – the longest – legs and big feet came out, sang in a high nervous tenor about the bard of Armagh, then tripped over the music stand and fell flat on his face. That act was much appreciated. A little girl in a white frock and with spangles or something shining in her hair, tiptoed out, curtsied, holding the hem of her skirt out wide in her hands, danced a jig to the fiddle, then sang a song in Irish that meant: There are two little yellow goats at me, courage of the milk, courage of the milk. This is the tune that is at the piper, Hielan laddy, Hielan laddy. And more of the same. A fat bald man sang: While I'm jog jog jogging along the highway, a vagabond like me. Then there were tin whistles and concertinas, six sets of Scottish and two of Irish or Uillean pipes, piano accordions, melodeons, combs in tissue paper and clicking spoons, cornet, fiddle, big bass drum something, something and euphonium. As the song says.

He lost interest. His insteps ached. He would unnoticed have slipped away only a crowd and girls hoaching was always better than a lonely room. Surveying the crowd from China to Peru he saw in the far corner the man from Lurganboy, like the old priest Peter Gilligan, asleep within a chair, his legs out like logs, hands locked over splendid stomach and watch-chain and velvet waistcoat, chin on chest, black hat at a wild angle but bravely holding on to his head. No angels, as in the case of Peter

Gilligan, hovered over him, none that Hugh could see. Five other adults sat in a row beside him, all awake except Lurganboy. Angels that around us hover, guard us till the close of day. Singing that, the Knockatatawn choir had once won a first prize in Derry city.

As Hugh watched, Lurganboy awoke, pulled in his legs, raised his head, gripped the arms of his chair and hoisted himself to sit erect. The ballroom was silent. Was it the oddness of the silence made the sleeper awake? No, not that, but something, Hugh felt, was going to happen. The drummer was back on the stage. He struck the drum a boom that went round the room, echoing, shivering slowly away. Then the compère said: Ladies and gentlemen.

He said it twice. He held up his right hand. He said again: Ladies and gentlemen, while the judges, including our old, true, tried and stalwart friend from Lurganboy are making up their minds, adding up points, assessing the vast array of talent, not to mention grace and beauty, we will meet again an old friend, a man who needs no introduction, a man who many a time and oft has starred on this stage and who, in days gone by but well remembered, has worn more laurels for music than—

The cheers hit the roof, and out on the stage like a released jack-in-the-box stepped the wee master from Knockatatawn, sober as a judge, lively as a cricket, dapper as a prize greyhound, fiddle in one fist, bow in the other. When the cheering stopped he played for fifteen minutes and even the gigglers, resurfacing after gin and vodka, kept a respectful silence. Lord God Almighty, he could play the fiddle.

It could be that the way to get the women is to be a bachelor and play the fiddle, and drink all day and pay no attention to them. For I declare to God, the schoolmaster from Corcreevy said long afterwards, I never saw anything like it before or since, flies round the honeypot, rats round a carcase, never did I see hoaching like that hoaching, and in the middle of it and hopping about on the stage like a wound-up toy, a monkey on a stick, the red Scots girl from the windowsill, and her shoe in my pocket. Radar or something must have told her where it was. She saw me, isolated as I was, standing like a pillar-box in the middle of the floor, for the crowd was on the stage or fighting to get on the stage, and the drum was booming and the compère shouting and nobody listening. She came towards me slowly and I backed away and then ran for the beach, and then stopped. The moon was out between clouds. There was a mizzle of rain.

He stopped running and looked at the moon and the moonlight on the water. This was destiny and he had no real wish to run from it. The moon shines bright, on such a night as this. As he is now, a moonlit beach always reminds him of loneliness, a crowded beach of faceless death. She was a little monkey of a girl and she crouched her shoulders and stooped when she talked. Her red hair was down to her hips. She said: Wee laddie, will ye no gie me back ma shoe?

He was learning the language.

—I'm as big as ye are, yersel.

—Will ye no gie me back ma shoe?

She wasn't pleading. She wasn't angry. He knew by her big eyes that it was all fun to her, all part of the holiday. She really wasn't any taller than himself and her foot fitted into his pocket.

—It's no here. It's in ma room.

—You'll bring it tae me.

—For sure. It's no awa tae bide away.

—Guid laddie. Do ye dance?

—Thon's my uncle wi' the fiddle.

—Ye're like him. Ye were quick away wi' ma shoe. I'll no tell him ye're here.

The red shoe was his ticket of admission to the wild happy house. Nothing much, naturally, came of that except a lot of singing and some kisses in the mornings from a sort of elder sister. He learned to talk and understood Scots and to this day, and in his cups, can sing that he's no awa tae bide awa with the best Glaswegian that e'er cam doon frae Gilmour hill. Like his uncle he enjoyed his double life. Not for years, though, not until he had been through college and had his own school, in Corcreevy or the Branchy Wood, did he tell the tale to the old man, who by that time was retired and able to drink as he pleased. The old fellow, mellow at the time, laughed immoderately and said: Seemuldoon, I always hold, is a land of milk and honey if you keep your own bees and milk your own cow.

That was a favourite and frequently irrelevant saying of his. Seemuldoon, meaning the dwelling-place of the Muldoons, was, in all truth, the place he came from, and not Knockatatawn. Nor did the man from Lurganboy really come from Lurganboy: I used the name just because I like it, and when people ask me to go to Paris and places like that I say no, I'll go to Lurganboy. Because you don't *go* to Lurganboy, you find yourself there when you lose the road going somewhere else.

# The Night We Rode With Sarsfield

That was the house where I put the gooseberries back on the bushes by sticking them on the thorns. It wasn't one house but two houses under one roof, a thatched roof. Before I remember being there, I was there.

We came from the small village of Dromore to the big town of Omagh, the county town of Tyrone, in the spring of 1920, bad times in Ireland (Violence upon the roads/Violence of horses) particularly bad times in the north-east corner of Ulster. There have been any God's amount of bad times in the north-east corner of Ulster. There were no houses going in the big town and the nearest my father could find to his work was three miles away in the townland of Drumragh and under the one roof with Willy and Jinny Norris, a Presbyterian couple, brother and sister. They were small farmers.

That was the place then where I put the gooseberries back on the bushes by impaling them on the thorns. But not just yet because I wasn't twelve months old, a good age for a man and one of the best he's ever liable afterwards to experience: more care is taken of him, especially by women. No, the impaling of the gooseberries took place seven to eight years later. For, although we were only there six or so months until my father got a place in the town – in the last house in a laneway overlooking the green flowery banks of the serpentine Strule – we went on visiting Willy and Jinny until they died, and my father walked at their funeral and entered their church and knelt with the congregation: a thing that Roman Catholics were not by no means then supposed to do. Not knelt exactly but rested the hips on the seat and inclined the head: Ulster Presbyterians don't kneel, not even to God above.

It was a good lasting friendship with Willy and Jinny. There's an Irish proverb: *Nil aitheantas go haontigheas.* Or: You don't know anybody until you've lived in the one house with them.

Not one house, though, in this case but two houses under one roof which may be the next best thing.

Willy and Jinny had the one funeral because one night the house burned down – by accident. Nowadays when you say that a house or a shop or a pub or a factory burned down, it seems necessary to add – by accident. Although the neighbours, living next door in our house, did their best to rescue them and to save the whole structure with buckets of water from the spring-well which was down there surrounded by gooseberry bushes, they died, Willy from suffocation, Jinny from shock, the shock of the whole happening, the shock of loneliness at knowing that Willy was dead and that the long quiet evenings were over. However sadly and roughly they left the world, they went, I know, to a heaven of carefully kept harvest fields, and Orange lilies in bloom on the lawn before the farmhouse, and trees heavy with fruit, and those long evenings spent spelling-out, by the combined light of oil-lamp and hearth fire, the contents of *The Christian Herald.* My three sisters, who were all older than me, said that that was the only literature, apart from the Bible, they had ever seen in the house but, at that time, that didn't mean much to me.

The place they lived in must have been the quietest place in the world. This was the way to get there.

The Cannonhill road went up from the town in three steps but those steps could only be taken by Titans. Halfways up the second step or steep hill there was on the right-hand side a tarred timber barn behind which such of the young as fancied, and some as didn't, used to box. My elder brother, there, chopped one of the town's bullies, who was a head-fighter, on the soft section of the crown of his head as he came charging like a bull, and that cured him of head-fighting for a long time. Every boy has an elder brother who can box.

The barn belonged to a farmer who would leave a team of horses standing in the field and go follow a brass band for the length of a day. Since the town had two brass bands, one military, one civilian, his sowing was always dilatory and his harvests very close to Christmas. He owned a butcher shop in the town but he had the word, Butcher, painted out and replaced by the word, Flesher, which some joker had told him was more modern and polite but which a lot of people thought wasn't exactly decent.

If you looked back from Cannonhill the prospect was really something: the whole town, spires and all, you could even see clear down into some of the streets; the winding river or rivers, the red brick of the county hospital on a hill across the valley, and beyond all that the mountains, Glenhordial where the water came from, Gortin Gap and Mullagharn and the high Sperrins. Sometime in the past, nobody knew when, there must have been a gun-emplacement on Cannonhill so as to give the place its name. Some of the local learned men talked vaguely about Oliver Cromwell but he was never next or near the place. There were, though, guns there in 1941 when a visit from the Germans seemed imminent and, indeed, they came near enough to bomb Belfast and Pennyburn in Derry City and were heard in the darkness over our town, and the whole population of Gallowshill, where I came from, took off for refuge up the three titanic steps of the Cannonhill road. It was a lovely June night, though, and everybody enjoyed themselves.

If any of those merry refugees had raced on beyond the ridge of Cannonhill they would have found themselves, Germans or no Germans, in the heart of quietness. The road goes down in easy curves through good farmland to the Drumragh River and the old grave-yard where the gateway was closed with concrete and stone long before my time, and the dead sealed off for ever. There's a sort of stile made out of protruding stones in the high wall and within – desolation, a fragment of a church wall that might be medieval, waist-high stag-nant grass, table tombstones made anonymous by moss and lichen, a sinister hollow like a huge shellhole in the centre of the place where the dead, also anonymous, of the great famine of the 1840s were thrown coffinless, one on top of the other. A man who went to school with me used to call that hollow the navel of nothing and to explain in gruesome detail why and how the earth that once had been mounded had sunk into a hollow.

That same man ran away from home in 1938 to join the British navy. He survived the sinking of three destroyers on which he was a crew member: once, off the Faroes; once, for a change of temperature, in the Red Sea; and a third time at the Battle of Crete. It may be possible that the crew of the fourth destroyer he joined looked at him with some misgiving. A fellow townsman who had the misfortune to be in Crete as a groundsman with the RAF when the Germans were coming in low and dropping all sorts of unpleasant things to the great danger of life and limb, found a hole in the ground where he could rest unseen, and doing no harm to anybody, until he caught the next boat to Alexandria.

When he crawled into the hole, who should be there but the thrice-torpedoed sailor reading *The Ulster Herald*. He said hello and went on reading. He was a cool one, and what I remember most about him is the infinite patience with which he helped me when, impelled by a passion for history, I decided to clean all the table tombstones in old Drumragh and recall from namelessness and oblivion the decent people who were buried there. It was a big project. Not surprisingly it was never completed, never even properly commenced, but it brought us one discovery: that one of the four people, all priests, buried under a stone that was flat to the ground and circled by giant yews, was a MacCathmhaoil (you could English it as Campbell or McCarvill) who had in history been known as the Sagart Costarnocht because he went about without boots or socks, and who in the penal days of proscribed Catholicism had said Mass in the open air at the Mass rock on Corra Duine mountain.

For that discovery our own parish priest praised us from the pulpit. He was a stern Irish republican who had been to the Irish college in Rome, had met D'Annunzio and approved of him and who always spoke of the Six Counties of north-east Ulster as *Hibernia Irredenta*. He was also, as became his calling, a stern Roman Catholic, and an antiquarian, and in honour of the past and the shadow of the proscribed, barefooted priest, he had read the Mass one Sunday at the rock on Corra Duine and watched, in glory on the summit like the Lord himself, as the congregation trooped in over the mountain from the seven separate parishes.

This ground is littered with things, cluttered with memories and multiple associations. It turns out to be a long three miles from Gallowshill to the house of Willy and Jinny Norris. With my mother and my elder sisters I walked it so often, and later on with friends and long after Willy and Jinny were gone and the house a blackened ruin, the lawn a wilderness, the gooseberry bushes gone to seed, the Orange lilies extinguished – miniature suns that would never rise again in that place no more than life would ever come back to the empty mansion of Johnny Pet Wilson. That was just to the left before you turned into the Norris laneway, red-sanded, like a tunnel with high hawthorn hedges and sycamores and ash trees shining white and naked. My father had known Johnny Pet and afterwards had woven mythologies about him: a big Presbyterian farmer, the meanest and oddest man that had ever lived in those parts. When his hired men, mostly Gaelic speakers from west Donegal, once asked him for jam or treacle or syrup or, God help us, butter itself, to moisten their dry bread, he said: Do you say your prayers?

—Yes, boss.

They were puzzled.

—Do you say the Lord's prayer?

—Yes, boss.

—Well, in the Lord's prayer it says: Give us this day our daily bread. Damn the word about jam or treacle or syrup or butter.

When he bought provisions in a shop in the town he specified: So much of labouring man's bacon and so much of the good bacon.

For the hired men, the imported long-bottom American bacon. For himself, the Limerick ham.

He rose between four and five in the morning and expected his men to be already out and about. He went

around with an old potato sack on his shoulders like a
shawl, and followed always by a giant of a gentleman goat,
stepping like a king's warhorse. The goat would attack
you if you angered Johnny Pet, and when Johnny died
the goat lay down and died on the same day. Their ghosts
walked, it was well known, in the abandoned orchard
where the apples had become half-crabs, through gaps in
hedges and broken fences, and in the roofless rooms of
the ruined house. Nobody had ever wanted to live there
after the goat and Johnny Pet died. There were no relatives even to claim the hoarded fortune.

—If the goat had lived, my father said, he might have
had the money and the place.

—The poor Donegals, my mother would say as she
walked past Johnny Pet's ghost, and the ghost of the goat,
on the way to see Willy and Jinny. Oh, the poor Donegals.

It was a phrase her mother had used when, from the
doorstep of the farmhouse in which my mother was
reared, the old lady would look west on a clear day and
see the tip of the white cone of Mount Errigal, the Cock
o' the North, 60 or more miles away, standing up and
shining with shale over Gweedore and the Rosses of
Donegal and by the edge of the open Atlantic. From that
hard coast, a treeless place of diminutive fields fenced by
drystone walls, of rocks, mountains, small lakes, empty
moors and ocean winds the young Donegal people (both
sexes) used to walk eastwards, sometimes barefoot, to
hire out in the rich farms along the valley of the Strule,
the Mourne and the Foyle – three fine names for different stages of the same river.

Or the young people, some of them hardly into their
teens, might travel as far even as the potato fields of
Fifeshire or Ayrshire. They'd stand in the streets at the
hiring fairs to be eyed by the farmers, even by God to

have their biceps tested to see what work was in them.
The last of the hiring fairs I saw in Omagh in the early
1930s but by that time everybody was well dressed and
wore boots and the institution, God be praised, was
doomed. There was a big war on the way and the promise of work for all. But my mother, remembering the old
days and thinking perhaps more of her own mother than
of the plight of the migratory labourers, would say: The
poor Donegals. Ah, the poor Donegals.

Then up the sheltered red-sanded boreen or laneway –
the Gaelic word would never at that time have been used
by Ulster Presbyterians – to the glory of the Orange lilies and the trim land and in the season, the trees heavy
with fruit. Those gooseberries I particularly remember
because one day when I raided the bushes more than
somewhat, to the fearful extent of a black-paper four-
teen-pound sugar-bag packed full, my sisters (elder)
reproved me. In a fit of remorse I began to stick the berries back on the thorns. Later in life I found out that
plucked fruit is plucked for ever and that berries do not
grow on thorns.

Then another day the three sisters, two of them
home on holidays from Dublin, said: Sing a song for
Jinny and Willy.

Some children suffer a lot when adults ask them to
sing or recite. There's never really much asking about it.
It's more a matter of get up and show your paces and
how clever you are, like a dancing dog in a circus, or
know the lash or the joys of going to bed supperless. Or
sometimes it's bribery. Sing up and you'll get this or that.

Once I remember – can I ever forget it? – the reverend mother of a convent in Dublin gave me a box of
chocolates because in the presence of my mother and

my cousin, who was a nun, and half the community I
brazenly sang:

> Paddy Doyle lived in Killarney
> And he loved a maid named Bessy Toole,
> Her tongue I know was tipped with blarney,
> But it seemed to him the golden rule.

But that was one of the exceptionally lucky days. I
often wondered, too, where the reverend mother got the
box of chocolates. You didn't expect to find boxes of chocolates lying around convents in those austere days. She
dived the depth of her right arm for them into a sort of
trousers-pocket in her habit, and the memory of them and
of the way I won them ever after braced me in vigour (as
the poet said) when asked to give a public performance.

—Up with you and sing, said the eldest sister.

Outside the sun shone. The lilies nodded and flashed
like bronze. You could hear them. On a tailor's dummy,
that Jinny had bought at an auction, Willy's bowler hat
and sash were out airing for the Orange walk on the
twelfth day in honour of King William and the battle of
the Boyne. The sash was a lovely blue, a true blue, and
the Orangemen who wore blue sashes were supposed to
be teetotallers. Summer and all as it was, the pyramid
of peat was bright on the hearth and the kettle above
it singing and swinging on the black crane, and Jinny's
fresh scones were in three piles, one brown, one white,
one spotted with currants and raisins, on the table and
close to the coolness of the doorway.

—Sing up, said the second sister. Give us a bar.

—Nothing can stop him, said the third sister who was
a cynic.

She was right. Or almost. Up I was and at it,
with a song learned from another cousin, the nun's

brother, who had been in 1920 in the IRA camp in the Sperrin mountains:

> We're off to Dublin in the green and the blue,
> Our helmets glitter in the sun,
> Our bayonets flash like lightning
> To the rattle of the Thompson gun.
> It's the dear old flag of Ireland, boys,
> That proudly waves on high,
> And the password of our order is:
> We'll conquer or we'll die.

The kettle sputtered and spat and boiled over. Jinny dived for it before the water could hit the ashes and raise a stink, or scald the backs of my legs where I stood shouting treason at Willy and the dummy in the bowler and the teetotaller's blue sash. It may have been a loyal Orange kettle. Willy was weeping with laughter and wiping the back of his left hand sideways across his eyes and his red moustache. In the confusion, the eldest sister, purple in the face with embarrassment, said: If you recited instead of singing. He's much better at reciting.

So I was – and proud of it. Off I went into a thundering galloping poem learned by heart from the *Our Boys,* a magazine that was nothing if not patriotic and was produced in Dublin by the Irish Christian Brothers.

> The night we rode with Sarsfield out from Limerick to meet
> The wagon-train that William hoped would help in our defeat
> How clearly I remember it though now my hair is white
> That clustered black and curly neath my trooper's cap that night.

This time there was no stopping me. Anyway Willy wouldn't let them. He was enjoying himself. With the effrontery of one of those diabolical little children who have freak memories, even when they don't know what the words mean, I let them have the whole works, eight verses of eight lines each, right up to the big bang at Ballyneety on a Munster hillside at the high rock that is still called Sarsfield's Rock.

It is after the siege of Derry and the battle of the Boyne and the Jacobite disaster at the slope of Aughrim on the Galway road. The victorious Williamite armies gather round the remnants of the Jacobites locked up behind the walls of Limerick. The ammunition train, guns, and wagons of ball and powder, that will end the siege rumble on across the country. Then Sarsfield with the pick of his hard-riding men, and led by the Rapparee, Galloping Hogan, who knows every track and hillock and hollow and marsh and bush on the mountains of Silver Mine and Keeper and Slieve Felim, rides north by night and along the western bank of the big river:

'Twas silently we left the town and silently we rode,
While o'er our heads the silent stars in silver beauty glowed.
And silently and stealthily well led by one who knew,
We crossed the shining Shannon at the ford of Killaloe.

On and on from one spur of the mountains to the next, then silently swooping down on the place where, within a day's drag from the city's battered walls, the well-guarded wagons rest for the night. For the joke of it the Williamite watchword is Sarsfield:

The sleepy sentry on his rounds perhaps was musing o'er
His happy days of childhood on the pleasant English shore,
Perhaps was thinking of his home and wishing he were there
When springtime makes the English land so wonderfully fair.

> At last our horses' hoofbeats and our jingling arms he heard.
> 'Halt, who goes there?' the sentry cried. 'Advance and give
>     the word.'
> 'The word is Sarsfield,' cried our chief, 'and stop us he who can,
> 'For Sarsfield is the word tonight and Sarsfield is the man.'

Willy had stopped laughing, not with hostility but
with excitement. This was a good story, well told. The
wild riders ride with the horses' shoes back to front so
that if a hostile scouting party should come on their
tracks, the pursuit will be led the wrong way. The camp
is captured. Below the rock a great hole is dug in the
ground, the gunpowder sunk in it, the guns piled on the
powder, the torch applied:

> We make a pile of captured guns and powder bags and stores,
> Then skyward in one flaming blast the great explosion roars.

All this is long long ago – even for the narrator in the
poem. The hair is now grey that once clustered black and
curly beneath his trooper's cap. Sarsfield, gallant Earl of
Lucan, great captain of horsemen, is long dead on the
plain of Landen or Neerwinden. Willy is silent, mourn-
ing all the past. Jinny by the table waits patiently to pour
the tea:

> For I was one of Sarsfield's men though yet a boy in years
> I rode as one of Sarsfield's men and men were my com-
>     peers.
> They're dead the most of them, afar, yet they were Ireland's
>     sons
> Who saved the walls of Limerick from the might of
>     William's guns.

No more than the sleepy sentry, my sisters never recov-
ered from the shock. They still talk about it. As for myself,

on my way home past the ghosts of Johnny Pet and the gentleman goat, I had a vague feeling that the reason why the poor girls were fussing so much was because the William that Sarsfield rode to defeat must have been Willy Norris himself. That was why the poem shouldn't be recited in his house, and fair play to him. But then why had Willy laughed so much? It was all very puzzling. Happy Ulster man that I then was I knew as little about politics and the ancient war of Orange and Green as I knew about the way gooseberries grew.

It wasn't until after my recital that they found out about the black-paper fourteen-pounder of a sugar-sack stuffed full of fruit. The manufacturers don't do sacks like that any more in this country. Not even paper like that any more. It was called crib-paper, because it was used, crumpled-up and worked-over and indented here and bulged out there to simulate the rock walls of the cave of Bethlehem in Christmas cribs.

For parcelling books I was looking for some of it in Dublin the other day, to be told that the only place I'd come up with it was some unlikely manufacturing town in Lancashire.

# Bluebell Meadow

When she came home in the evening from reading in the park that was a sort of an island, the sergeant who had been trounced by the gipsies was waiting to ask her questions about the bullets. He had two of them in the cupped palm of his right hand, holding the hand low down, secretively. His left elbow was on the edge of the white-scrubbed kitchen table. The golden stripes on his blue-black sleeve, more black than blue, were as bright as the evening sunshine on the old town outside. He was polite, almost apologetic, at first. He said: I hate to bother yourself and your aunt and uncle. But it would be better for everybody's sake if you told me where you got these things. People aren't supposed to have them. Least of all girls in a convent school.

There had been six of them. The evening Lofty gave them to her she had looked at them for a whole hour, sitting at that table, half-reading a book. Her uncle and aunt were out at the cinema. She spread the bullets on the table and moved them about, making designs and shapes and patterns with them, joining them by imaginary lines, playing with them as if they were draughts or dominoes or precious stones. It just wasn't possible that such harmless mute pieces of metal could be used to kill people. Then she wearied of them, put them away in an old earthenware jug on the mantelpiece and after a while forgot all about them. They were the oddest gifts,

God knew, for a boy to give to a girl. Not diamonds again, darling. Say it with bullets.

This is how the park happens to be a sort of an island. The river comes out of deep water, lined and overhung by tall beeches, and round a right-angled bend to burst over a waterfall and a salmon leap. On the right bank and above the fall a sluice-gate regulates the flow of a millrace. A hundred yards downstream the millrace is carried by aqueduct over a rough mountain stream or burn coming down to join the river. Between river and race and mountain stream is a triangular park, five or six acres, seats by the watersides, swings for children, her favourite seat under a tall conifer and close to the corner where the mountain stream meets the river. The place is called Bluebell Meadow. The bluebells grow in the woods on the far side of the millrace.

When the river is not in flood a peninsula of gravel and bright sand guides the mountain stream right out into the heart of the current. Children play on the sand, digging holes, building castles, sending flat pebbles skimming and dancing like wagtails upstream over the smooth water. One day Lofty is suddenly among the children just as if he had come out of the river which is exactly what he has done. His long black waders still drip water. The fishing-rod which he holds in his left hand, while he expertly skims pebbles with the right, dips and twiddles above him like an aerial. The canvas bag on his back is sodden and heavy and has grass, to keep the fish fresh, sticking out of the mouth of it. One of the children is doing rifle-drill with the shaft of his net. She has never spoken to him but she knows who he is.

When she tires of reading she can look at the river and dream, going sailing with the water. Or simply close

her eyes. Or lean back and look up into the tall conifer, its branches always restless and making sounds, and
going away from her like a complicated sort of spiral
stairway. She has been told that it is the easiest tree in
the world to climb but no tree is all that easy if you're
wearing a leg-splint. She is looking up into the tree, and
wondering, when Lofty sits beside her. His waders are
now dry and rubbery to smell. The rod, the net and the
bag are laid on the grass, the heads of two sad trout protruding, still life that was alive this morning. Her uncle
who keeps greyhounds argues that fishing is much more
cruel than coursing: somewhere in the happy river are
trout that were hooked and got away, hooks now fes-
tering in their lovely speckled bodies. She thinks a lot
about things like that.

Lofty sits for five minutes, almost, before he says: I
asked Alec Quigley to tell you I was asking for you.

—He told me.

—What did you say?

—Did he not tell you?

—He said you said nothing but I didn't believe him.

—Why not?

—You had to say something.

—If I said anything Alec Quigley would tell the whole
town.

—I daresay he would.

—He's the greatest clatter and clashbag from hell to
Omagh.

—I didn't know.

—You could have picked a more discreet ambassador.

The words impress him. He says: It's a big name for
Alec Quigley. I never thought of him as an ambassador.

—What then? A go-between? A match-maker? A
gooseberry?

215

They are both laughing. Lofty is a blond tall freckled fellow with a pleasant laugh. He asks her would she like a trout.

—I'd love one. Will we cook it here and now?

—I can roll it in grass for you and get a bit of newspaper in McCaslan's shop up at the waterfall.

—Who will I tell my aunt and uncle gave me the trout?

—Tell them nothing. Tell them you whistled and a trout jumped out at you. Tell them a black man came out of the river and gave you a trout.

He left his bag and rod where they were and walked from the apex of the triangular park to the shop at the angle by the waterfall. He came back with a sheet of black parcelling paper and wrapped up the trout very gently. He had long delicate hands, so freckled that they were almost totally brown. The trout, bloody mouth gaping, looked sadly up at the two of them. Lofty said: I'd like to go out with you.

—I'm often out. Here.

So he laughed and handed her the trout and went on upstream towards the falls, casting from the bank at first, then wading knee-deep across a shallow bar of gravel and walking on across a green hill towards the deeps above the falls. She liked his long stride, and the rod dipping and twiddling above him, and the laden bag – even though she knew it was full of dead gaping trout. She knew he was a popular fellow in the town. Yet she didn't tell her aunt and uncle who exactly it was had made her a gift of the trout. She said it was an elderly man and she wasn't quite sure of his name, but she described him so that they'd guess he was a well-known fisherman, a jeweller by trade and highly respected in the town. Not that Lofty and his people were disrespectable.

The gipsies who trounced the sergeant hadn't been real Romany gipsies but tinkers or travelling people from the west of Ireland, descendants, the theory was, of broken people who went on the roads during the hungry years of the 1840s and hadn't settled down since. Five of them, wild, ragged, rough-headed fellows, came roaring drunk out of a pub in Bridge Lane. The pub was owned by a man called Yarrow and the joke among those literate enough to appreciate it was about Yarrow Visited and Yarrow Revisited. There was also an old English pishogue about girls putting Yarrow, the plant, between two plates and wishing on it and saying: Good morrow, good morrow, good yarrow, thrice good morrow to thee! I hope before this time tomorrow thou wilt show my true love to me.

One of the five fell with a clatter down the three steps from the door of the pub. In their tottering efforts to pick him up two of the others struck their heads together and began to fight. The remaining two joined in and so, when he was able to stand up, did the fellow who had fallen down the steps. The sergeant was walking past and was fool enough to try to stop them. In the west of Ireland the civic guards had more sense and stood as silent spectators until the tinkers had hammered the fight out of each other.

The five of them, united by foreign invasion, gave the sergeant an unmerciful pounding. He had just enough breath left to blow his whistle. More police came running. More tinkers came shouting, men, women and children, out of the pub, out of dark tunnels of entryways between houses, out of holes in the walls. The battle escalated. More police came. The tinkers made off on two flat carts. One old man was so drunk he fell helpless off a cart and was arrested. The police followed in a tender.

At their encampment of caravans a mile outside the town the tinkers abandoned the carts and took in the darkness to the fields and the hedgerows and even, it was said, to the tops of the trees. The police wisely did not follow, but set a heavy guard on the camp, caravans, carts, horses, scrap metal and everything the tinkers owned. Sober and sheepishly apologetic they reappeared in the morning and gave themselves up and half a dozen of them went to jail. But for a long time afterwards when the sergeant walked the town the wits at the street-corner would whistle: Oh, play to me gipsy, the moon's high above.

Thanks to Arthur Tracy, known as the Street Singer, it was a popular song at the time.

In spite of all that, the sergeant remained an amiable sort of man, stout, slow-moving, with a large brown moustache and a son who was a distinguished footballer.

Yarrow is a strong-scented herb related to the daisies. It has white or pink flowers in flat clusters.

One Sunday in the previous June in an excursion train to Bundoran by the western sea she had overheard Lofty's mother telling funny stories. As a rule Protestants didn't go west to Bundoran but north to Portrush. The sea was sectarian. What were the wild waves saying: At Portrush: Slewter, slaughter, holy water, harry the papishes every one, drive them under and bate them asunder, the Protestant boys will carry the drum. Or at Bundoran: On St Patrick's day, jolly and gay, we'll kick all the Protestants out of the way, and if that won't do we'll cut them in two and send them to hell with their red, white and blue.

Nursery rhymes.

She sat facing her aunt in the train and her uncle sat beside her. They were quiet, looking at all the long beauty of Lough Erne which has an island, wooded or pastoral, for every day in the year. Her aunt, a timid little woman, said now and again: Glory be to God for all his goodness.

Her uncle said just once: You should see Lake Superior. No end to it. As far as the human eye can see.

Then they were all quiet, overhearing Lofty's mother who had no prejudices about the religion of the ocean and who, with three other people, sat across the corridor from them, and who had a good-natured carrying voice and really was fun to listen to. She was saying: I'm a Protestant myself, missus dear, and I mean no disrespect to confession but you must have heard about the young fellow who went to the priest to tell him his sins and told him a story that had more women in it than King Solomon had in the Bible and the goings-on were terrible, and the priest says to him, Young man are you married?, and the young fellow says back to him, dead serious and all, Naw father but I was twice in Fintona.

The train dived through a tunnel of tall trees. The lake vanished. Sunlight flashing and flickering through leaves made her close her eyes. Everybody on the train, even her aunt, seemed to be laughing. A man was saying: Fintona always had a bit of a name. For wild women.

Lofty's mother said, I was born there myself but I never noticed that it was all that good, nobody ever told me.

She opens her eyes and the sunlight flickers down on her through the spiralling branches of the great conifer. There's a book in the public library that has everything, including pictures, about all the trees of Great Britain and Ireland. Lofty is on the very tip of the peninsula of sand and gravel, demonstrating fly-casting to half a dozen children who are tailor-squatting around his feet.

She is aware that he's showing off to impress her and the thought makes her warm and pleased, ready to laugh at anything. But to pretend that she's unimpressed she leans back and looks up into the tree in which the sunlight is really alive, creeping round the great bole, spots of light leaping like birds from one branch to another. She thinks of the omú tree which grows on the pampas of South America. Its trunk can be anything up to 40 or 50 feet thick. The wood is so soft that when cut it rots like an over-ripe melon and is useless as firewood. The leaves are large, glossy and deep green like laurel leaves – and also poisonous. But they give shade from the bare sun to man and beast, and men mark their way on the endless plains by remembering this or that omú tree. She has read about omú trees. Her own tree is for sure not one of them. She sits up straight when her book is lifted from her lap. Lofty is sitting by her side. The children are pointing and laughing. He must have crept up on hands and knees pretending to be a wild animal, a wolf, a prowling tiger. He's very good at capers of that sort. His rod and net lie by the side of the burn.

It was April when he first sat beside her. It is now mid-June. Her school will close soon for the holidays and she will no longer be compelled to wear the uniform: black stockings, pleated skirt of navy-blue serge, blue gansey, blue necktie with saffron stripes, blue blazer with school crest in saffron on breast-pocket, blue beret, black flat-heeled shoes. Even Juliet, and she was very young, didn't have to wear a school uniform. If she had, Romeo wouldn't have looked at her.

Not that they are star-crossed lovers or Lofty any Romeo. They haven't even crossed the millrace to walk in the bluebell woods as couples of all ages customarily do. She isn't shy of walking slowly because of the leg-splint but she knows that Lofty hasn't asked her because he thinks she might be: that makes her feel for him as she might feel, if she had one, for a witless younger brother who's awkward. And a bit wild: for a lot of Lofty's talk doesn't go with the world of school uniforms mostly blue for the mother of God. What the saffron is for, except variety of a sort, she can't guess. Lofty's rattling restless talk would lift Mother Teresa out of her frozen black rigidity.

Lofty with great good humour fingers the saffron stripes and says that, in spite of everything, she's a wee bit of an Orangewoman. They hold hands regularly. Lofty can read palms, a variant reading every time. They have kissed occasionally, when the children who are always there have been distracted by a water-hen or rat or leaping fish or a broken branch or an iceberg of froth from the falls.

—Don't look now, he says one day, but if you swivel round slowly you'll see my three sisters in action.

Beyond the millrace and against the fresh green of woods she can see the flash of coloured frocks, the glint of brass buttons and pipe-clayed belts. In those days it was only the wild ones who went with the soldiers: it wasn't money and security they were after.

—They're hell for soldiers, he says, between the three of them they'd take on the Germans.

Lofty himself reads a lot of military books, campaigns and generals, Napoleon and Ludendorff, all the way from Blenheim to the Dardanelles. When he doodles as he often does on the writing-pad she always carries with her – to make notes on her reading, to transcribe favourite poems – he doodles uniforms, every detail exact. Yet he listens to her when she reads poetry or the splendid prose of a volume of selected English essays, Caxton to Belloc.

—They're advancing on us, he says. They have us surrounded, enfiladed, debouched and circumnavigated.

—We'll tell Maryanne, the three sisters say, that you're with another.

Two of them, Mildred and Rosemary, are plump, laughing, blonde girls, and Mildred who is the youngest is as freckled as her brother. Gertie, the eldest, is olive-faced, with jet-black hair, wrinkles on the forehead and around the eyes like her mother. She is never to see the father of the family but the gossip of the town is to tell her that he's away a lot in Aldershot and India and that Lofty's mother, that merry woman, is friendly with more soldiers than the one she's married to.

The three British soldiers who are with the sisters are, one of them from Sligo, one from Wexford and one actually from Lancashire, England. They all talk and laugh a lot and she likes them. The Lancashire lad climbs right up to the top of the tree and pretends to see everything that's going on in the town and tells them about it: he has a lurid imagination. Then they go away towards the waterfall, still laughing, calling back about telling Maryanne. She asks him who Maryanne is. Lofty, who clearly likes his sisters, is not in the least embarrassed by the suggestion that he has another woman.

—Oh Maryanne's nobody or nobody much.

—She has a name. She must be somebody.

She's not really jealous, just curious.

—Maryanne's a girl I met one day on the road beyond McCaslan's shop.

—You met nobody on the road?

—She was wheeling a pram.

—She's married to Mr Nobody?

—It wasn't her pram. She's the nursemaid in Mooney's, the fancy-bread bakery. There was a lovely smell of fresh bread.

—Had you a good appetite, apple-jelly, jam-tart?

But since the rest of that rhyme to which children, Protestant and Catholic, rope-skip on the streets, is tell me the name of your sweetheart, she doesn't finish it and finds herself, to her annoyance, blushing. Lofty doesn't seem to notice.

—There were twins in the pram. I pushed it for her up the hill to the main road. Then she said I bet you wouldn't do that for me if it was in the town on the court-house hill where everybody could see you. I said why not and she said Christian Brothers' boys are very stuck-up. I've met some that would do anything they could or you'd let them if they had a girl in the woods or in the dark, but that wouldn't be seen talking to her on the street, maids aren't good enough for them. I didn't tell her I was a Presbyterian and went to the academy.

—Why not?

—She mightn't like a Presbyterian pushing her pram.

They laugh at that until the playing children turn and look and laugh with them. Cheerful voices call from beyond the millrace where soldiers and sisters are withdrawing to the woods.

—We have girls at the academy, on the house, what Harry Cassidy and Jerry Hurst and the boys don't have at the Brothers. Harry and the boys are mad envious when we tell them about the fun we have feeling Daisy Allen under the desk at school. All lies of course.

—I hope Daisy Allen doesn't hear that.

—Och Daisy, she's well handled anyway, she's going about with a bus-driver and he's a married man as well, he ruined a doctor's daughter in Dungannon. Harry and the Catholic boys think the Protestant girls are wilder because they don't have to tell it all in confession. That isn't true either.

One other funny story she had heard Lofty's mother telling that day as the train in the evening left Bundoran station and the great romantic flat-topped mountains diminished into the distance. This time the story-teller faced her aunt and sat beside her uncle who had been talking about jerry-building in a new housing estate. Lofty's mother agreed with him. She had a shopping-bag of sugar to smuggle back into the Six Counties where it cost more. The sugar was tastefully disguised under a top-dressing of dulse. With content and triumph Lofty's mother sang a parody popular at the time: South of the border down Bundoran way, that's where we get the Free State sugar to sweeten our tay.

She was great fun. She had bright blue eyes and a brown hat with a flaring feather, and a brown crinkly face. She said: Those houses are everything you say and worse. Fancy fronts and ready to fall. When you flush the lavatory in them the noise is heard all over the town. Only the other day the lady who lives in number three sent down to River Row for old Mr Hill, the chimney-sweep, and up he came and put the brush up the chimney and then went out, the way sweeps do, to see if the brush was showing out of the top of the chimney. No brush. In he went and screws on another length of handle on the brush and pushes for dear life, and out again to look, but no brush. In again and screws on the last bit of handle he has, and he's pushing away when the lady from number eleven knocks on the door. Have you the sweep in, missus dear, she says. I have, missus dear, says the lady from number three. Then please ask him to be careful, missus dear, she says, that's twice now he's upset our wee Rosy from the lavatory seat.

Because of her happy carrying voice passers-by in the corridor stop to join the fun. The smuggled sugar is safely across the border.

Remembering Lofty's laughing mother makes it easier still to like Lofty. The three sisters also look as if they'd be good for a lot of laughs.

Her uncle is a tall broad-shouldered man with a good grey suit, a wide-brimmed hat, two gold teeth and a drawl. Years ago he was in the building trade in the United States and knows a lot about jerry-building. He gets on very well with Lofty's mother.

It was well on towards the end of August when the black man sat on the bench beside her. She was looking sideways towards the bridge over the millrace, and laughing: because two big rough young fellows were running like hares before Mr McCaslan's boxer dog. Mr McCaslan who owned the shop was also water-bailiff and park-keeper. The rough fellows had been using, brutally, one of the swings meant for small children, so brutally that the iron stays that supported it were rising out of the ground. Mr McCaslan had mentioned the matter to them. They had been offensive, even threatening, to the old rheumatic man so he hobbled back to his shop and sent the boxer dog down as his deputy. The pair took off as if all hell were behind them. It was funny because the dog didn't bark or growl or show hostility, didn't even run fast, just loped along with a certain air of quiet determination and wouldn't (as far as she knew) savage anybody. But he was a big dog even for a boxer and the retreat of the miscreants was faster than the Keystone Cops. She laughed so much that the book fell on the grass. The black man picked it up and sat down beside her.

She thought of him as a black man not because he was a Negro but because her uncle had told her that he was a member of the black preceptory which was a special branch of the Orange Order. She had seen him walking last twelfth of July in the big parade in memory of the battle of the Boyne, which happened a long time ago, and in honour of King William of Orange who was a long time dead and had never been in this town. He had worn the black sash, with shining metallic esoteric insignia attached, as had the other men who marched beside him. The contingent that followed wore blue sashes and were supposed to be teetotallers but her uncle said that that was not always so. One of the blue men, a red-faced red-headed fellow was teetering and might have fallen if he hadn't been holding on to one of the poles that supported a banner.

The drums drummed, the banners bellied in the breeze, the pipes and fifes and brass and accordions played:

> It is old but it is beautiful
> And its colours they are fine,
> It was worn at Derry, Aughrim,
> Enniskillen and the Boyne.
> My father wore it in his youth,
> In bygone days of yore,
> And on the Twelfth I'll always wear
> The sash my father wore.

The name of the black man who sat beside her was Samuel McClintock and he was a butcher. It was said about him for laughs that if the market ran out of meat the town could live for a week on McClintock's apron: blue, with white stripes. That August day and in the public park he naturally wasn't wearing the apron. He had a black moustache, a heavy blue chin, a check cloth-cap, thick-soled boots, thick woollen stockings and whipcord knee-breeches. The Fomorians, the monsters from stormy seas had, each of them, one arm, one leg and three rows of teeth. He said: The dog gave those ruffians the run.

The way he said it took the fun out of it. She said: Yes, Mr McClintock.

She wished him elsewhere. She half-looked at her book. She was too well-reared to pick it up from her lap and ostentatiously go on reading. The river was in a brown fresh that day, the peninsula of sand and gravel not to be seen, nor Lofty, nor the children. The black man said: Plenty water in the river today.

She agreed with him. It was also a public park in a free-and-easy town and everyone had a right to sit where he pleased. Yet this was her own seat under the tall tree, almost exclusively hers, except when Lofty was there. The black man said: The Scotchies have a saying that the salmon's her ain when there's water but she's oors when it's oot.

He explained: That means that often they're easier to catch when the water's low.

He filled his pipe and lighted it. The smell of tobacco was welcome. It might have been her imagination but until he pulled and puffed and sent the tobacco smell out around them she had thought that the resinous air under the tree was polluted by the odours of the butcher's shop and apron. He said that the salmon were a sight to see leaping the falls when they went running upstream. She said that she had often watched them.

—I'm told you're very friendly with a well-known young fisherman of my persuasion.

—Who, for instance?

—You know well. That's what I want to talk to you about. It's a serious matter.

—Being friendly with a fisherman?

—Don't play the smarty with me, young lassie. Even if you do go to the convent secondary school. Young people now get more education than's good for them. Lofty at the academy and you at the convent have no call to be chumming it up before the whole town.

—Why not?

But it occurred to her that they hadn't been chumming-up or anything else before the whole town. What eyes could have spied on them in this enchanted island?

—His uncle's a tyler, that's why.

—I never knew he had an uncle.

—His mother's brother is a tyler and very strict.

—What's a tyler?

—I shouldn't repeat it, lassie. But I will, to impress on you how serious it is. A tyler he is and a strict one. Wasn't it him spoke up to have Lofty let into the B Specials?

—Don't ask me. I never knew he was a B Special.

But one day for a joke, she remembered, he had given her a handful of bullets.

—The nuns wouldn't tell you this at school but the B Specials were set up by Sir Basil Brooke to hold Ulster against the Pope and the Republic of Ireland.

The nuns, for sure, hadn't told her anything of the sort: Mother Teresa, who was very strong on purity and being a lady and not sitting like a man with your legs crossed, had never once mentioned the defensive heroisms of the B Specials who, out in country places, went about at night with guns and in black uniforms, holding up Catholic neighbours and asking them their names and addresses – which they knew very well to begin with. The Lofty she knew in daylight by this laughing river didn't seem to be cut out for such nocturnal capers.

—If his uncle knew that the two of you and you a Catholic girl were carrying-on there'd be hell upon earth.

—But we're not carrying-on.

—You were seen kissing here on this bench. What's that but carrying-on?

—What does he level?

—What does who level?

—The uncle who's a leveller or whatever you called him.

—Speak with respect, young lassie. A tyler, although I shouldn't tell you the secret, is a big man in the Order at detecting intruders. His obligation is this: I do solemnly declare that I will be faithful to the duties of my office and I will not admit any person into the lodge without having first found him to be in possession of the financial password or without the sanction of the Worshipful Master of the Lodge.

Then after a pause he said with gravity: And I'm the worshipful master.

He was the only one of the kind she had ever met or ever was to meet and she did her best, although it was all very strange there by the river and the rough stream and under the big tree, to appear impressed, yet all she could think of saying was: But I'm not interfering with his tyling.

Then she was angry and close to tears, although it was also funny: For all I care he can tile the roofs and floors and walls of every house in this town.

The big man hadn't moved much since he sat down, never raised his voice, but now he shouted: Lassie, I'll make you care. The B Specials are sworn to uphold Protestant liberty and beat down the Fenians and the IRA.

—I'm not a Fenian nor an IRA.

—You're a Roman Catholic, aren't you? And there isn't any other sort. Sir Basil Brooke says that Roman Catholics are 100 per cent disloyal and that he wouldn't have one of them about the house.

—Sir Who's It?

—No cheek, lassie. Didn't he sit up a tree at Colebrook all night long with a gun waiting for the IRA to attack his house? Didn't he found the B Specials to help the police to defend the throne and the Protestant religion?

What was it to her if Sir Somebody or Other spent all his life up a tree at Colebrook or anywhere else? The Lancashire soldier had climbed her tree and been as comic as a monkey up a stick. The black man calmed himself: Your own clergy are dead set against mixed marriages.

—We weren't thinking of marriage.

—What of then? Silliness and nonsense. The young have no wit. What would Mother Teresa say if she heard you were keeping company with a Protestant?

—Who would tell her?

—I might. For your own good and for Lofty.

He knocked the ash out of his pipe and put it away. The pleasant tobacco smell faded. She smelled blood and dirt and heard screams and knew, with a comical feeling of kindness, that she had been wrongly blaming him for bringing with him the stench of the shambles. There was a piggery at the far end of the field beyond the river and the wind was blowing from that direction.

—That's the piggery, she said. It's a disgrace.

—Time and again I've said that on the town council. You must have read what I said in the papers. It's a sin, shame and scandal to have a piggery beside a beauty spot. Not that I've anything against pigs, in my business, in their own place.

He stood up and patted her on the shoulder. He was really just a big rough friendly man: You don't want him put out of the Specials or the Lodge itself.

—Why should he be?

—These are deep matters. But they tell me you read a lot. You've the name for being one of the cleverest students in this town, Protestant or Catholic. So I'll talk to you, all for the best, as if you were a grown-up and one of my own. It is possible but very difficult for a convert to be accepted as a member of the Orange Order.

He was as good as standing to attention. He was looking over her head towards the waterfall.

—A convert would have to be of several years standing and his background would have to be carefully screened. His admission would have to be authorized by the Grand Lodge. They'd have to go that high, like Rome for the Catholics. No convert can get into the Black Preceptory if either of his parents is still living, in case the Roman Catholic Church might exert pressure on a parent.

He was reciting. Like the sing-song way in which in school the children learned the Catechism.

Q: What are the seven deadly sins?
A: Pride, covetousness, lust, gluttony, envy, anger and sloth.
Q: What are the four sins that cry to heaven for vengeance?
A: Wilful murder, sodomy, oppression of the poor and defrauding the labourer of his wages.

Dear Sacred Heart it was a cheery world.

—A convert who was even a Protestant clergyman was blacked-out because one of his parents was still living, and there is automatic expulsion for dishonouring the Institution by marrying a Roman Catholic.

The great tree creaked its branches above them. The brown water tumbled on towards the town.

—You see what I mean, lassie.

She supposed she saw. In a way she was grateful. He was trying to help. He shook her hand as if they were friends for ever. He went off towards the waterfall so that, without turning around, she could not see him walking away and he could not, thank God, see her face laughing, laughing. For, sweet heart of Jesus fount of love and mercy to thee we come thy blessings to implore, but it was comic to think of him marching up the convent grounds (he should wear his black sash and have a fife and drum before him) holy white statues to left and right and a Lourdes grotto as high as Mount Errigal, to relate all about the love-life of Lofty and herself to Mother Teresa who had a mouth like a rat-trap – and a mind. A worshipful master and a most worshipful reverend mother and never, or seldom, the twain shall meet. She was an odd sort of a girl. She sat around a lot and had read too many books. It was funny, also, to think of his daughter, Gladys, a fine good-natured brunette with a swinging stride, a bosom like a Viking prow, and a dozen boy friends of all creeds and classes. Nothing sectarian about Gladys who was one of his own kind and the daughter of a worshipful master. Somebody should tell the tyler to keep an eye on her. But she was too clever to be caught, too fast on her feet, too fast on her feet.

Walking slowly past the Orange hall on the way home she thought that the next time she met him she would have a lot to tell to lazy, freckled, lovable Lofty. The Orange hall was a two-storeyed brownstone building at a crossroads on the edge of the town. High on its wall a medallion image of William of Orange on an impossibly white horse rode forever across the Boyne. The two old cannon-guns on the green outside had been captured from the Germans in the Kaiser war. In there, Lofty's lodge met and it was a popular joke that no man could become a member until he rode a buck goat backways up the stairs. Sometimes in the evenings bands of music played thunderously in there, practising for the day in July when they marched out, banners flying. It was crazy to think that a man on a white horse, riding across a river 200 years ago could now ride between herself and Lofty. Or for that matter – although Mother Teresa would have a fit if she thought that a pupil of hers could think of such things – another man on a chair or something being carried shoulder-high in the city of Rome.

All this she meant to mention to Lofty the next time he came to the seat under the tree. But all she could get around to saying was: Lofty, what's a tyler?

He had no rod and net and was dressed, not for fishing, in a new navy-blue suit. The children called to him from the gravel but he paid no attention to them. At first he didn't pretend to hear her, so she asked him again. He said that a tyler was a man who laid tiles. That was the end of that. Then it was winter. One whole week the park was flooded. She couldn't exactly remember when it was that Lofty had given her the bullets.

It was also crazy to think that Lofty's laughing mother could have a brother who went about spying on people and nosing them out. What eyes had spied on Lofty and herself on the enchanted island? What nosy neighbour had told somebody who told somebody who told the sergeant that she had bullets in the earthenware jug?

—If you don't tell me, the sergeant says, it will be awkward for all concerned. What would Mother Teresa think if she thought you had live bullets in an earthenware jug?

It wasn't possible to control the giggles. What, in the holy name of God, would Mother Teresa think, if the sergeant and the worshipful master descended on her simultaneously, what would she say, how would she look? Keeping live bullets in a jug must be one of the few things that she had not warned her girls against.

—You'll have to come down to the barracks with me. I'll walk ahead and you follow just in case the people are passing remarks. They might think I'm arresting you.

—What are you doing?

—Och, I'd just like you to make a statement. It's not a crime to have bullets. Not for a young lady like you who wouldn't be likely to be using them. But we have a duty to find out where they came from. My son Reggie speaks highly of you, Reggie the footballer you know.

She knew. It was a town joke that the sergeant couldn't speak to anybody for ten minutes without mentioning Reggie who parted his hair up the middle, wore loud scarves and played football very well: it was clear that the sergeant thought that to be thought well of by Reggie was a special distinction.

Old low white houses line the hill that goes up from the brook and the co-operative creamery to the centre of the town. The sergeant plods on, twenty yards ahead of her. The town is very quiet. His black leather belt creaks and strains to hold him together. The butt of his pistol, his black baton case shine. She has never noticed before that Lofty has a stutter. Another sergeant sits behind a desk in the dayroom and makes notes. Two young constables are laughing in the background. The black man comes in and says: I warned the two of them.

Her own sergeant says: There wasn't much harm in it.

—Not for the girl, says the man behind the desk. But for him a breach of discipline.

Lofty has surely never stuttered when he talked to her by the meeting of the waters.

—Did you tell them I gave you the bullets?

—Dear God, it wasn't a crime to give me bullets.

—Did you tell them?

—I did not.

—They said you did.

—So.

Her own sergeant looks ashamed and rubs his moustache. The other sergeant says: Case closed.

Then her uncle walks in, and so hopping mad that he seems to have a mouthful of gold teeth. He talks for a long time and they listen respectfully because he's a famous man for keeping running dogs which he feeds on brandy and beef. He says over and over again: You make a helluva fuss about a few bullets.

—A breach of discipline, says the man behind the desk.

—My ass and yours, says her uncle. A helluva fuss.

And repeats it many times as they walk home together.

—But all the same they'll put him out of the Specials, he says. And I dare say he shouldn't have been assing around giving away government issue.

Over the supper table he remembers the time he had been a policeman in Detroit: Some Negro trouble then and this rookie policeman from Oklahoma was on patrol with a trained man. The rookie has no gun. So they're rushed by twenty black men and the first rock thrown clobbers the trained man unconscious. But the Oklahoma guy he stoops down, takes the pistol out of the other man's holster and shoots six times and kills six black men, one, two, three, four, five, six. He didn't waste a bullet.

—Sacred Heart have mercy, says her aunt.

—What did the other black men do, uncle?

—They took off for home and small blame to them. He was a cool one, that rookie, and a damned good shot. Here in this place they make a helluva fuss over a few bullets. I told them so.

Lofty came never again to the tall tree. They met a few times on the street and spoke a few words. She left the town after a while and went to work in London. Once, home on holidays, she met Lofty and he asked her to go to the pictures, and she meant to but never did. The Hitler war came on. She married an American and went to live in, of all places, Detroit. Her uncle and aunt and the sergeant and the worshipful master and the tyler and, I suppose, Lofty's mother and old McCaslan and his dog died.

Remembering her, I walked, the last time I was in the town, to revisit Bluebell Meadow. The bridge over the millrace was broken down to one plank. Rank grass grew a foot high over most of the island. The rest of it was a wide track of sand and gravel where the river in fierce flood had taken everything before it. The children's swings and all the seats were gone, smashed some time before by reluctant young soldiers from the North English cities doing their national service. Repair work had been planned but then the bombings and murders began.

No laughing Lancashire boy in British uniform will ever again climb the tall tree. For one thing the tree is gone. For another the soldiers go about in bands, guns at the ready, in trucks and armoured cars. There are burned-out buildings in the main streets – although the great barracks is unscathed – and barricades and checkpoints at the ends of the town. As a woman said to me: Nowadays we have gates to the town. Still, other towns are worse. Strabane, which was on the border and easy to bomb, is a burned-out wreck. And Newry, where the people badly needed shops and factories, and not ruins. And Derry is like Dresden on the day after.

When I wrote to her about this she said, among other things, that she had never found out the name of that tall conifer.

# Bloodless Byrne of a Monday

Three tall men excuse themselves politely, close the door gently behind them, hope he doesn't mind. But they are exhausted putting fractious Connemara ponies on a boat for a show and sale in Britain. Odd caper to be at so early on a Monday morning, they admit. And, as well, they're all Dublinmen by accent, and may never have seen the Twelve Bens or Clifden or the plains of Glenbricken.

—Fair enough, they admit.

They are most courteous.

The tallest of the three says he knows the West of Ireland well, and knows the song about Derrylee and the greyhounds and the plains of Glenbricken and about the man who emigrated from Clifden to the other West, the Wild West, to hunt the red man, the panther and the beaver, and to gaze back with pride on the bogs of Shanaheever.

The tallest man also says that from an early age he has been into horses, the big ones; his father drove a four-wheeled dray. Then into hunters with a man on the Curragh of Kildare. Then, on his own and by a lucky break, into ponies. A bleeding goldmine. He is not boasting. The colour of his money is evident in three large whiskys for himself and his colleagues, and a brandy and ginger for the stranger up from …

—Sligo, he says.

—On a bit of a blinder, he adds.

To be civil and companionable. They are three very, civil, companionable men. And he craves company. The need of a world of men for me. And round the corner came the sun.

To the tallest man the fat redheaded man says: Bloodless Byrne was a friend of your father.

The smallest of the three, the man with the peaked cloth-cap, says: Bloodless Byrne of a Monday morning. The brooding terror of the Naas Road. Very vengeful. Bloodless drove a dray for the brewery.

—Bloodless Byrne of a Monday morning, the tallest man repeats. He wears strong nailed boots and black, well-polished leather leggings.

—It became a sort of a proverb, he explains. Like: Out of the question, as Ronnie Donnegan said. Bloodless. A face on him like Dracula without the teeth. They tried calling him Dracula Byrne. But it didn't stick. He didn't fancy it. He was vengeful. Vindictive. He'd wait a generation to get his own back. He didn't mind being called Bloodless. They say he wrote it when he filled in forms.

—Mad about pigeons, says the stout redheaded man.

—Bloodless Byrne of a Monday. My father told me how that came about.

Carefully the tallest man closes the other door that opens into the public bar, cuts off the morning voices of dockers on the way to work, printers on the way home.

—Bloodless, you see, is backing his horse and dray of a Monday into a gateway in a lane back of the fruit and fish markets in Moore Street. Backs and backs, again and again. Often as he tries, one or other of the back wheels catches on the brick wall. So finally he takes his cap off, throws it down, puts his foot on it, stares the unfortunate horse full in the face, and says: You're always the same of a fuckin' Monday.

—Deep voice he had too. Paul Robeson.

The shortest man removes his cloth cap to reveal utter baldness. A startling transformation, forcing the strange gentleman from Sligo to blink tired eyelids upon tired eyes. The shortest man says: Bloodless Byrne of a Monday.

—Pigeons, says the stout redheaded man.

Bangers, the barman, belying his nickname, steps in most politely, making no din, to gather up empties and hear requests: so the gentleman from Sligo places the relevant order. These men are true companions. And prepared to talk. And what he needs most at the moment is the vibration of the voices of men. And he wants to hear more about those pigeons. And Bloodless Byrne. And why Ronnie Donnegan said it was out of the question, and what it was that was. Drinks paid for, he has five single pound notes to survive on until the banks open and he can acquire a new chequebook.

—Out of the question, he says tentatively.

But the emphasis is on pigeons and the tallest man is talking.

—Fellow in America, Bloodless says to me, wrote a play about a cat on a hot tin roof. Bloodless never saw it. The play. He saw the poster on a wall. Could you imagine Bloodless at a play? Up above in the Gaiety with all the grandees. A play. Bloodless tells me the neighbour has three cats on a black tin roof, hot or cold, and says he wouldn't like to tell me what they're at, night and day. Bloodless has no time for cats.

—Pigeons, says the stout redheaded man.

—No time for the neighbour either. No love lost. No compatibility. No good fences. So one day …

—Cats and pigeons, says the stout redheaded man.

—One day the neighbour knocks on the door and says very sorry there's your pigeons, and throws in a potato sack, wet and heavy. Dead birds.

It is difficult not to join in the chant when the stout redheaded man says again: Cats and pigeons.

—What does the bold Bloodless do? Nothing. Simply nothing. He bides his time. He waits and watches. June goes by, July and August and the horse-show, and one day in September he throws a plastic sack, very sanitary, in at the neighbour's door and says sorry mate, them's your cats. Just like that. Them's your cats. In a plastic sack.

There is nobody in the snug, nobody even in the packed and noisy public bar but Bloodless Byrne, nothing to be seriously considered but his vengeance: Sorry mate, them's your cats.

Face like Dracula without the teeth, he broods over the place for the duration of several more drinks which must have been bought by the ponymen: for the five pound notes are still intact and the ponymen are gone, and never in this life may he know what it was that was out of the question. His clothes are creased and rumpled. He needs a bath and a shave and a long rest. The noise outside is of water relaxing from shelving shingle. The snug is silent. The old boozy Belfast lady fell asleep in the confessional and when the priest pulled across the slide, said: Another bottle, Peter, and turn on the light in the snug.

His eyes are moist at the memory of that schoolboy joke.

June, July, August, and then in September: Sorry, mate, them's your cats.

He should telephone his wife and say he is well and happy and sober. Anyway he wouldn't be here and like this if she hadn't been pregnant so that, to some extent, she is at fault: and he laughs aloud at the idea, and rests his head back on old smoke-browned panelling, and dozes for five minutes.

How many years now have we been meeting once a year: Niall and Robert, Eamonn and little Kevin, Anthony and John and Sean and big Kevin, and Arthur, that's me? Count us. Nine in all. Since two years after secondary school ended in good old St Kieran's where nobody, not even the clerical professors, ever talked about anything but hurling and gaelic football, safe topics, no heresies possible although at times you'd wonder a bit about that, only a little blasphemy and/or obscenity might creep in when Kilkenny had lost a game: but no sex, right or wrong, sex did not enter in. No sex, either, on this meditative morning. As you were. That wash of waves retreating in the public bar is now as far away as the high cliffs of Moher on the far western shore of the county Clare.

Day of a big game in Dublin, Kilkenny versus Tipperary who have the hay saved and Cork bet, the nine of us come together by happy accident: a journalist and a banker, a student of law, a civil servant, a student of art and theatre, another journalist, a student of history, an auctioneer and valuer, that's me. There's one missing there somewhere. Count us, as they do with the elephants at bedtime in Duffy's circus. *N'importe.* Bangers looks in and pleasantly smiles, but the glass is still brimming and the five pound notes must be held in reserve until Blucher gets to the bank. Nine old schoolfriends meet by happy accident and vow to make the meeting annual. Tipperary lost. How many years ago? Ten? More than ten. Twenty? No, not twenty. Then wives crept in. Crept in? Came in battalions, all in one year, mass madness, Gadarene swine, lemmings swarming to the sea: and college reunions and laughter and the love of friends became cocktails and wives who don't much like each other: and dinner dances. So nothing to worry about when this year Marie is expecting, and all I have to do is meet the men and make excuses and slip away, odd man out: which seemed a good idea at the time, late in the afternoon yesterday, or early in the evening, for in this untidy town afternoon melts un-noted into evening and, regrettably and returning as the wheel returns, it is now in a day as we say in the Irish when we say it in the Irish: and here I am, here I am, here I'm alone and the ponymen are gone, and five pound notes is all between now and the opening of the banks ...

Outside, the translucent stream, as he once heard some wit call it, slithers, green and spitting with pollution, eastwards to the sea. The sun is bright without mercy. His eyes water. His knees wobble. Where had he got to after he left the lads to get with their good, unco guid, wives to the dinner dance? The sequence of events, after their last brandy and backslapping, is a bit befogged.

This town is changing. For the worse. Nothing to lean on any more. Where, said Ulysses, where in hell are the pillars of Hercules. The Scotch House is gone. Called that, I suppose, when a boat went all the way from the North Wall to Glasgow, and came back again, carrying Scotsmen who would look across the river and see the sign and feel they were at home. Scotsmen were great men for feeling at home anywhere, westering home with a song in the air, at home with my ain folk in Islay, home no more home to me whither must I wander, and the Red Bank Restaurant gone, it's a church now, and the brewery barges that used to bring the booze downstream to the cross-channel cargo boats gone for ever and for a long time. He's just old enough to remember when he first made a trip to Dublin and saw the frantic puffs of the barges when they broke funnels to clear the low arch, and the children leaning over the parapet, just here, and yelling: Hey mister, bring us back a parrot. A monkey for me, mister. A monkey for me.

And slowly answered Arthur from the barge the old order changeth, yielding place to new. That went with a drawing in a comic magazine at the time: a man in frock-coat and top-hat standing among the beerbarrels on a barge, Arthur Guinness of course, immortal father of the brewery, bring me back a monkey, bring me back a parrot. And God fulfils himself in many ways, over from barges to motor-trucks.

Sorry, mate, them's your cats.

There in that small hotel the nine of us met the day Tipperary lost the match, and met there every year until the hotel wasn't grand enough for the assembled ladies. Then it descended lower still to include a discotheque: and that was that. Nine of us? Dear God, that was why this morning I counted only eight the second time round, for Eamonn who discovered that little hotel and liked it, even to the ultimate of the discotheque, Eamonn up and died on us and that's the worst change of all.

Somewhere last night I was talking mournfully to somebody about Eamonn, mournfully remembering him: and God fulfils himself in many ways.

Out all night, and cannot exactly remember where I was, and did not get home to my own hotel which, and this is another sign of the times, is away out somewhere in the suburbs. Once upon a time the best hotels were always in the centre. Like America now, the automobile rules okay, the centre of the city dies, and far away in ideal homes all are happy, and witness a drive-in movie from the comfort and security of your own automobile: and the gossip and the fevers of the middle-ages, middle between which and what, fore and aft, I never knew, are no more: and I am dirty and tired now, and want a bath and a shave and sleep. Samuel Taylor Coleridge emptied the po out of a first-floor window. While admiring the lakeland scenery.

But this other hotel outside which he now stands is still, and in spite of the changing times and the shifting pattern of urban concentrations, one of the best hotels in town. At this moment he loves it because he knows it will be clean, as he certainly is not. In the pubs of Dublin the loos can often be an upset to the delicate in health.

So up the steps here and in through the porch. There is a long porch. Jack Doyle, the boxer, used to sit here with an Alsatian dog, and read the papers and be photographed. That was away back in Jack's good days. As a boy he used to study those newspaper photos of handsome Jack and the big dog, and envy Jack because it was said that all the girls in Dublin and elsewhere were mad about him.

He has heard that a new proprietor of this hotel has Napoleonic delusions: and, to prove the point, *l'empereur* in a detail reproduced from David and blown up to monstrosity, is there on the wall on a horse rearing on the hindlegs, pawing with the forelegs. The French must fancy that pose or position: Louis the Sun King on a charger similarly performing is frozen for ever in the Place des Victoires.

Tread carefully now, long steps, across the foyer for if that horse should forget himself, I founder.

A porter salutes him, a thin sandy man, going bald. He nods in return.

Were we here last night? Could have been, for the nine of us used to meet here: and the eighteen of us, until that changing city pattern swept the dinner dance away somewhere to the south.

This morning anything is possible. He raises his left hand to reinforce his nod, and passes on. Upstairs or downstairs or to my lady's chamber? Destiny guides him. So he walks upstairs, soft carpets, long corridors, perhaps an open, detached bathroom even if he has no razor to shave with. Afterwards, a barber's shave, oh bliss, oh bliss. He finds the bathroom and washes his face and those tired eyelids and tired eyes, and combs his hair and shakes himself a bit and shakes his crumpled suit, and polishes his shoes with a dampish handtowel. A bit too risky to chance a bath and total exposure, although he has heard and read the oddest stories about deeds performed in hotel bathrooms by people who had no right in the world to be there. Bravely he steps out again. A brandy in the bar, and the road to the bank and his own hotel and sobriety, and home: Bright sun before whose glorious rays.

Sorry, mate, them's your pigeons.

Before him in the corridor a door opens and a man steps out.

This man who steps out is in one hell of a hurry. He swings left so fast that his face has been nothing more than a blur. A black back to be seen as he hares off down the corridor to the stairhead. Hat in one hand, brief-case in the other. Off with quick short steps and down the stairs and away, leaving the door of the room open behind him. His haste rattles me with guilt. That man has somewhere to go and something to do.

To sleep, to die, to sleep, to sleep perchance to dream, and his eyes are half-closed and a mist rolling at him, tumbling tumbleweed, up the corridor from the spot where the man has vanished: and the door is open and the devil dancing ahead of him. There is no luggage in the room, not in wardrobe nor on tables, racks nor floors, no papers except yesterday's evening papers discarded in the waste-basket, no shaving-kit in the bathroom: and the towels, all except one handtowel, all folded as if they have not been used. No empty cups nor glasses nor anything to prove that the robin goodfellows or good-girls of roomservice have ever passed this way. That's odd. The blackbacked hurrying man must carry all his luggage in that briefcase: but, now that he remembers, it was a big bulging briefcase, brown leather to clash badly with the black suit, big enough to hold pyjamas but scarcely big enough to accommodate anything more bulky than a light silk dressing-gown. Woollen would not fit. *N'importe*. There are two single beds, one pillowless and unused, all the pillows on the other, which is tossed and tumbled. That man must have had a restless night. But who in hell am I supposed to be or what am I play-ing at? Sherlock Holmes?

The phone on the table on the far side of the rumpled bed would do very well for his expiatory call to Sligo. He reaches across first for it and then, the most natural thing in the world it seems for him to subside, not just to subside but to allow himself to subside, gravity and all that: and to close his eyes. The bed is quite cold even to a man with his clothes on, and that's also odd because the man with the brown briefcase had moved so fast that his couch should not yet have had time to cool. Perhaps he had genuinely passed such a restless night that he had tumbled on the bed for a while, then sat up or walked the floor until dawn. To hell with Holmes and Dr Watson or Nigel Bruce and Basil, Basil, the second name eludes me. Pigeons fly high over a black roof that is crawling with spitting cats.

Opening his eyes again he reads seventeen in the centre of the dial and, with the phone in his hand, says not Sligo but: Room seventeen speaking, room service could I have, please, a glass of brandy and a baby ginger, not too well this morning, a slight dyspepsia, nervous dyspepsia, something I'm liable to.

The explanation perhaps was an error, too long, too apologetic, never apologize, like Sergius in the Shaw play, just barge ahead and hope for the best. Not too late yet to cut and run but, to hell with poverty we'll kill a duck, here's a pound note for a tip on the table between the beds, charge the brandy to the blackbacked man's bill, any man who moves so fast would need a brandy: now down, well down under the bedclothes, nothing to be seen but the crown of my head: and your brandy, sir, the ginger sir, will I pour it sir, do please, mumble but be firm, and thank you, that's for yourself and have one on me, and thank you, sir. It was a man's voice. A porter, not a chambermaid. You can't have everything. And where is the chambermaid? as the commercial traveller said in the Metropole in Cork when his tea was carried to him in the randy morning by, alas, the nightporter. Can't say, sir, about the chamber but the cup and saucer are the best Arklow pottery. Oh God, hoary old jokes: but then my mind is weakening or I wouldn't be here.

The door closes. This is the sweetest brandy he has ever tasted and cheap at a pound. Four notes left. Let me outa here. But gravity strikes again and, eyes closing, he is drifting into dreams when the phone rings and, before he can stop himself, he picks it up and the voice of the female switch says: Call for you, sir.

—Thanking you.

—That you, Mulqueen? Where the hell are you?

A rough, a very rough, male voice.

—Room seventeen.

—Balls. What I mean is what the hell are you up to?

That would by no means be easy to explain to a man I've never seen and on behalf of a man I've never really met.

Mumble: Up to nothing.

—Can't hear you too well. You sound odd. Are you drinking? A bloody pussyfoot like you might get drunk in a crisis.

That's the first time, the reely-reely first time, I was ever called a pussyfoot. Say something. Mumble something. What to say? What to mumble? Have another slow meditative sip. Never gulp brandy, my uncle always told me, it's bad for your brain and an insult to a great nation.

—Mulqueen, are you there? Are you bloody well listening?

—Everything's fine. Not to worry.

—Never heard you say that before, Mulqueen. You that worried the life out of yourself and everybody else. But I should bloodywell hope everything is fine. Although I may as well tell you that's not what the bossman thinks out here in the bloody suburbs. He's called a meeting. You'd better be here. And have the old alibis in order.

—I'll be there. When the roll is called up yonder I'll be there. I'll be ...

Perhaps he shouldn't have said that, but the brandy, brandy for heroes, is making a new man out of Pussyfoot Mulqueen or whoever he is. Anyway, and God be praised, it put an end to that conversation for the phone at the far end goes down with a dangerous crash that echoes in his ears, if not even in the bedroom. He finishes the brandy, beats time with his left hand and chants: I'll be there, I'll be there, when the roll is called up yonder I'll be there, oh I wonder, yes I wonder do the angels fart like thunder, when the roll is called up yonder I'll be there!

Sips at the empty glass and draws his breath and continues: At the cross, at the cross, where the jockey lost 'is 'oss: send down sal, send down sal, send down salvation from the lord catch my flea, catch my flea, catch my fleeting soul.

And orders another brandy and ginger, and plants another pound, and submerges, and all goes well, and surfaces and drinks the brandy, and realizes that he must not fall asleep, must out and away while the going is good and the great winds westward blow, and is about to get on his feet when the phone is at it again. Here now is a dilemma, emma, emma, emma, to answer or not to answer, dangerous to answer, more dangerous not to answer, the ringing may attract attention, the not answering may bring searchers up. It is a woman's voice.

—Is that you, Arthur.

Arthur is my name.

—Who else?

—You sound odd.

—The line is bad.

—Your hives are flourishing.

My hives? I don't have hives. Good God, the man's a beekeeper, an apywhatisit.

—But Arthur, I'm worried sick about you. What is it? What is wrong?

She is crying.

—O'Leary rang looking for you. I told him where you might be.

—That was unwise.

—I had to. He said things were in a bad way.

251

—He would.

—Arthur. You sound very peculiar.

—I feel very peculiar.

—What were you up to?

He still doesn't know what he was up to. He says: these things happen. So does Hiroshima. So does the end of the world.

—Arthur, how can you talk like that? You don't sound in the least like yourself. And there is something wrong with your voice.

Best put the phone down gently and run. But she will only ring again before he can get out the door and away.

—Laryngitis. Hoarse as a drake.

He coughs.

—Don't do anything desperate. Promise me.

—Promise.

—In the long run it will be better to face the music. Think of the children.

—I always do.

—You have been a good father. You were never unkind.

She is crying again and he feels like the ruffian he is for bursting in on the sorrows of a woman he has never seen, may never see, pray God. Then his self-respect is restored and his finer feelings dissipated by a male voice, sharp and clear and oh so nasty: You blackguard. Mary is much too soft with you. She always has been.

Nothing better to say than: Who's speaking?

—Very well you know who is speaking, you dishonest automaton, this is your brother-in-law speaking, and a sorry day it was that you ever saw Mary or she ever saw you, or that you brought a black stain, the only one ever, on the name of this family, get over to your office this

252

minute and face the music, it will make a man of you, a term in jail...

Christ save the hastening man who has this faceless monster for a brother-in-law. I am shent, or somebody is, Pussyfoot the automaton is shent as in Shakespeare. But what to say? So unable to think of anything better he says: Bugger off.

Somebody must stand up for Mulqueen who is not here to stand up for himself.

—Filthy language now to make a bad job worse, your father and mother were decent people who never used words like that ...

—They never had to listen to the like of you.

—I'll offer up my mass for you, as a Catholic priest I can think of nothing else.

And slam goes the phone and the gates of hell shall not prevail, and the Lord hath but spoken and chariots and horsemen are sunk in the wave: sound the loud timbrel o'er Egypt's dark sea: and he is halfway to the door when the loud timbrel sounds again. Let it sound. Divide the dark waves and let me outa here. And the bedroom door opens and in steps the thin sandy porter, going bald, with a third brandy and ginger on a tray, and puts the tray down carefully, and picks up the phone and says hello and listens, and cups his hand carefully over the mouthpiece and says: It's for Mr Mulqueen, sir. It might be as well to answer it. Just for the sake of appearances at the switch below.

Sounds, he means. Appearances do not enter into this caper. It's a wonderful world. As the song assures us.

A woman's voice, husky, says: Arthur, this is Emma.

Emma, dilemma, dilemma, dilemma.

He says: Emma.

—Arthur love, don't bother about what they say. Come over here to me.

Which at the moment he feels he might almost do, if he knew where she was. Or who. That voice.

—Arthur, do you read me?

—Loud and clear.

—Are you coming?

—Pronto.

And puts down the phone, and turns to face the porter and the music.


So the porter pours the ginger into the brandy and hands it to him and says: You sat here for a while last night, sir. After the others had gone.

Remembering Eamonn. Now he begins to remember something of the night.

—Nine of you used to meet here.

—Eamonn Murray and the rest of us.

—Poor Mr Murray, God be good to him. One decent man. He thought the world and all of you.

A silence. The phone also is mercifully silent.

—About Mr Mulqueen, sir.

—Who?

—Mulqueen, sir. His room, you know.

—Of course. Face the music, Mulqueen.

—You know him, sir?

—Not too well. A sort of passing acquaintance.

—You'll be glad to hear he's well, sir. They fished him safely out of the river. Nobody here knows a thing about it yet. An errand boy came in the back and told me. I sent him about his business. No harm done.

Another silence. He puts the last three notes on the table between the beds, flattens them down under an ashtray: That's for your trouble, Peter Callanan.

Memory, fond memory brings the light.

—How much do I owe you for the brandy?

—It came out of the dispense, sir.

—The name's Arthur.

—They won't miss it for a while.

—But we can't have that. I'll be back as soon as the banks open.

—No panic. No panic at all. You're old stock. Nine of you. And Mr Murray. The flower of the flock.

—What did he do that for? Jump?

—God knows, sir. He seemed such a quiet orderly man. Never touched a drop. And in broad daylight. Stood up on the wall and jumped with the city watching. He couldn't have meant it. Missed a moored dinghy by inches. But he did miss it.

—He had luck, the dog, 'twas a merry chance.

—What's that, sir?

—Oh, nothing. A bit of an old poem. How they kept the bridge of Athlone.

—Athlone. It's a fine town. I worked there for a summer in the Duke of York. Mr Murray was a great man for the poetry. He could recite all night. Under yonder beechtree. And to sing the parting glass.

He leads the way along the corridor and down the backstairs to the basement, then along a tunnel with store-rooms like treasure-caves to right and left. They shake hands.

—Many thanks, Peter.

—Good luck, sir.

—Them's your cats.

Two cats are wooing in the carpark across the laneway.

—What's that, sir?

—Oh, nothing. Just a sort of a proverb where I come from.

—Like out of the question as Ronnie Donnegan said.

—Something like that.

Bloodless Byrne to the right, Ronnie Donnegan to the left, he walks away along the laneway. He hasn't had the heart to ask Peter Callanan what it was that was out of the question. Ahead of him Eamonn walks, forever reciting: Under yonder beechtree, single on the green-sward, couched with her arms beneath her golden head, blank a blank a blanky, blank a blank a blanky, lies my young love sleeping in the shade.

He must ring Sligo and tell her that all is well. All is well. Somewhere poor Pussyfoot Mulqueen is being dried out through the mangle. All may not be well. The music is waiting.

There is a group of seven or eight people by the river-wall. One young fellow points. As if Mulqueen had made a permanent mark on the dark water.

He has never seen the man's face. Shared his life for a bit. Shared it? Lived it.

And he goes on over the bridge to the bank.

# Afterword

## Anthony Glavin

It seems to me that my first twenty-four hours in Ireland some fifty years ago might have been lifted straight out of a Benedict Kiely short story. Not alone the Scottish whisky and cigarettes lorry in which I had thumbed a lift on the morning of my twenty-first birthday to the Larne ferry in Stranraer, nor solely the kindness of Brian, a gentle lad not much older than myself who, with considerable drink taken, gave me a lift some hours later outside Cookstown, County Tyrone, only for his right-rear tyre to go flat. As Brian had no tyre iron, we flagged down a passing motorist who, upon my request for 'a sharp instrument' with which to prise off the hubcap, promptly produced from his boot the sword and scabbard he had only just purchased from an antique dealer, proudly pointing out the royal seal of Prince Edward on its hilt. He fortunately followed that with a wrench, however, which proved far better suited for the task at hand.

Flat tyre changed, I persuaded Brian to head for home, before catching another lift with Harry and Vera, a couple somewhere in their forties heading for Ben's Omagh, where they kindly brought me home for a cup of tea which then segued into supper, followed by several hours of chat, during which they inquired about my preconceptions of their fellow Northern Irish Unionists whom, they feared, were notorious 'for keeping the rest of Ireland down'.

Such candid openness vis-à-vis matters sectarian reflected what I would later learn from Ben of their shared hometown, how such divisions had not been entirely the practice in the Omagh he grew up in: 'In that town, we did, and do, go easy on the likes of that'. Indeed, his masterly story 'Blue Bell Meadow' is further testimony to such, with its beguiling storyline of a secondary school convent girl courting a Presbyterian (and prospective B Special) schoolboy in a spacious park, only to be prudently cautioned by a town butcher, who also belongs to the Orange Order.

Having slept that night on Harry and Vera's sitting-room sofa and after a hearty breakfast, I thanked my generous hosts and resumed my journey towards Donegal. However, I would not encounter Ben Kiely, neither his writing nor the man himself, until I returned to Ireland some eight years later in 1975 for a longer stay, when I happened first upon his remarkable radio presence, described by Ben himself as 'my mournful Scots-Irish voice'. 'I learned Ben's voice before I learned his name!' a friend recently told me, and down the years I've heard more than one chancer from Ballyshannon to Boston attempting to take off that mellifluous Tyrone accent. And a truly marvellous voice it was, capable of raising you from the dead sleep of a Sunday morning in order to follow him down the memory lane that was the 'Sunday Miscellany' programme on Radio Éireann.

It is however Kiely's voice as a master of the short story that concerns us in this new selection by New Island Books, which marks the centenary of his birth in 1919. And a singular narrative voice it is, one that patently echoes an Irish oral storytelling tradition, while simultaneously reflecting the encyclopaedic erudition of the man himself. Except that erudition is arguably too dry a word for Ben, better suited to a cloistered academic, say, because it fails to convey the energy and passion with which he writes of what he knows, crafting stories that assuredly blend song, anecdote, myth, history and place in an allusive storyline, all of which is simultaneously underpinned by a masterly organising principle which manages to deftly bring such seemingly disparate digressions home.

To be sure, beg, borrow and steal in magpie fashion is arguably what fiction writers do. Ben, for his part, procured the title of another of the stories here, 'The Shortest Way Home', from the aphorism 'The Longest Way Round is the Shortest Way Home', which is uttered by Leopold Bloom in Joyce's *Ulysses*, who likely lifted it himself from a sermon by the nineteenth-century Scottish, non-conformist minister Alexander Maclaren. Another saying halfway through the story,'I would give you some violets but they withered when my father died', turns out to be the only line our young, unnamed narrator liked out of the book of proverbs which his class had to copy out in order to practise their penmanship, though none of them 'knew what it meant or who said it or who died or who wanted to give violets to whom'. And while there's scant chance Ben wouldn't inform you of its provenance – a line spoken by Ophelia in Shakespeare's *Hamlet* – were he quoting it in conversation, Ben the writer is far too artful to reveal anything further about the line within the story. As the French painter Marcel Duchamp famously observed, 'It's not what you see that is art – art is the gap' and in fiction knowing what to leave out can be as vital as knowing what to put in.

The plot of 'The Shortest Way Home' is itself decep-
tively simple: a young schoolboy is befriended by a
nine-year-old girl, Big May, who brings our smitten,
unnamed, five-and-half-year-old narrator home each
afternoon via a circuitous route from the girls' school
in which his mother had enrolled him. When he finally
manages to railroad his mother into transferring him,
underage et al, into the Christian Brothers, he is again
befriended, only this time by four older boys, known as
the Four Horsemen of the Apocalypse, who once school
is out, also take it upon themselves to see him – again by
the longest way round – back home.

As it happens, Big May reappears to save the day at
the close of the story with a typical gesture of unbounded
generosity. However, this kindness is only part of the tour
de force finish to a love story of sorts, which not only
tells of friendship and discovery, but also of darker matters in its final lines: marital discord, psychosis and early
death. And so, what we might have taken for a neatly
wrought story, suffused with affection for an Omagh
childhood, transforms itself at its close into a universal
tale of loss, longing and mortality, positing those facts
of life and death which the poet Wordsworth tells us can
often lie 'too deep for tears'.

The longest way round is also a fair description of
Ben Kiely's own narrative style, if not his gift and genius
both on the page and in person, as all who were ever
in the company of this veritable past-master of the
segue can testify. Indeed, the American novelist Thomas
Flanagan observed how it was 'almost surrealism' to be
in the company of Ben. To my ears and eyes, he seemed
to function like a seed crystal in a saturated solution,
around which the most remarkable constellations of
characters and circumstance would subsequently form.

Consider, for example, the afternoon of a very slow pint at Ben's Donnybrook local, Madigan's, where, as if beamed up by the magnetic force field of his resonant voice and personality, two young lads rigged out in 1940s' style three-piece suits, ties and fedoras, asked if they might join us. They were two members of that seminal Irish punk band The Radiators, about to head off to play in Berlin. And yes, the ensuing chat was only mighty, not unlike sitting beside a sparkling stream in full flow – a spate of anecdotes, occasions, events, quotations and allusions – literary, geographical, genealogical or musical.

The Irish writer Seán O'Faoláin who, like Ben Kiely, placed some of his short stories in *The New Yorker*, wrote a superb study of short fiction entitled simply *The Short Story* wherein he quotes the French novelist Flaubert on how writing proceeds from 'a personal way of seeing and feeling, and that is everything!' According to O'Faoláin, writing a story takes 90 per cent personality and only 10 per cent craft, for what we ultimately set down on the page is not so much our subject as it is ourselves.

Such is a persuasive argument for a masterly writer like Ben Kiely, whose personality arguably informs his fiction to the degree that you can often all but hear him speaking as you read him. And 'voice', I'd warrant, is a reasonable synonym for what O'Faoláin meant by the personality that informs the short story, itself a more personal genre than the novel.

There is also a vivid, salient sense of place in Kiely's fiction which arguably underpins much of the best writing anywhere. According to Patrick Kavanagh, a great writer starts from his roots in a particular locale and 'dreams from his tiny foothold of the Known to the

Unknown'. In doing so, the primacy of place gives way to the spirit of imagination, a process that seems to me to lie at the heart of Kiely's fiction. 'Every corner is a world', remarks a character in his novel *Nothing Happens in Carmincross*, as if quoting Kiely himself, speaking from the heart.

That same novel, of course, foreshadowed the horrific bombing atrocity that befell his beloved Omagh on his seventy-ninth birthday, on 15 August 1998. 'The object of terrorism is to terrorise', declares its protagonist, Mervyn Kavanagh. 'Kill or maim the people so as to set them free…. Meditate on the facts. Do not distort.' And this, too, is something for which we are in Kiely's debt: who so courageously down the years, and at some cost, espoused such home truths – that violence on behalf of any cause is a true obscenity, far more obscene than the sexual content which saw his first three novels banned in Ireland.

To close, then, with something of a metaphysical argument, if you like, on behalf of the power and importance of *story* itself – not alone the magnificent dozen within this new selection, but also those stories we hear from, and tell to, others – what the poet Peggy O'Brien calls 'the consolations of storytelling', the manner in which a particular story on a given day can sometimes seem to offer us a blessed means of making our way through, if not making our peace with, life itself. Though none of that would likely be news to Benedict Kiely, who, as the novelist Colm McCann observes, 'knew so well that everybody, even the most anonymous amongst us – is in the middle of a story'.

Last, but not least, a single, sweet memory of Ben making his way slowly towards the Shelbourne Hotel on St Stephen's Green in Dublin one day some forty years ago. His left knee was swollen from a rheumatic complaint, he explained, only for him to brighten up entirely as he recalled how 'Dean Swift hopped for miles on one leg!'

# Bibliographical Note

'The Dogs in the Great Glen' was first published in *The New Yorker* in 1960. 'The Heroes in the Dark House', was originally published in *The New Yorker* as 'The Heroes in Die Dark House' in 1959. 'A Journey to the Seven Streams' was first published in *The New Yorker* in 1961. 'Homes on the Mountain' was originally published in 1959 in *The New Yorker* as 'Houses on the Mountain'. 'The Shortest Way Home' was first published in 1962 in *The New Yorker*. These stories were published together for the first time in *A Journey to the Seven Streams* in 1963 by Methuen. 'A Room in Linden' and 'Maiden's Leap' were first published in *The New Yorker* in 1972 and were first published, together with 'The Weavers at the Mill', in *A Ball of Malt and Madame Butterfly* in 1973 by Victor Gollancz. 'There are Meadows in Lanark' was first published in *The New Yorker* in 1974. 'The Night We Rode with Sarsfield' was first published in *The New Yorker* in 1973. 'Bluebell Meadow' was first published in *The New Yorker* in 1975. These stories were published together for the first time in *A Cow in the House* in 1978 by Victor Gollancz. 'Bloodless Byrne of a Monday' was first published in *A Letter to Peachtree and Nine Other Stories* by Victor Gollancz in 1987.